"DID I HURT YOU?"

He shook his head, his eyes again dropping to her full lips. He breathed in deeply. "No."

She hadn't hurt him, but something about this woman was addling his brain. What the hell was he thinking finding her attractive? He didn't find mortals attractive. Ever.

She regarded him closely, and he wondered for a moment if he was vamping out in some way. Had his irises widened, making his eyes totally black? Or had his skin pulled taut over his bones? Was a fang hanging out of the corner of his mouth?

Not that she looked frightened. She actually looked . . . concerned?

REASON TO BELIEVE

JESSICA INCLÁN

ZEBRA BOOKS
KENSINGTON PUBLISHING CORP.
http://www.kensingtonbooks.com

ZEBRA BOOKS are published by

Kensington Publishing Corp.
850 Third Avenue
New York, NY 10022

All Kensington titles, imprints, and distributed lines are available at special quantity discounts for bulk purchases for sales promotion, premiums, fund-raising, educational, or institutional use.

Special book excerpts or customized printings can also be created to fit specific needs. For details, write or phone the office of the Kensington Special Sales Manager: Attn: Special Sales Department. Kensington Publishing Corp., 850 Third Avenue, New York, NY 10022. Phone: 1-800-221-2647.

ISBN-13: 978-0-8217-8083-1
ISBN-10: 0-8217-8083-2

First Zebra Trade Paperback Printing: October 2006
First Zebra Mass Market Paperback Printing: July 2008

10 9 8 7 6 5 4 3 2 1

Printed in the United States of America

Prologue

It's dark in the room, the lights off, but there is the hum of electricity in the air. He heard the call and traveled as fast as he could, the matter of the world bumpy and fraught tonight, as if the particles of life knew that something was very wrong.

All he'd heard from the distance that separated them was a cry, a deep guttural moan that he recognized instantly. Within minutes he was on his way and now he is here, guarded, ready, slipping quietly into the room, trying to find the man who called him.

When it hits him, he knows what the electrical sound was, the hum and whir of a sortilège du foudre, *a thin, whipcord lash of heat that wraps around his chest, picks him up, and throws him to the far wall, his clothes scorched, his body aching, all his limbs buzzing. His ears pound to the mad beat of the current in his blood.*

Even though his breath is short and uneven, he covers himself with a protection spell and tries to stand. Another flash of the spell hits him but bounces off, and in the illumination of the strand of heat and fire, he sees what he knew he would find in this dark room.

There is the man, hanging in the middle of the room, blood trickling from a wound on his head. He looks limp—from pain or exhaustion, it's hard to tell—and his hands dangle at his sides.

He takes a deep breath, tries to hide the ache that is radiating from his bones. But it's too late to hide anything. She laughs, softly, the familiar sound a tease, a taunt.

Where has he heard her voice before? And where is she?

He swallows, pushes the sound away, watching the man dangle in the glow of evil magic. Once again, he tries to contact him, to work into the unconscious man's mind. But the man is empty, dark, closed off.

He can't hear you, *she thinks.* Just give up on it.

And then she laughs again.

Another flash curls around the room, angling down to try to find a crack in his protection spell, but he wishes himself into matter and then appears on the other side of the room, the terrible view still there: the man, unconscious, weak, maybe ill. Maybe dying.

"Don't fret. Really. After all, you could come with me instead," her voice says, and he wants to weep when he recognizes her voice.

No, *he thinks.* How could you do this?

"How could I? you wonder. How could I not!" she replies to the ideas in his mind. "Why should I stay here with him when someone so powerful calls to me? Wants me. Needs me. A sorcier *who can change the entire world."*

She keeps talking, her words as sharp as poison forks. Another flick of spell cracks against his weak-

ening protection spell, and he feels the pulse of electric energy squeeze his heart. "I thought you loved him," he says, staring at the man in the middle of the room. "I thought . . . You never deserved him. You deserve nothing."

She moves into the dim glow of her own bad magic, her hair black lacquer, her eyes black diamonds.

"Come now," she says, laughing, the sound as sickening to him as the sulfury after-smell of her magic. "Don't be truculent."

Another whoosh of fire passes by him, and his protection spell wavers and then rebuilds itself.

Gathering his strength, he closes his eyes. He thinks of heavy objects, iron, steel, granite, and then he opens his palms and whispers, "Détruire," wanting her gone, destroyed, hating how she tricked the man in the room, himself, his family, all of them, all Croyant.

The room seems to bounce and sway to his magic, and he hears her scream as his power hits her. For a second—a second too long and too open—he drops his protection spell and from somewhere else, somewhere not inside the woman, he is attacked. His body is thrown up and over the other man, kicked by invisible giant feet, tossed up and down like so much trash.

As he is hit and cudgeled and broken, he feels his mind going, disappearing, leaving him. He needs to save the man, he needs to fight back, but before he can really even think these things, everything is darkness and everything is gone.

Chapter One

By nightfall, the man was still slumped on the corner stoop, bent over, his head sunk in his hands, his elbows dug hard into his knees. Every so often, he would look up, gaze around him blankly, and then put his head back in his hands, his dark hair in long, loose strands. Even from her flat window, Fabia Fair could feel the dark blue of the sad air around him.

She had first seen him in the morning when she walked to the corner of Thistle and Hanover, desperate for her first cup of hot, black coffee, barely taking the time to brush her long blond hair into a thick ponytail before running out of her flat. She'd assumed he was a drunk on a bender, sitting it off on Mrs. Macatee's immaculate front step. He didn't know how lucky it was that the carnaptious Mrs. Macatee was in Bents in West Lothian visiting her sister Drusilla for a week. He'd have had a broom to his back end by now, Mrs. Macatee screeching, "Blootered, are ye? A fine thing. A drunk on the steps in the morning? I hae it in me mind to call the authorities."

As Fabia had passed him—having to whisk by his knees because of the tiny sidewalk—she'd quickly noted his long hair, matted and wet from the heavy morning condensation, and his strong, slender hands, the fingernails rimmed with dark moons of dirt. Fabia had put out a tiny feeler from her mind to see if he was awake, but his thoughts were shut down, closed, dark as pitch.

She'd almost stopped, unused to *Moyenne* protecting their thoughts. Most ordinary people's minds were completely open, thinking in one long, constant stream from morning till bedtime. They hadn't learned to find the silence inside them. "Sixty thousand thoughts a day," Adalbert Baird, the *Croyant* armiger, told her when she was a girl. "A full sixty thousand thoughts a day. If you listened to one person for even an hour, you'd go daft! You have to pick and choose what to listen to."

So it was odd to find a *Moyenne* so still in mind, but—needing her coffee and already late for the clinic she worked at—Fabia made the decision to leave him alone. If he had enough presence of mind to block someone reading his thoughts, he'd know when someone was trying to look in. And Fabia didn't want to call attention to herself. Not now, when she was so close to finding Caderyn Macara, who was only one thought away from her grasp.

Five years ago, Macara was the leader of *Le Société Pour Intégration des Tous*, the same group that Fabia's twin brother, Niall, worked for now. Macara had been the major proponent of developing ties between the magical *Croyant* world and the ordinary world of the *Moyenne*. He believed that if the magic and the real were brought together, the world would be that much richer, better for everyone. Together they could heal the environment, end violent conflict, unite humanity in one peacefully coexisting tribe. He was eloquent, impassioned, his red hair waving behind him as he spoke, his face bright, his eyes full of fire.

"Integrate. Share. Bring the cultures together," he'd said and written, publishing article after article in the *Informations du Croyant Matin*. He was a featured speaker at council meetings and festivals that celebrated *Moyenne* life. Conservative *Croyant* hated him, leveling him in editorials in the *Sommaire*, castigating him as a hater of *Croyant* culture in *Croyant Tous Les Jours*. When Macara brought groups together to rally for *Moyenne* safety, he was bombarded with illegal spells that took him weeks to recover from. How Fabia had cried when she read about the spells, his twisted limbs, his memory emptied time and time again, the many times he'd lost his vision, his voice, his ability to talk.

But no matter the spell or the length of his recuperation, he had always come back to fight once again for what he believed in.

Cadeyrn Macara had once been Fabia's hero.

But suddenly, he disappeared. No articles. No rallies. No pleas to the *Croyant* Council. There were rumors of burnout, of some conservative *Croyant* mischief or another.

"What else but a woman?" Niall had said, while Fabia pined.

But then *Moyenne* began losing their property, their money, their lives in ways that would suggest that whoever was committing the crimes knew the *Moyenne* better than most *Croyant* ever would. All evidence led to Macara. Who else understood *Moyenne* life so well? And as the problems escalated, the *Croyant* Council knew that there was another force involved, another *sorcier*. Quain Dalzeil, the man who wanted to change the *Croyant* world, the whole world, everything.

Finally at one crime scene, *Croyant* officials momentarily caught Macara, had him for seconds, before he whiffed away in a flare of blue smoke, taken to safety by Quain,

From that point on, feeling betrayed and confused, Fabia knew what she wanted to do with her life, becoming a *chasseur*, a searcher, as soon as she'd graduated from Bampton Academy.

Now she needed to stay open, mindful, alert, ready for the thought that would lead her to him and then to Quain, the man who'd challenged the magical world *Les Croyants de Trois* and wanted to destroy all *Moyenne*.

So rather than irritate or alert the drunken man on the corner stoop with her thoughts this morning, she'd walked by him, and within minutes, her steaming cup of coffee in her hands, had forgotten him.

But now it was night and cold, desperately so, the short Edinburgh summer turning into winter without bothering with autumn at all. From the window, Fabia saw that the man hadn't moved an inch, though he no longer held his head in his hands. Instead, he seemed to be looking forward, his head unmoving, his body still. He hadn't been wearing a coat—she'd noticed that this morning—and now it must be less than eight degrees outside, the sky full of wet chill.

Fabia turned away from the window, her hand absently on her cheek, her teeth biting softly on her bottom lip. Maybe she should call the authorities, just as Mrs. Macatee would have. At least, then the man would be warm and someone would feed him, even if it was powdered eggs and white bread toast. If he was a drunk, he could go through the DTs in a cell rather than on the street below as the night turned slick with frigid ocean air.

Then Fabia shook her head. Why was she worrying about one stray man? There were homeless everywhere, it seemed, men, women, and children huddled in dirty blankets, dressed only in dirty clothes, sleeping roughly, pressed tightly against walls to encourage some warmth. At the Care Now clinic Fabia volunteered at three times a week, she met all the homeless, gave them vouchers for meals and baths, rang the Housing Services Programme to see if rooms were available for the night. Only after they were tended to did she read their thoughts for stray, useful comments about Quain or Macara they might have picked up on the street unintentionally.

She pushed back the curtain again. The man sat still, unmoving, a dark stone in the fading light, a statue of sadness and despair. His bones must be frozen solid, she thought, almost feeling the ache from his long chilled legs. Cautiously, she put out another feeler, and his mind was still shut to her, like an iron wall against invaders.

"Shit." Fabia turned from the window and grabbed her gloves, putting on her coat, pulling on her hat, and picking up her keys. *It's not like I'm good at saving anyone anyway*, she thought to herself.

Aye, you are, came the answer from Niall, who lived in Paris and had a habit of casting his mind out at night to see what she was doing.

Maybe I could save you, Niall, she thought back. *But you're my baby brother. Not a strange man on the sidewalk.*

Baby brother! By two minutes!

Fabia laughed. *That counts. And you know it, so let's not get in a row about it again. I need to help this man.*

Don't get crabbit with me, lassie.

I'm not crabbit. You're just driving me crazy, as usual. I'm going to help him whether you like it or not.

Niall sighed so loudly she could hear it from Paris. *Well, you know you won't sleep a minute now that you've got him in your sights. You can't hear his thoughts?*

No, Fabia thought, sighing. *He's closed down.*

Well, go talk to him, at least.

Fine, she thought back. *And then I'll call you here to help me.*

I never need an excuse to visit. But I'm watching that daft Survivor *show on the telly. If you need me, wait an hour.*

Fabia cut off the communication and opened her door, quickly running down the hall and stairs and then pushing out onto the street. The temperature had dropped even more than the report had predicted; Fabia's cheeks flushed from the slick slap of cold air. Rubbing her gloved hands together, she walked toward the man, slowing as she neared him.

"Hello," she said softly, blinking against the streetlight.

He stared at her—no, past her—his face expressionless. His face was smudged with dirt, a deep, dark red scratch running from temple to jaw, one eye blackened. Blood swelled the skin under his eye and hung in a painful purple moon over his cheek. As Fabia moved closer, she realized that his hair wasn't so much matted from the wet, dank air as from dried blood. There was a clear, perfect circle of reddish, broken skin around his neck, and she noticed now that the dirt she'd seen under his nails this morning was actually blood.

Whatever had happened, he'd fought back. Whoever he'd fought with probably looked as bad as he.

"Are you all right?"

The man turned to her, tried to look up, and then took a deep breath, his mouth trying to move. He was trembling, his arms tight against his body now, his black eyes filled with fog and sadness. Again, she tried to reach for his mind, but the iron wall was still there, planted solidly.

What do you think? Fabia asked Niall without even meaning to.

All that blood, Niall thought. *Maybe it's not his.* Moyenne *are messy murderers.*

He hardly looks capable of a right killing, Fabia thought.

True. He didn't do his level best, there. So he might be on the lam. Injured from the barbed wire he crawled under, Niall thought. *Just call the police.*

Fabia stared at the man, ignoring Niall for a moment. Maybe she couldn't read the man's mind, but there was something about him. Something kind even in his quiet, painful desperation.

Bloody bleeding heart, Niall thought. *But just be ready to escape. Be prepared to step into the gray, okay? Hop back to your flat.*

Yes, sir, Fabia thought, shaking her head. But Niall was right. It was easier to extend this kindness knowing that if the man grew strange or crazy or even dangerous, she could disappear in an instant, traveling through matter to the police station where she could report the crime she'd just escaped. The *Moyenne* she worked with at the clinic were always amazed that Fabia would go to flophouses and tenements and dark alleys looking for clients. What she couldn't tell them was that she was protecting them by doing so, keeping them away from danger from which they might not be able to escape.

Fabia bent down, trying to attract his gaze. But he wouldn't look at her, and she could feel the tension radiating from inside him.

"Hi, there," she said. "My name's Fabia Fair. I live at the flat just down a bit."

He didn't move his eyes, but he blinked, once, twice.

"Would you like to come with me?" Fabia said, crouching down farther and looking into the man's desperate, searching eyes. "How about a wee bit to eat?"

He licked his lips, breathing in, scanning the ground as if he'd dropped some change. *Not drunk*, Fabia thought. *Schizophrenic.*

Perfect, Niall thought. *Go from Cadeyrn to just another crazy. Get yourself into another fankle.*

Haver on, man! Would you mind affording me some space here? she thought back. *Go watch your bleeding telly.*

Fabia closed her mind to her brother and moved closer to the man. He was shaking, his knees hitting together. Again, he moved his mouth, but then shook his head, tears streaming from the corners of his eyes.

Fabia watched him, trying everything she knew to get inside his mind, but there was no opening, as if the block was put there on purpose. And not by the man, who clearly was in no shape to create or even maintain a block, even if he were *Croyant*, magic, like her. And there was something about him, even with his quaking gaze and his long, thin, dirty body. Fabia couldn't read his mind, but she could feel . . . kindness.

"All right," Fabia said. "That's it. Please, come with me."

She stood up straight and held out her hand. The man breathed in, looking at her hand and then her face, her hand, her face, and then slowly, he lifted his dirty palm from his knee, studying his movements with surprise as if he'd never moved before. His fingers quivered, shook, and Fabia took them in her small gloved hand, feeling how cold he was even through the leather and wool.

Shit, she thought to herself, hating how *Moyenne* treated their castaways, knowing that in her world, the world of *Les Croyants des Trois*, this man would have food and a bath and a bed, no matter what was wrong with him. Adalbert Baird made sure of that, finding places for the damaged and weak—the only people who escaped his care were the ones who disdained it. Like Caderyn Macara. Like Quain Dalzeil. *And what will happen if Quain wins?* she thought.

We'll end up like this poor sod, Niall thought.

Shut it, Fabia thought and clutched the man's hand more tightly.

"Come on," she said. "Don't be scared."

But the man was scared. More than scared. She felt his fear in the energy coming off his body, in the sizzling whites of his distracted eyes, in his stiff, hesitant walk. Who had done this to him? What had happened?

"It's all right," Fabia said, her hand holding his as they walked slowly to the door of her building. "You'll be fine.

He turned to look at her, his black eyes so dark she couldn't see the irises. His forehead was creased with worry, his face gray with cold and hunger and fear. Despite the filth on his clothing, the blood on his head and body, and his clearly distressed mind, Fabia wanted to stop, pull him to her, and comfort him.

For the love of God, Niall thought. *Soup is the better answer. Some hot water, soap maybe. But keep your flipping arms away from him.*

Fabia shook her head, keeping her face free of the annoyance she felt. Because they were twins, Niall had always known how to break through her blocks. His interruptions hadn't seemed bad when they were children, but as they grew older and there were things—and situations—Fabia would have liked to keep secret, Niall managed to find his way in and vice versa, if she were being honest. But neither of them seemed to know the way to cut it off, to separate from each other as they hadn't at birth.

Finally, they'd made a pact to tell each other when to turn off and back on the telepathy, though Niall was the only one with hours shut off and away from her lately. Nothing much had happened to her that was worth hiding.

Like that night with that nutter Timo, Niall thought. *Or that full-of-himself, so-called boyfriend Fletcher?*

Niall! Let's please not go there. Do you want me to bring up that date last week with what's-her-name? Stop gowking and go back to the show.

Fine, I'm leaving. But I'm checking in later.

When Fabia and the man reached her door, she let go of his hand to dig for her keys in her pocket.

"Here they are." She held up the keys—the metal clacking and jingling—turned to look at him, and gasped. Inching away slightly, he breathed fast, his chest moving up and down, his face even paler than it had been moments before, his entire body jolting with fear.

As she looked at him, Fabia knew without finding a way into his mind that he wasn't mad. He wasn't schizophrenic. But someone had hurt him—tortured him—to the point of madness. Someone had done something to this strong, solid, six-foot-three man and broken worse than bones.

"Come on," she said. "Let's go inside."

The man breathed in, his breath a rough, aching sound Fabia could hear, hard, and heavy, and full of anxiety. She reached down and took his hand again, squeezing the long, frozen fingers.

"You'll be all right," she said. "No one will hurt you now. I promise."

The man blinked, his mouth working again with words impossible for him to say. Then he gave her a quick nod and followed her into the building and up the stairs to her flat.

The minute the man was inside, her door locked behind them, Fabia realized how large he was and how uncomfortable he felt in his body and his mind. In the bright light of her small hallway, he wouldn't meet her eyes, shifting back and forth on his feet. She pulled off her coat and tucked her gloves in a pocket, putting her hands on her hips.

"First thing," she said, "is to get you out of those clothes and into the bath. I'll do a wash while you bathe and eat. Then I can call my friend Alan about getting you a place to stay." Alan Fyfe was her supervisor at the clinic, and he was used to Fabia's phone calls about homeless people she spotted at the bus station on Dublin Street and in St. Andrew Square. As he spoke to her about budgetary concerns, she read his thoughts, hearing his *She picks up every bloody stray in town!* each time.

But Alan always came to the rescue of those in need, and this man standing in front of her was in need, desperate need.

"I have some of my brother's things here. A bathrobe, pajamas, some T-shirts, the hale jing bang. We'll get you set up while I wash your clothes. Is that okay?" Fabia tried to meet his gaze, but though he wouldn't look at her, he nodded slightly.

"Okay, then. Let's go run you a tub." As she walked down to the bathroom, the man following slowly behind her, Fabia suddenly felt a scurry of nerves up her sternum. This, she knew, was probably taking the homeless cause a bit too far.

You think? Niall called out.

If you could see him, Fabia thought. *It's so sad. But he's a big man.*

Fabia, do you want me there? I could be there in seconds.

Looking behind her as she entered the bathroom, Fabia stared at the man. It was hard to get a good idea of what he looked like with his matted hair, bruised face, and the dirt and grime from his time on the street. But he was imposing, at least six feet two and powerfully built—his muscles tightly wrapped around his shoulders and arms. She could imagine him in his real life, moving smoothly, using his body for work or in sports, or sitting down, watching the telly, his long legs in front of him. At this moment, though, he was simply lost, his body weak with confusion.

No, I just went mad for a second. But thanks, Niall.

Okay, Fabs. I'm here.

She turned on the light and walked over to the long porcelain tub, the very object that had convinced her to take this flat over the others she'd looked at. It wasn't the showerhead that the bloke from America had installed when he'd lived in the flat but the long, lovely tub. Fabia could almost float in it, her toes not touching the end as she sailed in perfumed water. Nothing, she had to admit—not even a long night in bed with a man—gave her as much pleasure. So even this man would feel comfortable, able to stretch out, relax, find his way back to the world in its warm, wet heat.

Crouching down, Fabia turned on the water, testing it as the tub filled. Soon the bathroom was filled with steam, the mirror filmed over. She grabbed some foaming lavender bath salt from the edge and sprinkled in a bit, and then, thinking of his sore and potentially smelly skin, dumped in the rest of the bag.

She felt the hot water one last time and then stood up, wiping her hands on her jeans.

"Okay. So I'll leave. You can undress and then toss the clothes out for me. Take as long as you'd like," Fabia said slowly, hoping he was listening. "The shampoo and soap are right here on this table."

She looked up at the man, who stared at her. "Do you understand?"

He nodded slightly, or at least she thought he did. Shrugging, Fabia walked out of the bathroom, closed the door, and leaned back on it. Her heart was pounding in her chest. For a second, she had an image of something dark, as if the man's thoughts had been cast over her like a black net. Under the net she could see nothing, feel nothing, and she knew that's what he felt inside, right now, the net stuck on him, trapping his body and mind, everything inside him a buzz of emptiness.

Closing her eyes, she thought her way into the bathroom and saw that he was standing just as she left him, his hands dangling by his sides, his head lowered, his lower lip trembling. Fabia stood straight, opened her eyes, and breathed in deeply. This wasn't going to be as easy as she'd thought.

Fabia knocked on the door and then stepped back into the steamy bathroom. The man didn't notice her, standing just as he had when she left, still and nervous.

"You know," she began, nodding. "I have a twin brother, God bless him, and I've seen my share of male skin. So let me help you get undressed. Is that all right?"

Fabia! Niall almost seemed to shout.

The man's no more than a statue, Niall, she thought back. *If he's a rapist, he'd need a bit more spark, I'd say.*

Ahh, another dead one, just like your Fletcher.

Aye, and as dead as you are going to be if you don't leave me alone, Fabia thought as she moved toward the man.

But Niall didn't answer, and Fabia smiled at the man, reaching out for his shoulder. He flinched, stepped back, and Fabia dropped her hand.

"Don't worry. I won't hurt you. Just let me help you into this bath." She reached out for his arm again, but then the door swung open, and Niall was in the doorway, his blond-white hair on end, his face ruddy from traveling through matter, his blue eyes wide and expectant. Even with his hair in disarray and even though she could see how irritated he was that she pulled him from his show on the telly, Fabia smiled, pleased to see him in the flesh instead of listening to him in her mind.

Quietly, she urged Niall. *Don't move too fast.*

Niall stopped for a moment, taking off his robe and

putting it on top of the hamper. Smoothing his hair, he walked slowly toward the man, looking at him up and down. "Tough day at the office, lad? You look all toozy, to be sure. But so do I, so there you have it."

The man looked at Niall, and Fabia could see him relax, his shoulders slumping, his eyes gathering some heat and energy.

"So let's let Fabia wash your clothes. Say I help you out a wee bit."

That was the clue for you to leave, Fabs. Let me take care of him for now.

Fabia felt herself loath to go for some reason, and then smiled, shaking her head.

You fancy him? That's fine. No one I've fixed you up with in years has interested you, but this poor bloody sod does. What does that mean? Shall we call on the healers?

Shut it! Fabia thought, turning and leaving the bathroom, shutting the door behind her. In a long few minutes, Niall opened the door and gingerly handed her the man's dirty sodden clothes.

Use bleach, he thought. *Bug spray. Turpentine. Perhaps you should just burn them.*

Fabia shook her head and grabbed the bundle from him. She'd seen worse at the clinic, clothes that didn't even remotely look like clothes, men and women and even children covered in rags.

In the laundry room in the building basement, Fabia started the load of laundry, using just a smidge more soap than usual. As she'd put the man's clothes into the washer, she'd seen that despite their condition, they were of good quality, nicely made. The jeans were thick, well stitched, almost new. The shirt was a wondrous thick cotton, collar unfrayed. Whatever his life had been, it hadn't been one on the streets. This man—whoever he was—hadn't been homeless for long.

As she closed the washer door, she turned to find her upstairs neighbor, Liam Macmillan, standing in the doorway, his hand on his hip. Fabia sighed, shaking her head and then flicking her hair behind her shoulder. Liam had been a problem since she'd moved in. At first, she imagined that he was almost good-looking, his hair dark and curly, his brown eyes almost caramel colored, his body in fine shape from the runs he took in the evening.

Maybe for about half a week she thought she'd say yes to his immediate requests for a date, but there was something about his mouth, the way his lips were too thin, and his eyes, the way his gaze never stayed on her when they spoke at any length. And once she moved into his thoughts, well, she knew that Liam Macmillan only wanted one thing—or maybe three—and none of them involved her mind, personality, or character.

"Hey, Fabia," he said. "A little late-night laundry?"

Fabia sighed, letting Liam's overabundance of ego and sex drive float into her mind: *She doesn't have a date. Her lucky night. Neither do I. She's hot. Those breasts. Just the right size. Panties. She's wearing no panties, I reckon, thinking that I'd be down here. So what's her problem that she always says no to me? She has no idea what she's missing. How I could give it to her.*

And then there were a few explicit erotic images, both with Fabia underneath him, taking in what had to be his highly exaggerated male member, enjoying every one of his moves tremendously. She shook her head, pulling away from his highly exaggerated ideas.

"Aye, my big evening. Well," she said, moving toward the door.

Liam stood straight, blocking her exit. "How about we head to the pub for a wee one?"

"I'm working at the clinic tomorrow, Liam. Got to get some sleep."

Fabia moved closer to the door, expecting him to move aside, but he didn't, letting her almost hit his shoulder. She breathed in his too soapy smell and the chemical tang of his industrial-strength antiperspirant.

Do I have to come down there, too? Niall asked. *For the love of God, I've got one man up here to look after. How many gits are there in this building?*

Don't be thick. I can take care of him myself, Fabia shot back.

Turning her mind back to Liam's, easing past his new image of her sliding down his naked body, Fabia pressed into his mind as she'd had to before.

"You're going to let me go upstairs, Liam," she said aloud. "And you're going to be glad to do it. In fact, you can't move away from me fast enough."

Liam immediately moved aside despite his puzzled look.

"You're going to say good night," Fabia said as she passed by him. "And you're going to think that you need to leave me alone."

"Good night, Fabia," Liam said, his voice quavering with confusion.

"Good night, Liam," Fabia said, walking up the stairs, the detergent box in her hands.

Niall was sitting in a chair in the living room, a beer in his hand.

"You need to move in with me," he said. "The situation with the men in Edinburgh is out of control. Now they're showing up unannounced."

"So is he clean?" she asked, putting the detergent away in the cupboard. "Did you tend to his hair? And his face? All those cuts and bruises?"

His mouth opening slightly, Niall shrugged. "No. Bloody hell, Fabs. I got him in the tub."

Fabia stood in front of him, her hands on her hips. Ever since they were children, this was how it worked. The other taking over, until the first came back to finish. They'd shared schoolwork—until the teachers at Bampton Academy found out—and household chores, until their mother, Xanthe, figured out that if she gave a task to one, she was giving it to both. They'd learned magic the same way, trying out spells and charms at night in one of their rooms, Niall starting the chant and Fabia finishing it.

Once their father, Donoch, came in to find the dining room curtains on fire, Fabia's and Niall's hands scorched from an *incendie* spell they'd read about in a book, neither of them knowing how to put out the flames they'd started. Their father put out the flames, repaired the curtains, and transported them both to their rooms with a wave of his hands. But because Fabia could, she listened hard as she pushed through matter and then appeared in her room and she heard Donoch's laughter, his whispered "Those two!"

"Fine. I'll go wash his hair."

Niall started to stand up, but Fabia shook her head. "I'll be all right. I can call you if I need you, Niall. And anyway, he's not going to harm me."

"He's a big man, Fabs. Powerful. Just be careful."

Even though Niall was overly protective and bossy, she was glad he was here.

Damn straight, Niall thought, taking a sip of his beer.

"There's a lovely piece of pie in the fridge," Fabia said as she walked down the hall. "And maybe you can catch the last of that silly show of yours."

Fabia walked down the hall and stopped in front of the bathroom door, knocking gently. The man inside didn't say a word, so she opened the door slowly and stepped in. The room was clear of steam now, and the man sat hunched in the tub, lavender foam covering his body.

"I thought I'd give you a proper shampoo," she said, approaching him as she would a wounded animal, her steps quiet on the tile floor. "There's a lot of blood in your hair, and we might need to take a wee ride to the emergency surgery for stitches later."

Smiling, Fabia kneeled down to the tub, trying to catch the man's dark gaze. But he wouldn't meet her eyes, staring down at the soapy water.

She tested the water with her hand and then turned on the tap, letting a bit more hot water run in. The blood in her body seemed to be giving life a standing ovation, thrumming and bumping in her veins. Why this dirty man was evoking this feeling, she didn't know.

Probably because he's in the full scuddie in your tub, Niall thought from the living room. *Hey, they kicked Charlene off the atoll. They found out she was a complete liar. Can't wait for next week.*

Great, Fabia thought. *Watch Sky TV for a while, all right?*

She turned on a bit of cold water, adjusting the temperature, and switching the tap to the nozzle. "So I'm going to rinse your hair, okay?"

Fabia gently pushed his head back against the tub, and the man closed his eyes, more against her view of him, she thought, than the impending rinse. Slowly, she brought the water to his head, first rinsing off some of the lavender foam and then, in sections, the blood. The man made a muffled groan, catching the sound in his throat before it really left his mouth. Fabia pulled the water away and pushed away a wet piece of hair to reveal three long, thin cuts running from crown to forehead.

"Oh," she said. "Well, there are the culprits. But they're not deep. Just bleeding like scalp wounds do."

She brought the nozzle gently back to his head, rinsing away the rest of the blood and foam, the reddish water filling the tub. The man reclined quietly, his eyes still closed. With his hair slicked back on his head, the dirt gone, she saw that despite the bruises, he was a truly good-looking man, handsome really, his skin the color of almonds, his lips full and red.

Don't, she warned Niall, but even as she thought the word, she knew that Niall had fallen asleep in front of the television. She'd have to shout him awake (by either thought or throat) if she needed him.

"I'm going to have to drain this water," she said. "And then fill it up again so I can wash your hair. Do you, um . . . do you want a towel to cover yourself while I do that?"

The man opened his eyes, watching her. He blinked and then sat up, holding his knees tight and tucking his head down.

At that protective move, Fabia wanted to weep. She wanted to strangle whoever had done this to him. She hated when people inflicted their power on others, taking away strength and power and basic, flipping dignity. That's why she wanted to hunt down Macara. That's why she wanted to find Quain—to stop him before he turned one more person to him, creating more darkness than light. What had happened to this big man in the bathtub would happen to many, and it was wrong. It had to be stopped.

Leaning over the tub, Fabia pulled the plug and then turned the water back on, adjusting the temperature. The water drained, the tub emptying even as it filled with clean warmth. She didn't want to look at the man, but she couldn't help herself, especially because she knew Niall was asleep and wouldn't read anything into her gaze. The man was not stringy and thin like many tall men, but powerful, his arms and chest tight with muscles, his thighs rounded and firm. Fabia flicked her eyes toward his middle, but she couldn't see anything down there, his arms and body folded too tight.

You are a sick girl, she thought. *Sick and potentially dangerous.*

Once the tub was almost full, Fabia put in the plug and grabbed the shampoo. Squeezing a large dollop into one hand, she gently pressed the man back so she could wash his hair. As he leaned back, his arms lessening their grip on his knees, she forced herself to be polite, keeping her eyes on his face. Fabia smiled, letting her fingers slip gently on his scalp, avoiding the three scratches. Without meaning to, she began to hum the song Xanthe had always sung around the house, a made-up tune of light happy notes. It was the song her mother sang when she cooked and worked in the garden. This was the song her mother sang when she bathed them and fed them and came to their minds at night when they had nightmares. All her life, Fabia had known the melody, the light up and down of notes, and realized—with her hands in this man's hair—that it was a song about love and care.

The man moved under her hands, and she looked down. He was staring up at her with his black eyes, his lips trembling, and in a quick second, Fabia pulled his wet, soapy head to her chest, letting him lean against her, pulling him tight.

For a moment, the room was still, and then she heard his cries, harsh, deep, jagged sounds that seemed to cut his throat and mouth as they made their passage into the room.

"There, there," she said. "It's been terrible, hasn't it? I don't know what you've been through, but it was bad. So bad. But you're safe now. I won't let them hurt you. I'll make sure you're all right."

And then she began to hum again, her mother's song flooding the room, covering his cries, stilling him as he pressed himself tight against her.

Fabia finished washing the man's hair and then conditioned it, needing a comb to get through all the snarls and tangles. Wet, it hung almost to his waist, the dark strands curling even as they lay soaked on his skin. As she'd helped him out of the tub, she couldn't help but notice he was well built all over, letting her eyes linger on him for a moment before she felt her blush burning on her face. Now he sat safely wrapped in towels on the toilet as Fabia braided his hair.

"I never had a sister," she said, the slick wet hair sliding between her fingers. "So my braiding is a bit below par."

The bathroom door opened, and Niall walked in, yawning. "The beauty class over? Was it braiding tonight?"

Fabia nodded. "And now it's your turn. A right

shave. I'd do it, but I fancy he likes his throat whole."

Niall shrugged, and Fabia felt her brother try to get into the man's mind, searching for a thought to turn over and examine. But still, there was nothing but darkness, the man's mind only a conglomeration of the events in the past two hours, images of cold, heat, water, voices, smells, and, yes, comfort. When Fabia looked in, all she saw was emptiness and a few fleeting sensory images, one of them her own body, a warm fragment floating in his mind.

You've made a good impression, Niall thought. *But who did this to him*?

I have no idea. But it was one of us. Croyant. *This isn't amnesia or a knock on the head or mental illness. It's a* sortilège du blanc*, and a good one*. "So, Niall's going to give you a quick shave, and I'm going to fix you some soup."

Fabia let go of the man's long braid and moved away. As she did, he reached out for her, gently taking her wrist in his hand. She looked down at him, and his eyes were fixed on hers, scared, tense.

"Why don't you stay with us?" Niall said, opening the medicine cabinet. "It will only take a couple of minutes, and this way, he won't imagine I'm going to attack with the double blades." Niall looked at Fabia's razor. "Oh! Triple blades. How high-tech. I guess you need something intense for that thicket on your shins."

She rolled her eyes and sat down on the edge of the tub, patting the man's wrist. "I'll stay."

Niall brought him to the sink, the man watching Fabia as he stood before the mirror. Quickly, Niall filled the sink, lathered the man's face, and brought the razor to his throat, holding it just above the bright red circle there, evidence of someone trying to suck the very air from him.

Flinching, the man turned to look at Fabia, who unconsciously put her hand at her own throat.

"It'll be fine. I promise."

"Come on, man," Niall coaxed. "I usually only take off a pound of flesh a day."

Niall! Fabia thought, and in that instant, she thought the man heard her, his eyebrows raising, his mouth opening a bit, his mind trying to hold on to a thought, a memory, an idea. But then Niall had him turned to the mirror and ran the razor up the man's stubbly face.

As her brother worked, his blue eyes intense with the activity, Fabia looked at the man. She'd seen a *sortilège du blanc* once, years ago. Actually, she'd only heard about it, her father coming home to tell Xanthe about a *sorcier* so angry with his wife, he'd taken away the memories of their marriage and life together and then left her alone in their house, a numb, thoughtless shell. The husband's magic had been so strong, the wife didn't recover for months, long after their marriage had been severed, long after her husband was brought before the *Croyant* Council and sent to the *Bagne de Complet*, where the prisoners had no magic, no movement, no thoughts at all.

So was this man *Croyant*? Had he fallen in the way of a powerful *sorcier*? And what had he been before someone had wiped his mind completely clean? What would he be after?

"A vision!" Niall declared, rinsing off the razor and putting it away. He dried the man's face with the towel and then opened the medicine chest again, grabbing a bottle full of amber liquid. "I have a new calling. I will open a shop forthwith. But I need to top him off." Niall held out the bottle. "A little leftover aftershave? From that nutter Timo?"

Fabia rolled her eyes but smiled as Niall poured a little of the fragrance on his hands and then carefully patted the man's face.

Fabia stood up, looking at the man, who winced as the aftershave moved into his skin. Whoever or whatever he was, he *was* a vision, the lines of his face clean and defined and strong. He was gorgeous, his skin as smooth as his thoughts.

Just what you've always wanted, Niall thought. *A man with no baggage. Not even a wee rucksack. No mind either, but what's that compared to such brawn?*

Fabia shook her head and grabbed the bathrobe off the hook, helping the man into it, taking away the towels as soon as he was properly covered. And even though she could only read his confusion and random, here-and-now images, she knew he felt better, calmer, his body clean and warm, his fears put into a quiet corner, at least for now.

Thank you, Niall, she thought, smiling at her twin.

For once, Niall didn't crack a joke, his thoughts on the man's empty memory. *There's still work to do here, you know.*

I know. But he's hungry.

So am I. That pie wasn't near enough. Why don't you get some carryout? A poke of chips at least.

Fabia watched the man, who again seemed to hear them, his eyes on her. What was he in his life? she wondered. He seemed the kind of man who would care for others, not the type to be cared for. He was probably married and had children, his family destroyed by his absence.

Niall caught on to her thoughts. *Your Prince Charming is a mute nutter with ten children. Let's eat.*

Fabia sighed. *Okay. But no carryout.*

"Come have some soup," she said to the man, taking his arm and leading him toward the kitchen. For now, even if he was a caretaker and married and without a past, Fabia knew she wanted to help him, needed to. She felt connected to him, brought into his life by his black eyes, by his wet arms reaching around her waist and pulling her tight, pulling her into his story.

Chapter Two

He was tumbling, leaving something behind. His heart. His mind. Or someone. Who?

He was tumbling.

He was leaving a person behind, someone who mattered, someone he was supposed to protect.

He was flying through matter, being pushed by—by someone. Who?

He was cold.

All he could feel was his lungs, the air of this place crackling down his throat. After a while, the sun tapped on his skin like a tentative visitor and then left. People walked back and forth, the street filling and emptying in waves, a tide of noise.

His body shook with cold and nerves, every piece of him jangling on his skin.

Then she was leaning over him. Her? No. Not again. Not what again? He didn't know what she had done before or what she was capable of now, but his body clenched, everything pounding inside him. He blinked, wondering what he was supposed to do. Run? Go with her? Give up, letting something terrible happen, but he didn't know what the terrible thing was. Unformed answers buzzed in his head, his mind ringing with too much nothing.

He was cold.

Her voice was soft, though, and easy to follow. His legs believed her, so he followed his body down the street toward a building.

Suddenly, he wasn't cold. He was inside, and she was talking to him, filling a room with heat and sound, the thick, warm air deadening the buzz of confusion in his brain.

Was it her again? Again, he felt his body respond, his insides buzzing with memory. Was she coming after him? He didn't remember who she was, but this time, he would hurt, kill, fight. He would stop her from doing . . . what? He flinched, his muscles contracting, reading for release, but then he heard someone else, a man. Was it—was it . . . ?

He didn't know who the man was, but then he was warm, sitting in warmth, his bones filled with heat now. And then she was looking at him, down at him, inside him. He felt her lightly skimming his mind, and he wanted to tell her things but he didn't know what to tell her. Thoughts stuck on his tongue like dirt clods. His mind was a dark room.

Her fingers touched him, rubbing his hair, so softly, the pain leaving his mind and body. Reaching out, he pulled this feeling to him, and the feeling felt like flesh, warmth, a woman who held him back, saying soft words that slipped into his ears.

She sat him down, touching his hair, and he almost remembered something, another woman doing the same thing. An older woman, her voice so familiar he thought he could grab it out of the air.

The man came back into the room. But then there was metal. More metal, like before, jangling metal!

He felt his heart slam against his chest, but the woman said more words, and then there was the smell of forest and then flowers, and a swoosh of pressure on his face, tingling. The man and woman laughed, touched him, led him into another room.

The ache in his body left because of more warmth, this time inside him. He realized he was chewing, eating something that felt heavy and hot on his tongue and throat. He must have fallen into darkness, because then the man and woman were walking him to another room, laying him down, covering him up until he wanted to scream. *Not again! This won't happen again!*

The woman grabbed him, whispered the same comforting sounds, leaving his shoulders free this time. They both stood over him, the woman patting his arm, and as he somehow floated into sleep, he wondered who they were. Wondered, as he fell asleep, who he was.

Chapter Three

"Are you sure you'll be all right?" Niall put on his blue robe, fastening it around his neck. "I can huckle him out of here right now."

Fabia yawned and nodded, looking at the kitchen counter full of soup dishes and glasses, the cutting board dusty with brown bread crumbs. "Yes, I know I'll be fine because you never leave even when you're gone."

"You're not to be trusted. The minute I ignore you, you're off to some drug-infested flat or, even worse, dating some sad sod."

"One day we're going to have to stop it." As she said the words, she felt a flare of sadness move through her and then to Niall, who caught it and held it softly.

"I know. I know," he said, breathing in and sending her back a warm, soft feeling she let spread throughout her body, calming her. "But for right now, who else is going to protect you? This guy sleeping in the only bed in your house *seems* to be your basic insane case, but you going after Macara is what worries me. You keep waiting for the perfect lead, and what will happen when you finally find it? I keep thinking you'll go off by yourself and have a go at him. I imagine one night when I'm asleep you'll hear something and off you'll be."

Fabia turned on the tap, washing bowls and putting them in the drainer. Of course, Niall was right. Macara was dangerous, but finding people was what she was good at. She and Niall were only twenty-eight, but ever since she could remember, the world had opened up to her in a funnel of sound. As she lay in her childhood bedroom, she realized that not only could she hear her brother's every sleeping thought, but she could also hear her parents' dreams, their neighbor Mrs. McClellan's telephone fights with her daughter in the States, the farmers in the countryside calming animals in distress. The noise of the world flushed over her like a terrifying fever, intense and loud and hot.

When Niall fell asleep, he took away the buffer she was able to hide behind during the day. With him off and dreaming, all the chatter of the neighborhood and town would become so overwhelming that Fabia had invented a friend to talk with to drown out the drone of the world, a boy she called Tilly. One night, she'd called out to him, thinking, *Tilly, where are you? Where can you be? I know you're there!*

As she called out to him, she saw him sleeping on his twin bed, his brown eyes blinking into the darkness of his room. He'd been waiting for her, she knew it, and she called to him again.

"I see you, Tilly. Don't hide. Talk to me."

Fabia sat up in bed and leaned against the headboard, imagining Tilly closing his eyes and turning away from her call, but to her surprise, he answered, a bit shyly at first. "Who is it?"

"It's me," Fabia had said, almost laughing with relief. "Princess Sofia! And you're Tilly."

"Tilly?" Tilly said. "That's a dorky name. But okay. Just for dreams, though."

"How old are you?" Fabia asked. "What are you doing? Where do you live?"

"God, slow down. We have all night."

But Fabia didn't want to think about all night. Night was too loud.

"I just wanted to know," Fabia said, trying to keep her nervousness out of her voice, but Tilly seemed to understand. He always did.

"All right. I'm eleven. I'm at school."

"Where is your school?"

"Oh, in dragon country. I catch them. With me and my friends. Then we fly them on journeys to the Red Sea and the Himalayas and the Sahara."

"I've been to the desert," Fabia said, thinking of the time she and Niall dreamed the same hot dream and ended up in a tent with a horse. But Xanthe and Donoch found them before they'd even had a chance to push aside the fabric door to look outside at the Saudi sunrise.

"You have?" Tilly seemed confused. "Where do you live—"

"But I've never seen a dragon. But my brother told me they have bad breath."

"You believe in dragons?"

Fabia snorted. "Of course I believe in dragons. Who doesn't?"

Tilly was silent for a moment and then laughed. "A lot of people."

"They're dumb people," Fabia said. "Tell me more. Tell me everything."

And Tilly did. Every night, Fabia tried to find him and he told her more stories about dragons and trolls and goblins and scary magic tricks. He told her jokes like "I'm such a fat boy, I can only play seek." And he asked her questions about her life. Like him, she made up stories. She told him that her parents the king and queen were embarrassed by her because she had such enormous ears, she wasn't allowed to leave the house because people mistook her for an elephant. She had seven prince brothers who rode through the kingdom every day, guarding against bad knights. All of them were ten feet tall and had hair as red as cinnamon candy.

The strange thing was, even her imaginary friend Tilly seemed to fall asleep, and the night became agony. Sometimes if she listened really hard, she could wake Tilly, listen to him yawn and stretch, and pull one more story out of him about his brothers Ludo and Super Weasel, the amazing half boy, half animal child his parents adopted.

One night, she couldn't shut down any of the sound, the world like a horrible radio on full blast, the commercials for dishwashers and the daily news and the call-in shows and the music all going at once.

"Don't," Tilly said into the darkness. "Don't listen."

"I can't help it," Fabia cried out. "It's too loud. I hate it."

"I wouldn't like it either. But do this. Listen to your breathing," Tilly said. "You know, feel your chest and stuff. Watch it go up and down."

"I can't see it," Fabia wailed.

"Well, take off your blankets," Tilly said.

Fabia pulled off her covers and stared at her nightgown. There. She moved her chest. "I'm doing it."

"Okay. Keep breathing. Keep watching. You know, like *one, two, one, two*."

For a moment, the radio kept blaring, but then, as she watched her breath and the flannel of her nightgown going up and down, she relaxed, calmed, closed her eyes.

"I'm here," Tilly said. "Just breathe."

Fabia did what he said until she forgot she was doing anything. When she woke up in the morning, Tilly was gone.

But more often than not, she found herself alone in the early morning hours, unable to tune out the sounds. Panicked, she wanted to hide in her room all day, ineffective pillows clamped around her ears. But after some persuasion, Xanthe and Donoch convinced her to meet with Adalbert Baird. In his cozy lounge in his house at Rabley Heath in Kent, England, Adalbert sat her down and stared at her, his hand moving through his long gray beard.

"What are you scared of hearing?" he asked.

Fabia bit the inside of her cheek, wondering if she could tell him the truth. Not only was everything just too loud, she was scared of people's most personal secrets and whispers and fears, their deepest pains, their enormous sorrows. She wasn't sure how to say that their tears made her have some of her own, when she felt Adalbert pick out her thoughts and read it.

"A full human life can be a terrifying thing to witness," he said. "And to hear more than what you should at your young age is difficult. But you must learn to discriminate. To winnow out, to discern. You'll need to be a big girl and really work hard, or what I teach you won't work."

Fabia nodded. "I promise. I don't want to hear anything unless I want to. Unless I ask it in."

Adalbert petted the ancient black-haired dog that slept next to his feet. The dog sighed loudly, turned on its back for a good rub.

"If only we could be so easily content," Adalbert said, smiling at Fabia. "None of this training would be necessary at all."

For the next week, Adalbert taught her to focus, to let her mind twirl into a slim stream of concentration. He showed her that she could unfurl it whenever she wanted to, controlling when she wanted to open up her head like a satellite dish.

And by the time she came home from Adalbert's, Fabia didn't even think to look for Tilly, knowing now how to shut the world off when she wanted to. In later years, she was almost positive she made up Tilly out of her own upset, creating all those long discussions in order to distract herself.

When Fabia went to Bampton Academy at thirteen, she was an expert—opening and shutting her hearing as easily as a window—and promised her teachers she'd keep her hearing in check so as not to figure out what was on every test and quiz and exam. In her personal life, she learned she didn't want to know that Pelagia Solon thought she was a show-off and Dakka Duhamel thought her lips were fat.

So she opened up her ears and mind only when she was needed, only when it was useful. Like now as she tried to track down Macara.

I know, thought Niall, his long robe flowing around him as he walked toward her. *I know it's needed. This is important work. Macara must be stopped.*

He pulled her close. *You're amazing. But I worry.*

Don't stop worrying, she thought back, knowing that Niall's constant voice in her head stayed her loneliness. *Please. Even if we row all the time.*

Niall squeezed her, kissed her on the temple, and

then stood back. "Okay. I'm off. Let me know what happens with Cave Dude in there."

"Niall," Fabia said, laughing, but her brother was gone, whipped away into matter, already, she knew, taking off his robe at his apartment in the Latin Quarter in Paris, the lit-up Luxembourg Gardens just across the street.

After retrieving the man's dry clothing from the laundry room, Fabia cleaned up the kitchen, turning off the lights as she left. Next, she went into the bathroom to tidy up after the man's bath and shave. From the dark ring around the tub, it was clear he'd gone a long time without a wash. How long had he been wandering with his head as shut down as a locked cellar? Wasn't someone looking for him? Hadn't someone missed him and alerted the authorities, posting photos with details and reward information?

If I lost a man like that, she thought, thinking of him standing before the mirror, his body clean, his face smooth and dark and handsome, *I'd put out an all-points bulletin. I'd insist on a manhunt of epic proportions.*

Fabia laughed at herself and finished scrubbing the tub and then rinsed it down with the nozzle. She washed her face, brushed her teeth, and then wiped down the sink, everything restored to its former pristine state.

Shaking her head, Fabia sighed and flicked off the bathroom light. Her pristine state. Aside from her working at the clinic with Alan and Gillian and monitoring thoughts for any inkling of Macara or Quain, her life was smooth and clean and immaculate, unfettered by deep anything. She had relationships with Bridgit at the coffee shop, Connor at the market,

Basil at the newspaper stand, and Miko at the Tampopo Noodle Bar. Oh! and how could she forget Liam from downstairs? Where would she be without deflecting his shallow advances?

After Donoch retired from the *Le Banqué des Croyants* and Xanthe from her healing practice, they'd moved to Olympia, Washington, in the States two years ago to volunteer with a radical group promoting *Moyenne/Croyant* social integration. When she touched them with her mind, her parents' voices seemed younger, happier, and Fabia didn't like to yank them into matter and Edinburgh unless it was necessary. Sure, her mother's sister, Aunt Nessa, lived just across town, but she was often off on spontaneous world trips at a moment's notice, currently favoring Jamaica and a *sorcier* named Devon. Without Niall, Fabia would have no real relationship at all.

And dates? All of them were ridiculous, men she met for quick talks at teahouses or restaurants, well-meaning setups by Gillian or Alan or even Niall. She just didn't have the energy to invest a thought in a strange man, especially when her last two steady boyfriends turned out to be more than disappointing.

Sitting in the pity patch again? she thought, pulling blankets and pillows out of the hallway closet and tossing them on the sofa. She was glad that Niall was already asleep, or he'd be thinking back, *Watch out for thorns in your arse.*

Fabia locked the door, turned off the lights, lay down on the sofa, and shut her head down, wanting to only hear the noises in the apartment. There was the tick of the clock on the bookcase, the whine and bend of straining plumbing in the walls, the hum of Liam's constant television buzzing up through the floor, and the quiet, deep breathing of the man in her room. Nothing out of the ordinary. Nothing she couldn't deal with. No signs of Macara or Quain or the world falling apart. Nothing unusual, all right with this tiny corner of the planet, she thought, yawning, closing her eyes, and falling into a quick, deep sleep.

In the morning, Fabia woke early, before the sky had paled into gray. Automatically, she scanned the flat, the building, the surrounding area for sound, just as she had done her whole life. But as she did, she almost laughed, knowing that the only out-of-the-ordinary thing she would find this day was sleeping in her bed. The man with no name or no memory.

She pushed away her blankets and stood, walking quietly to the door, wanting to peek in before she went to the loo. After his long ordeal out in the clacking Edinburgh cold, she'd expected him to sleep all night and much of today, his body and mind shredded from whatever had happened to him. But as she looked into the room, she saw him sitting up, his arms clasped around his knees, his eyes wide and alert.

When he saw her, he jumped, pressed back against the wall, and she almost cried out, at the last moment tamping her sound down in her throat. Her distress would only add to his, so she walked slowly and softly to the bed, sitting on the edge of the mattress.

"Do you remember coming here last night? I found you on Mrs. Macatee's steps. Remember that, don't you?" Fabia spoke low, using the voice she'd cultivated at the clinic for children.

The man breathed out in a long exhale and

seemed to relax a bit, his hands loosening on his knees. He blinked, looked at her, and then nodded.

"I'm Fabia. Remember? And this is my flat. I'm not going to hurt you."

The man bit his lip, and then nodded again, scooting away from the wall but keeping his distance from Fabia.

"Would you like to use the loo?" she asked, knowing that she certainly had to. But he'd clearly been up for quite a while.

The man's face relaxed, and he nodded again. But he didn't move, his eyes now on the space between him and Fabia. She stood up from the bed and reached out a hand.

"Come on, then. You first." She moved her hand a bit, urging him to take it, and he finally did, pushing himself across the bed. When he sat on the edge, Fabia pulled him up until he stood next to her. He was so tall, and for a quick, weird second, she was afraid.

What now? Niall thought. *Don't be blate. You can handle him.*

That's not what you said last night, Fabia threw back. *You just want to stay in bed.*

Maybe so. Niall laughed, the happy sound a *ping, ping* in her head. *But are you all right?*

Aye, Fabia thought, pulling gently on the man's hand, leading him to the door. *We're just going to the loo.*

Christ, he's worse than a pet. Can you imagine the size of that kitty box?

For the love of God, Niall. Go back to bed, Fabia thought, cutting him off and heading down the hall, the man behind her.

Fabia walked into the bathroom, flicking on the light. She led the man in, let go of his hand, and began to back away, closing the door slowly as she edged out of the room. Before she had the door completely closed, she glanced up quickly, hoping that the man had moved toward the toilet. But, like last night, he seemed unable to figure out the basics, needing her or Niall to help him out.

Fabia closed her eyes. He wasn't even like a pet. He was more like one of the toddlers that she cared for at the clinic. Every day, she held pudgy hands as she walked them to the loo, explaining the magic of going tiddly in a big person's pot.

But he wasn't a toddler. He was a grown man someone had tortured and hurt, and here he was in her flat needing her help.

Fabia sighed, opened her eyes, and opened the door wide. He was overwhelmed, stunned as he stood on the cold tile floor, his brain full of static and buzz. Whoever had taken his memories had taken his basic human rights and abilities, too, stripping him down to a time just after birth.

"Well, come on, then," Fabia said, her face flushed. She would just go ahead and think of him like that little boy the other day at the clinic, Kieran.

"Look, I'm a fountain!" Kieran had squealed, his tiny yellow arc before him. The child had laughed at the noise he'd made, smiling wide at Fabia.

She walked toward the man and put a hand on his shoulder, pushing him gently toward the toilet. "Okay, let's pull down these pajamas."

He looked at her, his face blank, and Fabia shook her head. *Dear Lord.*

Taking in a swift breath, she undid the tie belt and let the pajamas fall to the floor, pulling her eyes away from him. But then she froze. There was no way she was going to hold it for him. But he had to hurry because she had to go, too, and she bit her lip, hoping that he would figure it out now. What had Niall done last night?

I sat him down like a lass, Niall thought. *Put him right down on his arse end and let him do his business.*

Without saying a word, Fabia turned the man and sat him down. And thankfully, all the right parts were tucked in proper.

"That's it. Now you can go. I'll just leave you to it." She turned, shaking her head, flushed and red and shamed for her and him. Angry, too, at whoever had done this.

She was just about at the door, when he seemed to speak, a harsh, split sound that echoed in the loo. Fabia looked back. His eyes were as wide as they'd been in the bedroom, his face pale.

Swallowing, Fabia turned and sighed. She sat on the edge of the bathtub, but she didn't look at him. "I'll stay. Go ahead."

The man didn't make another sound, nor did he do anything else. Then she remembered the trick she'd learned at school when all the girls giggled in the stalls, waiting for someone to do something embarrassing. Standing quickly, Fabia leaned over to the sink and turned on the tap, ignoring the call her bladder made to the flowing water.

She sat back down, and then in a minute, she heard the man do, as Niall said, his business. As soon as she was sure he was done, Fabia turned off the water and went to him, helping him stand, and pulling up his pajamas. Try as she might, she couldn't help glancing at his equipment again. He was such an exceptionally well put together man in all ways, tall and strong and—

Well hung? Niall thought. *Strapping? Fully endowed?*

You noticed, too? Fabia flipped back, tying the man's belt. *Jealous, are you? How do you stack up? Just a bit wee down there?*

Niall blew her a thought raspberry and thought nothing else.

Taking the man's hand again, Fabia walked him to the door. "Now it's my turn. Just stay here. I'm going to close the door. But I'll be out in a second."

The man stopped walking, and she could feel his quick, panicked pulse beat in his palm. Then he began to shake, and she rolled her eyes. "For the love of God! Fine. Sit here. Don't look."

She sat him down on the bathtub edge and turned the water back on. It would take her minutes to pee in these circumstances. Who knew what her water bill would be after a few days of living with this man?

Feeling red all over, she sat down on the toilet, letting her hair fall in front of her face. She hadn't gone to the bathroom in front of a man, ever. Even though Fletcher was a doctor, she'd never let him in the loo with her. He'd had no compunction about bursting in while she was putting on her makeup, and peeing loudly while she stroked on her mascara. And this was one thing she and Niall didn't share, not since she was about three and asked her mother, Xanthe, why Niall had a worm for a wee-wee.

Looking up through her hair, she saw that the man was obeying her, staring straight ahead of him. Sighing, she closed her eyes and thought about rivers and oceans and rain puddles. Finally, as she listened to the tap, she felt her body relax and do what it needed to.

Quickly, she stood up and pulled down her nightgown, pulling the chain on the toilet. She washed her hands, turned off the water, and faced the man, who looked up at her.

"We are going to have to figure a plan," she said. "Maybe this worked out, but I am not going to—I mean, I can't do anything else in here with you sitting on the bathtub. Or vice versa for that matter. Do you understand? Am I being perfectly clear about this?"

He blinked. For a second, Fabia saw words and ideas flicker across his face, a response, maybe even a smile begin to form on his lips. But then he shook his head and rubbed his eyes.

"Don't worry about it now," she said, sorry she'd been so firm. He wouldn't remember what she was telling him anyway. She took his hand and helped him up. "I just won't feed you much. How's that? No fiber, that's for sure."

He didn't seem to understand, but then he squeezed her hand, his fingers strong and tight on hers.

"Well, maybe some toast. Cheese. Lots of cheese," Fabia said, almost laughing. And she pulled him out of the loo and into the kitchen for breakfast.

Before she'd fallen asleep the night before, Fabia imagined that as soon as things opened, she'd take the man around to the clinic, to the police station, or to the Social Work Department. Someone would have missed this man and reported his absence to the authorities. But now as she watched him try to eat his buttered toast, she knew that he was in no state to go anywhere. As he lifted the bread to his mouth, his hand shook; when she stood up from the table, he flinched; when she laughed at something she read in *The Scotsman*, he put his hands over his eyes, cowering in his chair.

She tried to reach into his mind, but still it was a swirl of confusion and fear, no facts, no clues, no way to determine who he was or where he was from. So after she slowly cleared the breakfast things and did the dishes, trying not to make any quick movements, she took him into the living room and got him comfortable on the sofa. It was going to be a sick day—the kind Xanthe would let her have now and then when she was very little, before she went away to Bampton. Instead of having to do her lessons and practice magic, Fabia and her mother would curl up on the sofa and read, do crossword puzzles, and watch television. They never dressed, staying in their nightgowns all day, and made it a point to get up as few times as possible. When Fabia went to the academy, those sick days were one of the things she missed the most.

The man watched her as she arranged a pillow behind his head and then covered him with a blanket.

"So the thing is, we stay here all day. Nothing like a day of rest to set things to rights. You need to let me know, of course, when you have to go back to the . . . well, the loo. But otherwise, we watch TV or sleep or have a little tea." Fabia got herself cozy at the other end of the sofa, picking up a copy of *Hello!* Basil at the newsstand had slipped her a few days earlier. She flipped through a couple of pages, shaking her head at the strange things that *Moyenne* thought were worth two or three glossy pages. Movie stars' weddings or nonweddings. Prince This or That doing whatever. President, Prime Minister, Parliamentarian *Who's It* or *What's It* cheating on Spouse A or Spouse B or Spouse C. On and on it went through the whole magazine. Putting it down with a sigh, she was about to pick up *Informations des Croyant Matin*, when she noticed the man still looking at her, his expression unchanged since she put the blanket on him.

Of course he couldn't read now. He couldn't even

think. Fabia looked at her bookcase and then stood up, walking over to the shelf, and pulling down a copy of *The Mists of Avalon*. Xanthe had given it to her on her thirteenth birthday, just before she and Niall went to Bampton. At night, she'd created a little reading light spell and read it under her covers, loving that the magic in this *Moyenne* novel was almost right. What had her mother said? "This *Moyenne* writer got it. She knows her magic."

Fabia smiled. "Let me read this book to you," she said, sitting closer to him, tugging her blanket over her legs. "This is my favorite story."

She opened the book, spreading it on her lap. She glanced up at the man, who was staring at the pages, waiting. A strand of hair had come loose from his braid, and without thinking, Fabia reached out for it and tucked it behind his ear. At her movement, the man sucked in air, holding his large breath when she first touched him, and then releasing it as she smoothed his hair. Fabia ran her hand on his hair once more, his long dark hair so smooth, and again she felt such sadness for him. Underneath his confusion and fear, she could tell he was a good man. A strong man. A safe man.

Niall, she thought, still stroking the man's hair. *We have to help him find his family.*

I know, Niall thought. *Let him rest today and we'll figure it out tomorrow. I'll help you.*

Fabia slowly took her hand away from his hair, letting it fall to his shoulder. *If he's up to it. I might have to stay around the house another day with him.*

Let me know, Niall thought. *I'll poke about to see if I can come up with anything.*

Thanks, she thought, and then she felt Niall's thoughts move away.

Fabia tried to find the man's gaze, and she saw he was crying without sound, his cheeks wet.

"Don't," she said, empathetic tears building inside her chest. "Oh, don't."

She plucked a tissue from the box on the coffee table and tried to hand it to him, but he just stared at it. So she wiped his eyes, until he stopped crying.

"Listen, there's nothing better to mend a pain than a story," she said. "This one got me through leaving home, fights with Niall, and bad marks in school. Let's give it a try, why don't we?"

The man actually nodded, and Fabia smiled. "That's it. A good story. Nothing better."

He blinked, and she began to read, letting the words calm them both.

It was late afternoon and already dusk, the fall light hazy in the city sky. The man was asleep, and Fabia wasn't sure what to do. Somewhere around chapter 6, he'd leaned over onto her shoulder and fallen into a deep sleep, his breath heavy and regular. Now his arms were around her, his cheek against her chest. The remote for the telly was just inches away, but Fabia didn't dare grab for it, not wanting to wake him. If he awakened, they'd most likely have to go back to the loo, a trip she'd rather not repeat today. Just after lunch, he'd had to go, and this time, she turned on the shower head, wishing she could jump under the water while he went. He didn't seem to enjoy the experience that much either, but when she'd tried to leave, he'd begun to shake, just like in the morning.

By the time she had to go, she made him stand by the door facing it, and she'd turned on the shower and opened the window. Never in her life had she felt so ridiculous and stupid, and she'd had to ignore Niall's laughter from Paris at the same time. Thank God she was already potty trained or she would be scarred for life.

But this nap on the sofa she could handle. In fact, if she admitted it to herself, she liked it. He had no memories, but he did seem to know how to move into another person, his arms practiced, his want of a woman's body clear. She thought of the woman who was his wife. With some vestige of memory, he must be crying out for her flesh, for her arms. He was too comfortable next to Fabia to be unpracticed with intimacy.

Fabia settled herself a bit closer, not quite sure if she should enjoy this closeness. But his hand was only inches from her breast, and when he'd first settled his fingers on her, she'd had the desire for him to touch her.

Desperate, she thought to herself, making sure that Niall wasn't hovering in her mind somewhere. *Without a doubt, you are a nutter.*

But the man smelled good, still sweet with her bath salts, and his hair was soft on her neck. Sighing, she stared into the quiet lounge, sitting still as long as she could, knowing that this sleep would do him wonders. Maybe even now, his unconscious was wrestling with his demons—or, if this were a spell, the magic was wearing off, sleep erasing the evil incantation.

And in a way, this silence was good for her, too. She'd been so focused on finding Macara for years that she never really sat for no reason other than sitting. All day long, if she was at the clinic or not, she was listening. Both she and Niall as well as her parents wanted *Croyant* life to change. There had to be a way to bring *Moyenne* and *Croyant* together. *Croyant* needed *Moyenne* for all the infrastructure of the world—the roads and businesses and products and government systems. And the *Moyenne*, not having done such a great job with governments and societies—war after war after war—needed some magic, some way of realizing power without subduing another culture or bombing the hell out of a country. But it was people like Macara and Quain that fought this idea, wanting to hide magic from the other ninety-nine point five percent of the world's population. Really, they wanted to do away with the ninety-five percent so there was nothing to hide at all and they could have everything.

Without thinking, Fabia shook her head at the thought, and at her movement, the man shifted, yawned, moved his head off her.

She turned to him, smiling. "Well, that was a nice long nap."

And then he smiled back at her.

Fabia froze, not wanting to scare him out of his reaction, a normal reaction.

He didn't seem to notice that he'd done anything different, but instead, wiped his face with his hands and then looked at her again.

"So," Fabia began, noticing that he was pushing off his blanket.

The loo, she thought. *Here we go again.*

Without her help, he stood and waited for her to do likewise. Together, they walked into the hall and toward the loo. Behind him, Fabia was shaking her head, wondering how she would ever be able to tell anyone about this part of her adventure with the man. Gillian at the clinic would laugh so hard, her face would turn magenta and then she would tell Alan, who would pretend to take it all seriously and then laugh himself silly in the staff room. Niall already knew and would use it against her for the rest of her life.

But in the loo, the man didn't walk to the toilet, stopping instead at the tub. He cocked his head and almost seemed to shrug.

"You want a bath?" she asked.

He breathed in and pointed to the shower head.

"Ah, a shower. You're lucky an American bloke put in this plumbing. Otherwise, it would be the tub only." Fabia kept talking over her nerves. Seeing how the toilet issues had gone, she imagined she'd have to watch him shower as well. But they'd gone through this last night, and she'd survived.

Leaning over, Fabia turned on the water, letting it warm before she switched the stream to the showerhead. The man had pulled off his shirt by himself and was working his pajama tie. Finally, he undid the knot Fabia had tied earlier, and the bottoms fell to the floor.

Fabia averted her eyes, adjusted the water, and then held out her hand. But he was already stepping into the tub and then before she knew it, he'd pulled the curtain closed.

Well, she thought, standing still. *My.*

Our little lad's growing up, Niall thought. *Give him a wee bit of privacy.*

She wanted to protest. What if he fell or couldn't turn off the water or needed something? What if he became frightened or slipped or—

He's getting better, Niall thought. *His mind is coming back. Let the man have some space.*

Sighing, Fabia ignored Niall, but she picked up the man's pajamas and the T-shirt and put them on the counter and left the loo. She was about to close the door, but then she didn't.

He might need me, she defended herself to Niall, but something in Paris had caught his attention and he'd turned his mind away from her.

Fine, she thought, sitting down on a chair in the living room and crossing her legs. *Just fine.*

Chapter Four

Under the water, he thought he could remember something. Flashes of thought streaked through his mind, too quick to fully comprehend. But there was a woman—was it the woman who was with him all the time now? The blond one, the soft one, the warm one, the one who laughed and gave him things to eat?

And there was a man, a dark man. Not the man who had helped him the night before. Not that man who was blond like the woman and fair and full of laughter. This dark man was the one he'd hurt and betrayed and forgotten.

The man breathed in, sputtered as water poured into his mouth. *Stop it, stop it,* he thought. His mind settled for a moment as he undid his hair, struggling a bit with the band the woman had put in. But then he washed his hair, his body, feeling his skin, it almost seemed, for the first time. He ached, he tingled. His muscles were cramped and tight and sore, but this water, the woman's water, felt so good.

Under the showerhead, his mind seemed to make

sense, the images flowing in his thoughts in a constant current. He was in an apartment somewhere, with a woman who was caring for him. She had bathed him and fed him and talked to him. She'd talked to him as they sat together eating; she'd laughed with him. He was scared still, but not as much as he had been, even if he really didn't know why he'd been afraid in the first place. The woman was somewhere close, maybe just outside the curtain, and she would help him make sense of all of this. Her arms and voice calmed him, somehow, and he needed her *now, now, now*.

The man fumbled with the dials, trying to turn off the water, hearing a sound leave his mouth when the water dashed cold against him. He backed up, slipping slightly in the tub, but then she was there, pushing away at the curtain, turning off the water, holding out a towel.

He could breathe again. She was there, and then she was combing his hair as he sat, with long, steady, firm strokes. Then she was weaving strands back and forth, tugging at him with her fingers, fastening his braid with a band. She moved around the room, opening the cupboard, looking for something. She came back to him and then rubbed lotion on his arms, handing him the bottle, and he stared at it, seeing the black markings on it. He squinted, knowing the black markings meant something—they were the same shapes that had been on the thing the woman had looked at all day. The thing. A book. Words. Ideas. And this bottle had ideas on it, too, and he brought it to his face, seeing one suddenly make sense: moisture.

The woman smiled, took the bottle back, kneeled in front of him, and rubbed something on his legs, the smell like something from outside in his nose.

Maybe a plant of some kind. As she smoothed the stuff into him, he felt his body shift, change, heat pulsing up from his middle, and he turned away from her, knowing that this change was wrong. Very wrong.

She stopped rubbing him and said something to him, but he was too afraid to listen. She might make him leave her house and go back and sit outside. Maybe she would give him back to the other woman, the one who had hurt him. But then she had his face between her palms, and she was still smiling. Her eyes were a color he knew—blue—and her hair reminded him of hills he'd seen somewhere, dry hills in summer, blond and fine.

"It's all right, you know. Biology. Can't be helped. Don't think about it again. Let's dress you now and make some dinner."

He wanted to reach out and hold her face, too, tell her thank you, tell her *Bless you*, tell her to help the dark man he'd left. The man he had abandoned. But instead, he let her help him into a clean set of pajamas, watched her ignore the part of him that wanted her in a way his mind could not right now.

Later, he hoped he would remember to tell her what he was thinking now, to apologize. He needed to know how to make the sounds on his tongue that would thank her for everything she was doing. But now he would follow the woman into the room where they ate, listen to her talk, try to find the strand in his mind to make everything else make sense.

Chapter Five

Well? What have we got today? Niall said, the morning stretch in his voice making his voice lazy.

Fabia turned to the man who sat with her on a bench, a cup of coffee in his hands. They'd left the flat early, and she'd taken him on a short walk before going to the coffee shop. Bridgit opened up early, and she'd winked at Fabia as they walked in the door, bells ringing.

"So two coffees, is it now?" Bridgit asked. "What a change. What a surprise."

Fabia had felt her blush run down her face all the way to her chest. Thank goodness, she'd thought, that she was in a full coat and muffler.

The man had seemed to want his coffee, but now he simply held it to his lips. His eyes darted about so frequently, he hadn't managed to take one sip. He turned to her for a second, and she noticed that while his face was healing, he still had bruises, the welt under his eyes making him look more despairing.

He's nowhere near okay, she thought. *I was hoping that I'd be able to get him to rights today, but he's a wreck. I woke up with him standing next to the sofa this morning.*

Spiffy, he's after you already.

No, Niall, she thought. *He was scared. He was waiting for me to wake up.*

So what do you think? Moyenne *or* Croyant*?*

She looked at the man who had finally given up with his coffee, putting the cup on the sidewalk. He'd moved closer to her, his hand almost touching her thigh.

I don't know. If it's a sortilège du blanc, *it's the best one I've ever heard of, and the only one who could do that—*

Quain? What would he want with this man?

Exactly. He's just a lost man, Moyenne. *It's so sad. I should take him to the clinic and figure it all out.*

So why don't you? Get on with it, woman.

Fabia shook her head, trying to come up with some smart comeback, a struggle Niall heard.

You like him. You are clearly having some kind of nurse experience.

I am not. He's too scared. Bridgit's laugh almost made him run out of the store and into the street.

You fancy him.

I do not.

You do.

Fabia sighed, and the man looked at her, put his hand on her leg. She put her hand on top of his and bit her lip.

All right. I do a little. So bugger off and go to work.

Fine. But I'll be back later.

Fabia shut down her thoughts and turned to the

man. The man. What a horrid way of thinking about him, his existence being boiled down to an article and a noun. But he hadn't managed to say a word this morning, and she doubted that he had a clue what his name was. But to go on thinking about him like that was horrible. What about David? Or Paul? Or John.

"The thing is," she said. "I just can't tell what your name would be. Names are like symbols, you know. They mean something."

The man stilled, looked at her, gently squeezed her thigh.

"So you are tall and dark and, in a total cliché, handsome." She laughed, and his eyes widened.

"And you won't remember any of this. Or you don't even understand me now. So this is how I see it. Your name is something that invokes tall, dark, and handsome. What would it be?"

The man almost nodded, his eyes steady on hers.

"You get it, do you? Well, then, what about Rafe? Do you fancy that?"

He blinked and seemed to wait for her to say more.

"Okay, maybe not Rafe. What about Antonio? Jack? Jake? Adore that one. Or Fabrizio—wait, that's too precious. Fabrizio and Fabia. Gillian would never let me get over that if I turned up with a man named Fabrizio. I'd be the joke of the clinic."

Fabia sipped her own coffee, letting the dark taste float on her tongue for a moment. "I have it. Dante. Brilliant! Like the writer. It's perfect. You've clearly been through the levels of hell these past days, that's for certain."

Dante. She breathed in the name for a moment, and then sighed, knowing that she couldn't give this poor man a name until he could say it to her first. *A name is something you need to know in order to be who you are*, she thought. All her life, her name helped her understand how she was separate from Niall.

"Never mind," she said. "I'm being flipping ridiculous. You'll figure out your name, I know you will."

But when she looked at him, she knew that his mind was a far distance away from latching around a name, much less the story of how he ended up in Edinburgh and on Mrs. Macatee's stoop.

"Let's go back to the flat. We'll have another go at the novel."

Fabia stood up and reached out her hand. The man took a deep breath, took her hand, and stood up. It was going to be a long day, she knew, but at least he'd sorted himself out about the bathroom. He took care of himself right and proper today.

"Come on, then," she said, starting to walk, his hand tight in hers. "By tomorrow, everything will be just fine."

Fabia shot up, her hand at her throat. What was it? What was that sound?

She threw off the blankets, finding her breath, steadying her mind. A hoarse, sad cry filled the room, and she sat up from the sofa and then stood up. It was the man. Something was wrong.

She ran into the room and turned on the light. He was flinging himself in the bed, attacking something she couldn't see, his arms and fists beating away a strong and painful dream. Fabia felt her heart pulsing in her throat, her hands gripping her nightgown.

What should she do? A few more moments of screaming, and Liam would be sure to bang on his ceiling in a blind fit of jealousy. She closed her eyes and cried loudly, "*Arrêt!*"

But the man didn't stop, didn't rest, and from the apartment above, she heard the creak of Mrs. McLeod's irritated bedsprings.

Fabia bit her lip and moved forward, her hands in front of her, wondering what spell would work. Again, she tried to find her way into the man's mind, and though his thoughts heaved with energy and confusion, he was still blank.

"It's okay," she said, moving closer. "It'll be fine."

His eyes opened wide, and he shot up, his black eyes wild. "No," he cried, his voice crackling like foil paper.

"It's me, Fabia," she said, touching the end of the bed.

With a swift, fast move, the man had her in his grip and was pulling her down, his arms tight around her back and neck. For a second, she couldn't breathe, couldn't think of the proper spell to throw at him. In her mind, she cast about for Niall, but he wasn't answering her, off on a night of adventure with a woman.

Fabia knew she had to do something. The man could hurt her, his arms so powerful he was pushing all the air out of her body. She should just will herself into matter, but something made her stay in his tight, hurtful grip, made her listen to his hoarse cry of "Not again. Not this time. I won't let you have him."

Without knowing why, Fabia tilted her head and whispered into his ear, "I'm here," and then with the only part of her that she could move, she put her lips on his neck, pressing into him with the heat of her body, his pulse under her lips. Thinking about everything good that she knew—love, family, laughter, sunrise, a hot bath, a good book, a cup of coffee on a cold morning, this very press of flesh on flesh—

she moved into his struggling body and his empty mind, filling him with her thoughts, even as her breath grew weak and her head full of stars.

Slowly, so slowly, he stopped thrashing, his grip lessened, and he lay back against the pillow, breathing heavily. Fabia felt the tears dripping down his neck, and she moved away just a bit. At her retreat, he pulled her back, and she didn't fight him, keeping all the good thoughts flowing between them.

"She has him," he said, his voice scratchy and full of unuse. "She took him. She made him do what she wanted."

"Who?" Fabia asked, wishing she could sit up and look at his face, but his arm was still tight around her. "Who took whom?"

The man shook his head. "I don't know. I have no idea at all."

"Do you know who you are? Did you remember something?" Fabia asked, moving away slightly when he relaxed again, and yet again, he pulled her close, pulling her close to his skin, where she breathed in the whiff of lavender soap on his skin.

He shook his head against the pillow. Above them, Mrs. McLeod settled back to bed, her bedsprings creaking and then falling silent.

He cleared his throat, the noise rumbling in Fabia's ear. "Do you know who I am?"

"No," she said. "I don't."

"Why have you been so kind?" he asked, finally releasing her. Fabia scooted slowly over, not wanting him to feel alarmed or rejected. "Why didn't you send me somewhere, get rid of me?"

She opened her mouth, ready to talk about the clinic and her work there, how she and Alan and Gillian and the rest of the staff wanted to make sure every single person in Edinburgh had a bed and warm meal each day. But as she formed words in her head, she realized that her volunteer work wasn't necessarily why he was here in her bed, tended to by her own hand, smelling of her favorite Body Shop soap and lotion. She couldn't explain why his hair was carefully braided, the strands finally even. Something else had drawn her to him, and Fabia didn't know what it was.

So she shrugged and then smiled. "You looked cold out on the street. And in the past day or two, I knew that you were remembering things. All you need is time."

The man brought his hands to his face, wiping away his tears. He breathed in deeply and then sat up, leaning against the headboard. Even in Niall's baggy pajamas, he looked, well, sexy, his body strong and muscular, his dark braid whipping down his back.

Now that he was sitting, Fabia pushed herself up, smoothing her nightgown. "Are you all right?"

The man nodded and then stopped, his eyes wide. "Maybe. I don't know. I don't know how to judge. But at least I can speak. I know what things are. Simple things. Like nouns. I remembered colors. I remembered smells. For—I don't know—a long time, I couldn't even wrap my head around the idea of an object, and there was no way I could get my voice to work. My head wouldn't settle down into a place where I could concentrate on words."

The spell must be wearing off, she thought, remembering the hard, cold place in his thoughts. Or the drug he took was working its way out of his body or his mental illness was lessening or—or? What was the explanation that would make sense? If he was under a spell, how could she tell him that? If he was *Moyenne*, the idea of having a blank, empty space in his head might send him back into nightmare. And even if he were *Croyant*, in his current condition, he wouldn't understand, either.

"That's good," she said, letting her hand fall on his warm wrist. "That means you're getting better."

He looked up at her, his eyes black and glistening. "I'm sorry. I didn't mean to hurt you."

"You didn't," she said, feeling a blush spread up her neck. Fabia pulled her nightgown closed at the neck, rubbing a hand absently on her bedspread. He hadn't hurt her, and in a very sad, pathetic way, she'd felt alive in his grasp. Safe, even, as if she'd known all along he wouldn't do a thing to harm her.

When she glanced up, he was still watching her. Then he sighed, noticing his braid, running a hand over it. "You did this?"

"I wish I could say no because I can see that I still have something to learn about braiding, but yes. That's my third one, and I can see I'm not improving."

"Thank you," he said, nodding. Then the room filled with a silence that startled Fabia, no one in the building making a noise, the street outside quiet, the man's head clear of thought.

"You're welcome," she said, and then, from inside him, she felt the word *gratitude* beat out a swirl in his mind.

"Listen, I can go in the morning, if you want. Maybe I should go tonight. . . ." He trailed off, clearly not knowing who would be able to help a man who didn't know who he was, what he needed, or where he belonged.

"No." Fabia stood up. "Not until we can figure out what happened to you. We'll go to the clinic tomorrow, and they have some resources we can look into. If they don't, I have some other ideas that I'll tell you about later. But until then, you can stay here."

The man's face opened with relief and gratitude, but she noticed that he was shaking again.

"You're cold. Get comfortable," she said, leaning over and picking up the thrashed-away blanket off the floor.

"I'm not cold," the man said quietly. "I'm—I'm scared. Something very bad happened. I did—I hurt someone."

Fabia spread the blanket on top of the bed and stared at him in the yellow room light. She felt his warmth make her want to settle right down next to him. She took in a deep breath. "I don't know what you did, but I know you in a way. And I don't think you did anything wrong. I think someone did something to you. Or you were in, well, an accident of some kind. But you're a good man. You need to believe that."

The man sighed. "I don't know who I am, but whoever I was, I know I wouldn't feel scared. I know I am acting differently than who I really am. I don't know myself, my mind, my thoughts. And that scares me."

Fabia nodded, wondering if she could stand to be parted from Niall's mind, much less her own. For as long as she remembered her thoughts, she'd been paired with Niall's.

"It's horrible," she said to the man, meaning it.

He breathed out, the sound jittery and tentative, as if breath itself were likely to disappear.

As Fabia watched him, listened to his words, she felt something happen in her body. At first it felt like she was going to burst into panic, but then the push of adrenaline turned into warmth, filling her body with feeling, and then she was washed with a slight desire, the same that she'd had the day before as he'd slept against her body while she read to him on the sofa. Her mouth opened before she could think, the same problem she'd had in school, but instead of smarting off to a teacher, she said, "Do you want me to stay here with you? I mean, sleep here with you?"

Without pause, he said, "Yes."

Fabia blinked, her breath caught up in her ribs, her body stilled by his somber, still, slate eyes. She stared at him for a moment, and then she stood up from the bed, walked carefully across the bedroom to the light switch, and flicked it off, moving slowly back to the bed. She was glad to be in the dark. Her heart was beating so hard that in the light, the man could have seen it thumping through her nightgown.

She could feel his heat and scent as she got under the covers, warm and spicy and full of sadness.

"What do you remember about the man you left? About this woman who has him?" she asked, her voice covering her nerves as she settled herself on her bed—her bed that suddenly felt as strange and awkward as a hard, square motel mattress.

She felt him search the dark expanse of his thoughts, and then he said, "I don't remember much. A room. The man, well, there, in trouble. But what I remember best is you. You're all I can really remember."

Even though she knew it was ridiculous and slightly pathetic, Fabia smiled, liking the idea that she was his memory, the one thing he could find.

"We'll figure it out," Fabia said as they faced each other, their heads resting on the pillows. She watched him blink, his dark eyes full of light that seemed to come from inside him.

He reached out a hand, smoothing her hair away from her face. "Thank you, Fabia."

And then, he closed his eyes and fell asleep.

When Fabia woke up in the morning, the alarm beeping in her ear, she found herself scanning as usual. Below her, Liam was dreaming about a Mediterranean beach, water, a girl with amazing breasts, her face unclear. Above her, Mrs. McLeod was watching *Sky News* and slurping her Earl Grey tea. Outside the apartment, people walked by, filled with busy, random morning thoughts—paper, coffee, work. One woman fumed as she passed the building, wishing her husband would drink a wee bit of rat poison. *He never cleans the dishes. Never takes the kids to school. I must be daft to stay with him.*

Farther out, the city rang with people. Because she let herself, Fabia's hearing spread out like a ripple in water, and she listened for a moment before shutting out the din. No Macara. No Quain.

Suddenly, she realized she'd neglected to check herself, feel her body. What was this pressure around her middle? Fabia breathed in quickly, her heart slamming against her chest in a bad dance, and then she remembered. The man. She was sleeping with the man, and during the night, he'd pressed up against her, his arm thrown across her body, his hand cupping her breast, his fingers tight on the warm flannel of her nightgown. His hard chest, lean stomach, and powerful thighs were against her back and legs, and she could feel his breath and beating heart and . . . Fabia blushed, staring distractedly out at her cold, morning bedroom, knowing what exactly was against her, having seen it now repeatedly in the bath. She hadn't slept with a man in so long—Fletcher, going on two years ago—that she'd forgotten what happened in the morning, a man hard from some biological urge that beat back consciousness.

Responding to her slight moves, the man pushed in closer, and even through his pajama bottoms, she could feel his thick, hard length against her bum. Her nipples tingled, especially the one his fingers touched, and without wanting to, Fabia felt herself swim in warmth, wanting—irrationally—to turn to him and press her body against him, her breasts against his chest, opening up to him and letting that long, lovely portion of him inside her. She'd already touched his skin as she'd bathed him and then dried him and rubbed lotion on his skin, and knew he would be smooth and hard and tight against her, kissing her with those dusky lips, his hands moving all over her. She could feel the sleek length of his braid in her hand, his weight hovering over and then pressing onto hers, that lovely, so-ready part of him moving into her.

Fabia closed her eyes, wishing that she could believe that such an act wouldn't be sick and desperate at this point. Or would it? He had remembered a little bit, he could talk, he had his senses, didn't he?

For the love of God, she thought loudly, closing her eyes, her breath quick and light. *I don't seem to have any sense myself.*

What is it? Niall asked, his yawn a thought Fabia could hear.

Oh, just a moment of desperation, she thought back, winnowing out her heart rate, giddy head, and flushed insides from her brother's mind. She lifted the man's hand and arm away from her and slowly slipped out of the bed, not looking back at him.

How is our silent friend? Still improving?

Fabia stood up and walked out of the bedroom. *He's talking, now. Still has no clue who he is.*

I thought I'd ask around today, Niall thought. *I have a meeting with a Council group, and maybe one of them heard about a missing* Croyant.

In the kitchen, Fabia turned on the kettle, rubbing her hands together as she stood by the hob. *Sounds good. He's well enough to go to the clinic, so I'm taking him with me this morning. If he's a missing* Moyenne, *there's bound to be a poster there. Alan will know what to do.*

Okay, Niall thought. *Keep an eye on him, though. You still don't know anything about him. He could be some kind of, I don't know, monster. A beast.*

Fabia felt Niall leave her mind, and she smiled, shaking her head. Her brother had missed *her* being the beast, a woman about to take advantage of a sleeping, amnesiac man. And after being with the man for two full days, watching his dark eyes scan the book, her face, the apartment, the neighborhood, she knew he was only trying to figure out who and where he was. Inside, deep down, he was, well, simply lovely.

After she made some oatmeal, sliced bread for toast, and washed and cut up a tart green apple, Fabia went into the bathroom, needing some hot water to slap some sense into her. As she filled the tub and then sat down in its warmth, she wondered what was wrong with her. From the very first, there had been something about the man that had intrigued her. Even as she'd passed him that first morning as he'd sat on the steps, he'd called out to her, despite his mindless state. Her attraction wasn't just a Mother Teresa, Florence Nightingale experience. It was something about his eyes, his scratchy, unused voice, his willingness to trust her. And, if she was honest with herself, it was his body and face and strength.

But underneath her attraction was something else, ephemeral and scattered, like a conversation in a dream. Fabia was certain that she knew him, but she didn't know how or why.

She rubbed her eyes, almost snorting with laughter. Here she was, making up a connection because she'd reacted to his morning arousal. As usual, guilt made her do ridiculous things. She *should* feel guilty. Any man who so naturally turned to another body in a bed like that, pressing close, needing the feel of flesh under his hands, was clearly married or at least used to sleeping with a known, well-loved, trusted person.

He had to be married, and here she was sleeping with him. Fabia's stomach lurched, and she splashed her face, hoping that would still her thoughts, but all she could feel was his hand on her breast, his fingers just over her hard nipple.

Fabia dunked herself, holding herself under water for a moment, and then popped up, exhaling hard. No more. Enough was enough. She would wash her hair, dress, and give the man some breakfast. Then they would go down to the clinic and ask Alan for help. By noon, the man's people would be found, he'd have a place to go, and she would never have to see him again.

"My word, lass," Gillian O'Shanachan said, putting down her clipboard as Fabia and the man walked into the Care Now Clinic. Gillian's green eyes were wide with pleasure, and as she stared at the man, she unconsciously smoothed her red hair away from her broad pale face. Gillian seemed to want to say more, her mouth working over phrases Fabia could read in her mind: *She finally found a man? And a nice-sized one at that. Nothing wee there. Oh, it's about ruddy time.*

But before Gillian could push out sound, Fabia took her arm and led her away from the man.

"I found him three days ago. Amnesia, I think," Fabia said, her voice intense and low.

"Three days!" Gillian said, far too loudly, the man turning to look at them. "What have you been doing with a man like that for a full three days?"

Fabia felt her skin flare. "Gillian, shhh."

"Well," Gillian said, flicking her hair behind her shoulder and putting a hand on her hip. "I can tell you I wouldn't be knitting by the fire if I had one like him at home, lass. No, I'd have a wee plan for him. A very time-consuming wee plan. First I would—"

"Listen, Gillian," Fabia interrupted. "I was wondering if I could go through the missing fliers, that kind of thing. Maybe you could check the Lothian and Borders police reports. Someone should be looking for him."

"Indeed," Gillian agreed, nodding as she watched the man, approval in her gaze and her mind. "Just as I was trying to tell you. If I lost a man like that, I'd be keen to find him again. Though he looks a little peelie-wallie, actually. Right pale, in fact. Make sure Alan takes a look at him. And then I will, just to be certain. We'll go out for a stout and come back tomorrow."

"Gillian," Fabia said, shaking her head. "This is serious."

"Aye, I know that." Gillian put her clipboard down on a desk and walked to a file cabinet, opening a couple of drawers before pulling out two large manila folders. "I can see how serious it is already.

So serious that you kept him to yourself for three days before bringing him to us. I can see it in your eyes."

Even though she knew Gillian was teasing her, Fabia blushed again, grabbed the folders, and walked back to the man, taking him to a free desk. She opened the folders and pulled out stacks of fliers, names and faces on each.

"What was she saying?" he asked. "You looked like you were angry."

Fabia waved a hand, glad her hair was falling in front of her. She wasn't sure she was going to survive this very long day at the clinic.

"Nothing, really. Gillian is like—like the older sister I never had."

"All right," he said. "So what are we going to do?"

"I have a plan. Someone *must* have missed you," Fabia said, pulling out the chair and then dragging another over for the man. "Let's go through these. Gillian's looking through police reports."

He looked at her and then nodded, his face full of some kind of regret. Since breakfast, he hadn't said too much despite the fact that he had his words back. Over her protests, he'd washed the dishes, made her bed, and folded Niall's pajamas carefully and left them on her dresser. It seemed he knew she intended to leave him somewhere else. Fabia could read his sadness against the blank darkness of his memory, and her heart felt weighed down with bricks.

"All these people are missing?" he asked, touching the first flier carefully, his long fingers lightly grazing the photo of a young woman, blond and smiling for the camera.

"Afraid so," Fabia said. "Every year, so many

people disappear." Just saying the words made her grit her teeth. If the rules were different—if *Moyenne* had long ago let *Croyant* live with them in the world instead of hunting them down—*Croyant* magic could help find all of these people. In a few minutes, some of the most talented *Croyant* could spread their minds and ears over an area and find either the missing or those responsible for their disappearance.

So righteous, Niall thought. *You can't even help this poor sod. You have no idea where he belongs.*

Oh, shut up, Niall! she thought back, embarrassed to be caught in the truth. *I'm trying, though, to be sure.*

Okay, okay. I'll check in after my meeting, he thought, and then he was gone. *Don't worry. We'll figure it out together. Like we always do.*

"Where do they go?" the man asked. "What happens to them?"

Fabia shook her head as she picked up another flier and read it distractedly. "Some are runaways. Some wanted to disappear, to leave behind a bad situation. Maybe something violent in the home. Others are kidnapped. Some are—"

"Killed?"

Fabia nodded, passing over the last names of the lost: Nevin, Angus, Greer, Blane, Brendan. Not one of them remotely like the man. After a few minutes, Gillian held up a folder and shook her head, mouthing, "Nothing."

Shrugging, Fabia went back to her stack, hoping the next photo would be of the man, his eyes happy, his smile wide. Then as she moved on to the next photo, she hoped she wouldn't find him, knowing that then she could come back another day, sit with him like this, his body next to hers as they worked. She wouldn't have to hand him over to his joyful wife and family. She wouldn't have to go home to her flat alone.

Mad! she thought. *Daft!*

The man was silent, turning the fliers slowly, his hands moving over each. Fabia watched him, letting her gaze move from his eyes to his hands and back. He wasn't just reading the fliers, he was trying to read them the way he must have before he lost his memory. With his flesh, he was trying to pull in information, his index finger circling the figure on the flier, his eyes partially closed. In his mind, he was trying to read the clues that his body was giving to him.

For a floaty moment, Fabia was back in school, sitting in class as Mrs. Morna Crum taught them the secrets of *soulever du l'image*, the lifting of ideas from a photo or drawing, pulling up the captured feelings or information that intent left behind. It wasn't always easy, especially if the person taking the photo or drawing the picture and spelling the words didn't care about what he or she was doing. Sometimes only words and phrases like *piss off* or *boring* or *hurry up* or a sensation like *hunger* would come off the page. But if someone put feelings behind action, the truth was always just under the fingertips, a story of emotion and action pulling right up from the hand into the brain.

She remembered their homework of trading essays they'd written for any class. They were all sent back to the dormitories at night to read not what was written on the page but what was felt. Fabia hadn't been able to stop laughing when she realized that Matthew Dunlap's *Histoire de Sorcier* paper was really all about his crush on Milly Peele.

For a moment, Fabia watched the man and then she sat back in her chair, the breath whipped out of her lungs. They had to stop looking at the fliers right now and go home. The man was *Croyant*. Clearly. They would never find anything here at the clinic to help him.

"So," Alan said, suddenly in front of the desk. "Who's your friend, Fabia?"

Fabia blinked, looking up into Alan's kind face, trying to move past the surprise she still felt about the man and his true identity. Alan was a short, whip-thin, balding man with an energy that astounded Fabia. Secretly, she'd often wondered if he was *Croyant*, using a *potion du non endormi* to maintain a twenty-four-hour workday. Because from scratch and without much public support, Alan had started the clinic, ministering to the homeless and destitute, providing whatever help he could rustle up with limited funds. Nothing really surprised him, and as she lightly touched Alan's thoughts, Fabia found that he had no suspicions about the man but only curiosity and concern, Alan's staples. But then as she was about to pull away from his ideas, she found a twinkling glimmer of pleasure that maybe, just maybe Fabia had finally found someone, even if he was amnesiac and slightly bewildered.

"Well," Fabia said, her newfound talent for blushing in fine form, her throat and cheeks hot. "We're not quite clear on that part."

The man stood up and held out his hand. "I'm not sure exactly who I am yet. But Fabia has been helping me."

"I'm not surprised in the least," said Alan, as he took the man's hand and shook it. "You look well, but why don't we give you a once-over before you leave?"

The man looked at Fabia, waiting for her answer. "Thanks, Alan," she said, knowing that now she knew the man was *Croyant*, she needed to get him back to her apartment as soon as she could. Niall would meet them there, and they could contact Adalbert Baird, who would notify *Le Domaine du Santé* immediately, the proper people examining this man's mind. More than likely, in the time that the man had been with Fabia, someone had reported some trouble or someone missing or there had been a report about the person the man was so concerned about, the one the woman had hurt. Here, Fabia was helpless, though she could send a message to her parents or Adalbert or Niall—in fact, she shouldn't waste another moment.

But before she could even stand up from the desk and put the fliers away, a family came in, three sick children, the wife pregnant, the husband's face gray and hopeless. The woman sat down gingerly on the chair at Gillian's desk, the man brushing her brown hair away from her face. The three children huddled around their mother, as if they were expecting pain to come from any direction, her softness their only protection.

As she watched Gillian begin to take down initial information, Fabia stood slowly and put her hand on the man's shoulder. He looked up at her, but she forgot him for a moment and let her mind soften and open and move toward the front of the room. Focusing on the family, she could hear the husband's sorrow, feel the way he barely kept himself from jumping off the Forth Road Bridge each day.

For them, for them, for them, the husband thought, tightening his grip on his youngest child.

"I'm going to go talk with these people," she said to the man, pushing her chair in. "Could you put these fliers away for me, and we can go right after I'm done."

She looked down at the man, who studied her. "I'm not in these files, am I?"

Fabia shook her head. "No, you're not. Not in all the files in Edinburgh."

"What do you know?" the man asked. "What did you find out?"

Fabia let her hand linger for a second on his shoulder, feeling the steady warmth of his skin through his clothing. For a quick second, she swept his mind, finding the now familiar *sortilège du blanc* keeping her out.

"It's a long story. Or a short story with a long explanation. I'll tell you on the way home," she said. "I'll be just a minute, okay?"

The man looked up at her, his gaze so different from last night when he had panicked, his eyes then alive with fear and distrust. Now Fabia could tell he trusted her more than anyone else. Hearing her own thought, she laughed. Other than Niall, the man didn't *know* anyone else.

"Yes," the man said, and she breathed in sharply. Yes, what? Had he heard her thought? Was he a telepath?

"I'll clean this up," he continued, already organizing the stacks of lost faces.

"This won't take long." Fabia walked away from the man, her mind already on the family, her thoughts already filled with their cold and hunger and fear. And it wasn't until two hours later—after calls to shelters and work exchange programs—that she thought to look away from Mr. and Mrs. Addison to find the man. But he was gone. He wasn't at the desk or near the cabinets. Or with Gillian, who stood filing reports at the bank of filing cabinets. Or with Alan, who crouched next to a woman who had just stumbled in, shaking from withdrawal.

"Excuse me, Mrs. Addison," Fabia said. "I'll be right back."

Fabia went to Gillian and tapped her shoulder. "Where did he go? Did he leave? Did you see him?" She felt her questions flume into one long sentence, her throat tightening as she continued. What was going on with her? All she had to do was listen for him or cast her mind about to find him in a trice. And anyway, it would be so much easier for her if the man disappeared, taking care of his own problems. He was better now. Clean and fed and talking. In only a matter of days or even hours, his memory would return—or at least part of it. Someone would find him, right? His wife most likely already contacted the *Croyant* Council, and in no time, the man would be as safe as the Addison family was now.

"Miss him already, love?" Gillian turned to Fabia, smiling. "Can't bear to be without him for a moment? Longing for those deep, soulful eyes? That tall, lean body?"

"Gillian!" Fabia grabbed the woman's shoulder and relaxed, finding the humor in her friend's voice and thoughts, seeing, before Gillian could tell her, the man in the dormitory, reading to the youngest Addison boy.

"He's—" Gillian started, and then stopped, shaking her head as Fabia walked toward the dormitory. "You always do that! It drives me mad! Sometimes I think you can read minds!"

In the dormitory, the man sat in a chair by Ewan Addison's bed. Ewan's two little sisters, Anice and Sheila, were already asleep, but Ewan was pale, his hair slicked back from a quick, mandatory shower, his eyes still alert, as if he expected the bed, his clean body, and the man's lulling voice to vanish like smoke.

The man held a large picture book on his lap, reading softly, and Fabia stopped walking and closed her eyes. Overnight, he'd remembered how to read, the words flowing from him. But in his voice, she could hear the man's loss, a loss that mirrored Ewan's. He was reading for both himself and the boy, the words from the story filling the room: *Can you really love such an ugly creature as I am?* said the Beast faintly.

You're not ugly! Fabia thought before she could help it. *You're brilliant. And yes. Yes, I could.*

The man read on, Beauty recognizing the Beast as her prince, her true love, and everyone lived happily ever after.

The man smiled, closed the book, and put a hand on Ewan's head, saying something quietly. As he put the book on the bedside table, the man looked up, and Fabia felt the same warmth in her body she'd felt this morning as he pressed into her, aroused but unconscious.

And when he stood up, smiling at her as he walked toward her, Fabia's heart beat in a heavy rhythm of jungle drums. Biting her lip, she breathed in through her nose. She was in so much trouble. She was, as Niall would say, a nutter.

"Is the family going to be all right?" he asked as they walked together back into the main office.

"I think so," Fabia said. "They can stay here for a week or so, and we found them some public housing through the Transitional Housing Programme. The kids will get medical exams, and Mrs. Addison can obtain prenatal care." Speaking these facts seemed to calm her down, and Fabia took a big breath, letting her nerves simmer in a light, slow tingle. She wasn't sure how long she could take all this feeling, and she was glad they were on their way home, to where she could get Adalbert on the case. "Let me say good-bye to them, and then let's go home—to my flat."

The man nodded, and Fabia felt his eyes on her as she walked toward Mr. and Mrs. Addison. Opening her mind to his, she saw that while he didn't know whom he'd admired in the past, he admired her work at the clinic, her long blond hair, and her—her bum!

Fabia smiled, her face red, her eyes unfocused.

"What's the trouble?" Mrs. Addison asked when she looked up into Fabia's reddened face, her hand clasped tight on her belly. "Is it the children? Ewan?"

"Oh no! Nothing's wrong at all," Fabia said, turning back to look at the man, who was still watching her, his face smooth and untroubled by a past that was clearly too much trouble. "We'll have you taken care of in no time. I think it's all going to be just fine."

Chapter Six

Since Fabia had awakened him from his nightmare—that dark wrestling with fears he couldn't touch or understand—he felt better, calmer, the world falling into a pattern he could understand. For days, the light and the dark seemed irrational, the noise of people walking back and forth needles in his ears, the cold an old enemy he couldn't escape.

And always there'd been his fear that he hadn't done what he was supposed to do. Someone was in danger, needing him. He'd left that person in terrible danger. He'd failed that person and he'd failed himself. He'd let *her* take something important away from him. He'd let so many people down.

But now as he and Fabia walked down Grassmarket Street, his shoulder occasionally touching hers, he felt infused as if she passed him an electrical charge each time they bumped slightly, a current moving between them. When he had the chance, he turned toward her, taking in her lapis eyes, her smooth dark blond eyebrows, her small, full lips. Once when they passed a couple on the sidewalk, he put his hand on the smooth, tight dip at the small of her back, her soft, prairie-colored hair under his palm, and he'd wished that he hadn't had to take his hand away.

"So," she said. "I have some ideas. And they might make sense to you or not. Depending on how much you begin to remember. But at least I know who to contact."

He closed his eyes. If she could find his people, whoever they were, he would know whom he had failed, betrayed, let suffer.

Fabia put her hand on his arm and then let it slide to his hand, taking it gently with her fingers. For a few steps, she clutched him. "Whatever happened, we'll try to fix it. Maybe there's time to help this per—" She stopped and let go of his hand. "It might not be too late to set things to rights."

"So what do you know?" he asked. "Who do you think I am?"

A lorry passed, honking at two children who ran across the road at a red light. People passed them, holding bags and suitcases and black furled umbrellas, the clip of shoes ringing in his ears. It would be easier, he knew, to go back to the corner of Thistle and Hanover Streets, and stay cold and unclear and confused. At least then, he hadn't known that he was guilty.

Fabia cleared her throat. "When you were looking at the fliers, I noticed how you were 'reading' them—with your fingers, circling the image, closing your eyes, taking in information by touch."

He turned to her and shrugged. "And? Does it mean something more than I'm nuts?"

Smiling, she shrugged back. "Well, yes, of course it does. Most people, most *Moyenne,* don't read fliers through images. They use their eyes and memory and facts. Sometimes imagination. Sometimes intuition. But it's not their general course of action. But you were trying to pull energy from the photo that wasn't from you. You were using a technique called *soulever du l'image,* which is a way of pulling the energy from an image to see how the image came to be. What happens is that we can read the feelings of the person in the image. Or understand the ideas of the person who took the photo or who painted the picture."

He stopped, a pedestrian almost running into him as he did.

"Bloody stupid," the pedestrian muttered, moving past in an irritated flick.

For a moment, he recalled the fliers in his hands and remembered the joyful, missing-toothed smile of one particular boy. As he'd looked at the photo, he'd felt the boy's excitement about his birthday party, his mother's anxiety at the children pulling on Grandmother Conochie's tatted tablecloth, the rubbing swish of balloons floating above the dining room table.

Turning to Fabia, he nodded. "Oh. That's kind of hard to take in."

"I know. But that's what you were doing."

"I thought I was imagining it. Making it up. Just another one of the strange events of my very short life, at least the life I can remember."

Fabia bit her bottom lip, watching him carefully. Finally, she said, "You weren't making it up. Those were sensations and feelings from that boy's party. You took that information in as easily as if there had been a brilliant paragraph describing it."

He rubbed his forehead, and then realized he hadn't said anything about the boy to Fabia. "How did you know that? Can you read my thoughts?"

She took his arm again, and they started to walk,

turning onto a street lined with large Wych elms. "Yes," Fabia said. "I can. Many of us can, some better than others. Some choose to work at it, make it their lives' work. Others turn it off most of the time because it can be distracting and upsetting and sometimes just a wee bit embarrassing."

"I can imagine," he said, hoping that he'd not thought too often about the way Fabia's hair twirled around her waist as she walked, the way her breast felt under his hand. As he thought about his thoughts, he knew she might be listening. He turned to the stone wall and thought *wall*, thought *ivy*, thought *crowded sidewalk* until the image of her body left his mind.

Just when he felt all free and clear of her body and her face, there she was again next to him in bed.

Shit, he thought, and as he thought the word, she tightened her hold on his arm.

"Have you felt any of my thoughts? Did it ever seem like you heard words that no one actually spoke? What about right now?"

"How would I know? And how do I try?"

"You just listen," she said. "A word is a word even when it is thought. We interpret feelings in our brain through language, too. So when I feel cold, I think *I am cold*. When we learn to listen properly, we can read thoughts as easily as we can hear words. We can also pick up images and feelings, but we can talk with our minds just as easily as with our mouths. Try it. Listen."

Looking behind him this time, he stopped and pulled Fabia to the edge of the sidewalk closest to a building. Leaning against the sun-warmed stone, he closed his eyes, trying to seek out her thoughts.

There was so little inside him, so much that swirled black and confusing, only tiny bits of light breaking through, moments of clarity that only brought him pain.

"Relax," she whispered, reaching for his hand again. "Open your mind."

He squeezed her hand and then breathed out, stilling his thoughts. He tuned out the sun on his face, her hand in his, the sound of his own heart. For a minute, he felt nothing, heard nothing, and was about to open his eyes and tell Fabia it was hopeless, he was hopeless, when he heard a whisper.

What was that? he thought, feeling his mind lean toward the sound.

The word *worry* slipped into his view. The question, *What now?*

And then it was a rush, her thoughts in paragraphs, her fear for him, her concern about his health. She thought about the man walking by with his cell phone, talking and waving his arms, looking like a madman. Her hand felt good in his. She—she was hiding something else, a feeling that felt like warm butter, and she pulled it away from him, covering it with other thoughts about the clinic, Alan, Gillian, the Addison family.

You're there, right? she thought.

Yes, I'm here, he thought, wishing he could go into his own mind as far as he was into hers.

You will. The sortilège du blanc *will wear off. It's already wearing off. Look how much better you are today. This will all be over soon.*

When? he thought, opening his eyes and looking at her, amazed that he could hear her even though her mouth was closed.

Fabia stared at him, her eyes so amazing, so beautifully blue.

"Thank you," she said, her skin flushing a light rose.

He felt a push of blood under his own skin. "You're welcome."

She pulled him off the wall, squeezed his hand, and then let go as they started walking again.

"So who are we? I guess reading minds is not a normal activity in the world," he said. He missed her hand in his and then tried not to think about her long, smooth fingers, knowing she was still reading him. He had to be careful. She was the only person he knew now, and he didn't want to scare her away.

Fabia laughed. "That's a question with a long answer."

"Give me a quick summary," he said. "Of course, it seems slightly insane to tell me who we are when I don't even know who I am myself."

"Who we are *is* part of who you are. A big part," Fabia said. "We aren't that many. And I know who to go to for help."

They crossed the street and turned right, walking along the park. Above them in the ash trees, crested tits tittered, a crossbill cackling as it swooped overhead and then landed on the fence rail.

"Well," she went on, "we call ourselves *Croyant*, short for *Les Croyants de Trois*. The believers of three."

"That's French," he asked. "I can tell because your C is stuck somewhere in the back of your throat. And I can't really tell you why I even know that."

"See, you are getting better by the second. And you're right, I have excellent pronunciation," Fabia said, smiling. "Madame Lakritz always told me so."

The man nodded. "You do. And it's strange, but I think I can speak French. I mean, I know I can. *Je compre tout*."

"It's our second language. Our parents teach us, and then we study it at school."

"Go on, then," he said.

"Most of the people in the world are *Moyenne*. Ordinary. Average."

"Nice category to land in," he said. "I'd soon as not know that if I were them."

Fabia shrugged, kicking at a fallen leaf with her shoe. "It's not the nicest, is it? I guess I don't think about what it means."

"I would," he said. "I know the people I met today weren't average. That Alan was a regular saint. Gillian, too. They were wonderful to those people."

She put a hand on his arm and stopped him, smiling. "I'm with you on that. I think sometimes *Croyant* imagine we're better because we can do things *Moyenne* can't. In a lot of ways, we take better care of each other. We don't need a clinic like Alan's, but we've forgotten how to do some of the things they can. They do most of the hard work, too, like building bridges and roads and dams. We get lazy because some things come to us so easily. We can just appear in a place rather than think up tools or toys to get us there."

Fabia paused. "And it's a big problem. Too much to go into now, but there are a lot of *Croyant* who want *Moyenne* gone. They think we don't need their help. They think we've suffered too much by their hands in the past. There are *sorciers*. . . . Well, when you are healed, you'll likely already know what I'm speaking about here."

He looked at Fabia, letting her words fall around him, stuck on one phrase. *Can just appear in a place.* In a way, he felt that he *had* just appeared in a place, finding himself last night thrashing in Fabia's bed, as if waking from a horrible nightmare into yet another horrible nightmare but for one thing—her. As he looked around the street, people coming and going, cars and trucks passing by, no one else seemed to just appear anywhere. People pushed themselves into places by their own energy, using their own bodies or their vehicles. He didn't understand at all.

"What do you mean exactly about appearing somewhere?"

She gave him another smile. He wanted to bring his hands to her face, still her, so he could look at her for a long, long time. Why did he feel like he was trying to remember one particular thing, a tiny chip of memory that would pull together everything else? And why was this one piece about Fabia, someone he'd never met before—at least, according to her?

"It's kind of hard to explain," she said, as they continued to walk. "After a while, it's like walking—something you do without thinking but if you had to try to explain it . . ."

He nodded, thinking of his legs right now. What would he say? Swing one leg forward (but with what muscles? Did he even know the names?), bend at the knee, and put foot down. But was that the order of it? He laughed. "I don't think I can explain walking. But try with this other thing."

Fabia pushed her hair behind a shoulder. "Okay. The theory is this. We are all made up of energy. And not just people. Everything. Plants, animals, rocks, buildings. All atoms in movement. When you travel through matter, you just feel your energy becoming part of the energy of the world. It's all connected, all tied together. We aren't separate at all."

"Sounds religious. You know, people are all one. Or at least what I can remember about religion. Or what I think I remember about religion." He cocked his head. "So then what?"

"This is hard!" Fabia said, walking around a

planter of English ivy. "Okay. We learn how to concentrate to find this energy, to see it as spread out and open. And then we envision where we want to be and go. Because really, aren't we already there? If everything is connected, we are everywhere at once. All we have to do is believe it."

He nodded, keeping silent. Had he been able to do all this? If what Fabia said was true—and he couldn't disbelieve her, because at the moment, he knew nothing else—at one point, he'd been able to move from one part of the planet to another by thought. Not by foot or in a car or truck or plane. Maybe that was how he ended up here after whatever terrible thing had happened. And if that was the case, once he knew who he was, he could go back and make it right.

After a moment of quiet walking, he cleared his throat. "So aside from traveling through atoms, what do *Croyant* do, then, if I can ask? What do you do, Fabia?" He loved the way her name felt in his mouth, the sigh at the end of her name.

They stopped at a corner, waiting for a lorry to pass, the two men in the cab smiling as they drove by. He took her arm as they walked across the street, feeling for a second like he had a purpose, even if it was over in a flash.

She pushed her hair off her face. "I'm trying to work on what I was telling you about earlier. Our world is facing some turmoil these days. I'm part of the group trying to find the people who are mucking about."

"Oh," he said, wondering how she could be doing that while working at the clinic. Or what the clinic had to do with anything.

"I listen," she said, obviously listening to his thoughts. "I have ears like proper satellites. It nearly drove me daft when I was a girl. So the clinic gives me a good place to be unobtrusive, to listen to people who might not realize they'd heard anything. Sort of my 'cover,' as they say in the movies."

"So aside from finding troublemakers, what else do we do?"

Fabia shrugged. "Well, there's government—that's where I fit in. Money. Social groups. Teaching. Business. Same as *Moyenne*, but on a different level. We have some folks who are working on travel between worlds. And some space travel. Experimental stuff. A few artists. And then a lot of us fit into *Moyenne* life and pass on ideas that will help. But not too many or too frequently. We've been burned and tortured and imprisoned for less in the past. But most of us find work of some kind."

He sighed, wishing he could remember the work that he did. He must have had a job, a role, a place in this *Croyant* life. He must have a family and people who cared for him and whom he cared for. But if he had any work or family or life, it was all sucked into the black hole of his memory.

"So," he said as they started walking again. "What are the three things we believe in?"

"I feel like I'm back in school!" Fabia laughed again. "First science and now history. You're really testing me. I wasn't a very apt pupil."

"Give it a shot," he said.

"Okay," she said, her forehead lined with concentration. "There are three *plaques—Les Plaques de la Pensee*—that hold our forged energy. They represent earth, sky, water, and our ancients instilled them with the essence of everything. Creation. Fertility. The cycle of life. Alone, each is immensely powerful, but put together, they cause, well, creation. We believe in the elements of life, the magic of the cycle of being."

Fabia breathed out, shaking her head. "Ouch. All that thought hurt."

He put his hand on her forehead and smoothed away the effort. "You did great. Not that I really know what you are talking about, but at least I know what I should believe in."

"Oh," she said, "not everyone believes. Some *Croyant* just go on with their lives, knowing the *plaques* are there but not thinking or caring about them much. It's like with any belief system or religion, I suppose. Some people need it more than others."

"Do you need it?" he asked as they turned down Princes Street.

She blinked, bit her lip, and then shrugged. "I don't know. All my life I've been able to hear everything. Listening to all the people in the world sort of made me see how we are connected, the same, all of us just trying to live. And then there's my twin brother, Niall. If I ever was lonely or sad, he was right there with me in my thoughts. I guess not everyone has a connection for that long with another person."

"Niall's the man from the other night." He remembered the man's smile, the way he carefully shaved his face.

"That's Niall," Fabia said, smiling. Moving into her mind, he could almost see the place Niall took in it, a large, worn, comfortable place.

He nodded, a thought he couldn't grab pressing down on his chest. He knew he was connected to someone, to somebody, to people in the way Fabia described. He could almost hear the thoughts he'd shared with one person in particular, the pain and torment this person had passed to him. The person he'd failed. The person he'd left behind.

"What is it?" Fabia said. "You're so pale!"

"I . . . I," he began, something dark and red and evil floating through his body like nausea. "I left someone. He's in trouble. I need to find him."

Fabia took his arm, holding him against her body, her warmth slowly reaching him. After a short time, his worry turned into confusion and then into stillness, nothing as important as the feeling of this lovely woman next to him.

They walked in silence, past shoppers angling for deals and workers on lunch breaks. They turned on Hanover and then onto Thistle, Rufus following behind her on the small stone sidewalk. At her flat, she found her keys in her deep coat pocket and was about to unlock the door, when a man inside the building beat her to it, standing on the threshold, one hand on his hip.

Shit, Fabia thought, gripping him tighter.

Who is this? he thought

Don't ask. I'll get rid of him.

"So what's this?" the man at the door asked, his eyes slits, his mouth pulled down at the corners.

"Liam," Fabia said. "This is my friend . . . my friend Donald."

As she spoke the name Donald, something funny occurred to him, something he enjoyed, and he heard a list of names running through his thoughts.

"So that's why you didn't hang around the laundry room too long that night," Liam said, his voice bumpy with irritation. "You had a wee Donald date."

As he listened to Liam talk and felt Fabia's body tense, he found himself slipping into a remembered feeling, a need to strike out, hit, attack. He had to save Fabia. He had to save—he didn't know who else. Without knowing what he was really doing, he pulled away from Fabia and walked toward Liam, moving the man away from the door and against the wall of the building's foyer.

"Do you have an issue with me, man?" he said, staring into Liam's eyes. "Do you have a problem with a *wee* 'Donald date'? Or do you feel you have a prior claim?"

Liam didn't make a sound, his only reply the adrenaline and fear swirling in his head.

The man took a step closer, putting a hand on Liam's shoulder, gripping tight.

"I suggest, then, that you leave Fabia alone. If she wanted you to know about her life, she'd tell you." With one more tight squeeze, he moved away from Liam and turned to Fabia, who stared at him open-mouthed.

"Nice to meet you, Liam," he said. "Fabia?"

She looked at him, shaking her head. *Testosterone*, she thought.

Well, can't change biology, now, can we? he thought back. *I hope there isn't a spell that can!*

I think I'll start working on that directly, she thought, the humor in her idea ringing in his head.

"Bye, Liam," she said, as they headed up the stairs to Fabia's flat.

And then he remembered, heard her imagining his name.

"Donald, is it? That's not one of the names."

"What names?"

"Oh, that list of yours. What about Dante? I think that's much more to your liking."

Fabia turned back, her face shocked. "You heard that?" she said. "You remember that?"

"I must. I do have to say, though, that I'm a bit

partial to Fabrizio. Sounds more me, don't you think?"

"Oh!" She blinked, flushed, and then turned and ran up the stairs, her keys jangling.

Her flat looked the way his mind had felt the day before, a swirl of chaotic images, memories, objects, sensations, everything tossed together until they were unrecognizable. He pushed the door open after she'd unlocked it, and then stopped, holding Fabia back, not wanting her to see.

"What?" she asked, as she stood behind him. She brought her hands to his back and tried to push him forward. "What is it?"

"Fabia," he said softly and then moved aside, taking her hand. "Who would have done this?"

He turned to her, but her face was blank, pale, afraid, her eyes wide. Using what she'd taught him, he moved into her mind, felt her allow him in, and read her shock, her thoughts white and hollow and disbelieving.

Fabia's shock wasn't surprising. In the kitchen, it seemed that someone had taken every single fork, knife, spoon, spatula, dish, cup, and food item out of drawers and cupboards and shelves and the fridge and juggled it all, finally letting it fall to the floor and counters. Glass, smashed fruit, chunks of bread, cutlery, and plates were strewn everywhere like a terrible puzzle.

After finishing in the kitchen, the crazed invader had made his way to the living room, tipping back furniture, tossing books, breaking everything glass. All Fabia's trinkets were twisted, broken, crushed. The television was kicked in, its electronic insides hanging out of the broken glass. In the bedroom, the bed was ripped apart, the mattress cut open, drawers disgorged of clothing, the closets ransacked, shoes and hangers everywhere. The bathroom was slick with lotions and shampoos and ointments, makeup and powders and medicines smashed on the floor.

As they picked their way through the debris, Fabia made tiny moans, occasionally clutching at his hand. Finally, they stood in the hall, staring at the photographs on the floor, the frames cracked and broken, the captured smiles ironic as they looked up from the floor.

He took her shoulder and turned her to him. "Fabia, do you have any idea who did this? Could it have been Liam? I'll kill the bloody fool."

"I—I don't think so," she said slowly, her eyes flicking to the photos on the floor and then past him to the bedroom. "I didn't sense anything like this in him when we were talking. Just his usual nonsense."

"Is anything gone? Or is it all here but broken?"

Fabia rubbed her forehead. "I don't have much that anyone would want to steal. It was all just my personal stuff. Someone wanted to hurt me, but Liam doesn't have the backbone to do this."

Nodding, he breathed out. Liam had only been full of himself, nothing worse, full of himself as a ladies' man, the stud-about-town. "So we should call the authorities. Right now. This is worse than a robbery, then."

She stared at him, blank and wide, and he realized she was trying to contact her brother, Niall.

"I can't find him," Fabia said after a moment, rubbing her forehead. "I can't reach him at all. And he's always there. I haven't heard from him since this morning, but I didn't think anything about it until now."

"Maybe he's busy, Fabia. Maybe he had something he wanted to do without you knowing," he said.

"But he'd tell me that! He always lets me know before he tunes out! And it never goes on this long." She gripped his forearms, her voice ragged and full of worry. "It's our pact. We promised. And I can't find him."

He pulled her close, letting her lean against him, feeling her tears under his hands. If only he could access the magic he supposedly had to clean up this mess, he'd fix her bed and tuck her in, comforting her as she'd comforted him these past few days. Then he'd open his mind and find out who had done this and hunt him down, think his way to the man, and punish him.

"Cry it out, love," he said softly. "Just let it come. Then we'll take care of this mess. And we'll call the right people. We'll find who did this."

He'd righted a chair and put her in it and started cleaning up. After a few minutes, she wiped her eyes and breathed in. He looked at her, cupping the broken fragments of a porcelain teacup in his hands.

"You don't have to do that. There's a spell. I can fix all of this," she said. "Most of it."

He stood up and gently put the fragments on the bookcase. He pushed his hair back, watching her. Fabia seemed too exhausted to even speak, much less push out a spell that would clean up a mess like this.

"But," she went on, "I'll always know someone touched everything with their horrible thoughts. Everything. And I can't take that knowledge away."

"You probably could get rid of that information," he said, knowing that someone had done a pretty good number on him, wiping him free of anything personal. "I have a feeling it's very possible."

"Oh," she said, shaking her head. "I am pathetic."

She got up and walked to him, taking his hand. "You've lost more than this. This is really just stuff. Things. And I can fix it. I guess I'm just shocked. And scared about Niall."

"If this were my flat, I'd be upset, too," he said. "Niall—well, I can't help but wonder if he's met a lovely lady. If it were me, I don't think I'd want my sister hanging around."

Fabia looked up at him, her eyes lighter and filled with hope. "You're right. Enough mooning and wailing."

"Can we call the police now?" he asked, looking around him for where the phone was tossed.

"No, not the police. Or any of the authorities you're thinking of," she said. "I need to contact *Croyant* authorities. Adalbert Baird. I should have contacted him about you hours ago. Probably days."

For a quick second, he read her thought, saw her *But I wanted you here with me* rush through her mind followed by *I should have done better.*

He focused, reached in to her, and thought, *You did everything exactly right.*

Fabia looked up at him, bit her lip, and sighed.

"So," he said, "are you sure this wasn't a random break-in or a malicious joke that your pal Liam paid a hooligan to do?"

Fabia closed her eyes. She seemed to be feeling her way around the flat in her mind, picking up stray bits of information from the air.

"I don't know if a person actually even came into the flat at all," she said. "It might have been done from a distance."

"Oh." He wondered if he would ever figure out this world he supposedly belonged to, a world where things seemed to break all the rules he could see with his eyes, gravity being the first.

"So what's this spell?" he asked.

She breathed in, his hand still in hers. "I'll need your help. We're going to connect our energy, our minds. So you've got to be with me. And then I'll say the word."

"I'm ready," he said, knowing that after what Fabia had done for him, he would do anything for her. She'd been brave enough to bring a scary, bloody, sodden, incoherent man into her apartment, her home, to bathe and feed him. Today, while she hadn't discovered *who* he was, she'd discovered *what* he was. At this moment, he owed her everything.

"Oh . . . Donald!" she said, smiling. "You don't owe me a thing."

"So it's Donald for good, is it? You won't reconsider Fabrizio?"

Fabia laughed. "I guess I'm never going to hear the end of this, am I? Donald is better than thinking about you as him or he or that guy or what's-his-name, don't you think? And Fabrizio is just too much." Fabia blushed. He went into her mind and felt a wee block around a thought that then shimmered away.

"So," she said quickly. "Let's clean up this mess and get in touch with Adalbert."

"No time to waste," he said, squeezing her hand and closing his eyes.

In a second, he felt her mind flooding his, and he watched as she curled around his thoughts, pulling the two of them together. When they were one stream of thought and energy, he felt himself leave his body, pull into some kind of matter, a swirl of gray, and then he saw Fabia in front of him, her eyes a lapis fire.

"*Réparer!*" she cried. He felt his heat and energy

swirl with hers, focused into a beam that slipped into the flat, moving over all the broken objects and shattered furniture, pulling all the atoms of the mess back together until he knew that when he opened his eyes, things would be just as they'd been when he and Fabia had left for the clinic.

After everything was whole, he felt Fabia in the matter, and reached to her with the last of his energy, wrapping his arms around her shoulders and pressing her close. She hugged him back, and he felt himself soften. If only he knew who he was. He wasn't Donald, a normal guy that Fabia might go out with. He was homeless, nameless, untethered by the things that made people human—family, a past, love.

We'll find out who you are, Donald, she thought, as she pulled their energy into a stream and dropped them both back into the flat.

He nodded, hoping that when Fabia found out who he was, she would still hold him close, want him pressed next to her body, learn to call him by his real name, whatever it was. He hoped that when he found out his identity, there would be time to save the person he'd left behind. If there wasn't, he wouldn't be able to fathom himself, and there would be no chance that Fabia would either.

The old man put his hands on either side of his face, kissed him on the forehead, and then stood back smiling. He stared at the old man, feeling that he should recognize him, everything about him—his long gray hair, his rich purple robe, his strong, quiet gaze—so familiar. But there was really only a blank in his memory, a place the man might have filled. "My boy," the old man said. "Rufus, it's such a relief."

Fabia smiled. "Rufus! That's your name? That means 'red-haired one.' Doesn't quite fit, does it, Adalbert?"

The old man shook his head and smiled. "No, but it's the color of his good heart. My boy, I am so glad to see you. Your mother and Felix have been beset with the most furious worry. I'm going to have to contact them now."

Without thinking, Rufus grabbed Adalbert's arm, not wanting him to contact anyone until he knew what he had done. "I—something happened before I disappeared. I betrayed someone. I left someone who I'm sure was harmed. Who was it? I don't remember a thing. I don't even know who Felix is. And though you say I have a mother, I don't remember her, either."

Adalbert removed his glasses to wipe them on a corner of his silk robe. Rufus crossed his arms and looked at Fabia, who had suddenly become very interested in a stack of old magazines that only an hour before had been nothing but shreds. Letting himself slide next to her distracted thoughts, Rufus felt all her questions about his past, the biggest one about a wife. A wife? His wife? Did he have a wife? Oh God, was that whom he'd betrayed? He'd thought it was a man, a friend, a brother. But a wife? And were there children, too? He was certainly old enough to have some.

Rufus glanced up at Adalbert, panicked. Adalbert calmly put on his glasses, adjusting them on his long nose.

"Let's sit for a moment before I bring Felix and Zosime here," he said, pointing to two chairs.

Numbly, Rufus sat down, trying to ignore Fabia, feeling that a glance in her direction or a dip into her mind might send him over the edge.

"Your full name is Rufus Valasay," Adalbert began, smoothing his robe. "You are the oldest son of one of the best men I ever knew, Hadrian Valasay."

"Your verb tense," Rufus said slowly. "He's dead?"

Adalbert nodded. "Yes. Many years ago. His death had nothing to do with what has happened to your family recently. Your mother, Zosime, raised you and your two younger brothers, Sariel and Felix."

"Do you know what went on? Why I ended up here in Edinburgh with Fabia?" Rufus asked, his heart beating out a painful rhythm that had started the moment Adalbert said the name Sariel. He'd done something to this brother, he could tell. Adalbert hadn't mentioned him in the beginning of their conversation, so his brother, this Sariel, was dead, too. And it was Rufus's fault.

"Over a week ago, you went to the rescue of your brother Sariel. For over two years, Sariel has—"

"Has? You said has and not had," Rufus interrupted.

"Indeed, I did," Adalbert said. "He's not himself, but he's alive, Rufus. You did nothing to your brother but try to save him from one who would have done otherwise."

Rufus leaned back against the chair and closed his eyes. For days, he'd felt darkness slicing away at any comfort he'd been able to find: the sun on his face, a smile from the woman, Fabia, as she passed him by on the street, the warmth of Fabia's carefully drawn bath, the feel of her soft body in her bed. But now he knew everything was all right. Fine. All was set to rights, as Fabia would say.

"I wouldn't go that far, my boy," Adalbert said. "Sariel is recovering, just as you are, weak and despairing, for his heart was broken as well as his mind. But Kallisto, the woman who did this to both of you, has escaped."

From the corner of the room, Fabia spoke. "She's working with Macara, isn't she? She's the one all the chatter has been centered on? That's what my apartment was all about. They know Rufus is here, don't they?"

Adalbert put his hand on Rufus's arm and turned to face Fabia. "You are correct, Fabia, about Kallisto's present company. Your ears served you well. Both Macara and Kallisto have joined forces with Quain, and though I am not sure who is directly responsible for what happened here at your apartment, I think it was a warning from all of them."

The inside of Rufus's head felt filled with angry insects, the buzz a roar that moved into his body, making him want to run right out of the flat and back into the streets, where he could forget what he'd just learned. Rufus didn't know who Quain or Macara were; he didn't understand what he needed to do next. How could he help anyone if he still didn't know who he was? Sure, he knew his name and the names of his family members, but he didn't feel like Rufus Valasay. Or, he thought, maybe he did, but if this was what being Rufus Valasay felt like, he didn't want any part of it.

Suddenly, he felt a warmth pulse from Adalbert's hand, moving into his body and pushing away the flight of insane nerves.

"We will find a way to release your memories," Adalbert said. "And it won't be easy on you when your mother and brother arrive. You will want to feel what you assume you should feel for them, but they will be like strangers. But you can go into their memories and see yourself, find clues that might begin to open the door to your thoughts."

Rufus's head pounded as he imagined what it would be like to step into thoughts he couldn't understand, images of himself talking, laughing, working with people he knew he should love and respect but couldn't because he didn't bloody remember. The insects took flight again, swarming his body with pinpricks of fear. All he wanted was to get back inside Fabia's bed, press her against him just as she had been this morning, and fall asleep.

Adalbert watched him, nodding. "Hmm. I do think it might be best for me to go back home to alert them and have them meet me in Rabley Heath. Then we can come to you later. Maybe tomorrow morning. Though I'm not sure how long I can hold off Zosime."

Adalbert stood, and Rufus did so as well, not wanting to lose the warm connection the old man provided.

"My boy," Adalbert said. "You are in good hands here. I've known Fabia Fair since before she was born, and I've never had the opportunity to wish I did not."

Fabia. Fabia, Rufus thought, sensing her thoughts hovering just on the outskirts of his mind.

Did you ask him about Niall? Rufus thought.

Fabia jerked out of his mind, walking toward Adalbert. "And Niall, Adalbert. I know he's probably off doing something he shouldn't, but the lout never leaves me alone for this long. It's been hours. If it were anyone else, I wouldn't worry. . . ."

Rufus dropped back into her thoughts, feeling her accept him there, letting him share the heavy oval of fear hanging in her chest.

If you could find me, Rufus thought, *Adalbert can find Niall.*

Fabia gave him a quick smile, and Adalbert nodded as if hearing their thoughts.

"I will pass all this information on to Nala

Nagode," Adalbert said. "Now that Sariel is needing a rest, she's our most proficient *chasseur*. Rufus, soon you will remember how talented she is. You and she are well acquainted."

Fabia looked at him, and he heard her think, *Well acquainted, he says. Nice euphemism?*

Adalbert cleared his throat. "Nala is able to find almost anyone. And I will contact your parents later tonight if need be."

Rufus dropped his head, rubbing the bridge of his nose. His brother, this Sariel, needed a rest, was unable to work because of Kallisto, the woman who had taken away Rufus's mind. Somehow Rufus had to find her, make sure she never did this to anyone else again.

"I will be in touch shortly," Adalbert said, and in a twirl of flashing purple robe and swish of air, he was gone.

Chapter Seven

Without meaning to, Fabia kept trying to reach Niall. First she would picture him, his blond hair the same color as hers, his clear, wide, loving eyes, his laugh that punctuated almost every conversation they'd ever had. Then she would call out to him. Time after time, her mind obsessively found the smooth place his presence had worn in her mind, the ledge from which he provided quips and teasing and concern and advice. But every time she went there, the space was empty, airless, dead, no voice, no laughter, no thoughts.

Now she and Rufus—Rufus, not *he* or *him*, not *Donald* and certainly not *Fabrizio*—worked in the kitchen, cutting up vegetables for a stew. With each vegetable she sliced, she tried to focus only on her task—round wet wheels of carrots, white wedges of new potatoes, slick-skinned pearl onions—but all she heard was the absence of Niall's voice. And when she'd moved into Rufus's thoughts for a moment, all she heard was his running worry about Sariel, the brother he didn't remember but had barely been able to save, his mother and Felix, the other brother who would expect him to know how to act, what to say, how to be.

Fabia slapped down the knife and laughed, the sound harsh and brittle. "We are two of the sorriest people in the U.K. right now," she said. "Listening to us think would drive the daft daft."

Rufus put down his knife and looked up at her, wiping away onion tears. "You're right. But I can't stop imagining what happened. Where did I go wrong? What didn't I do? I made a very important mistake of some kind. And my brother Sariel. Will he recover?"

Without answering him, Fabia began to pace. "And Niall! Where did he go? If he's off seducing some woman or just fooling around with his mates conjuring magic they shouldn't be, I'm going to kill him, I am! He knows he's not supposed to leave me like this. He's not supposed to leave me without saying something. Since we were kids—"

Rufus walked around the counter and stood in front of her, putting his hands on her shoulders. "We've got to stop. This obsessive jabber isn't going to help either of our brothers."

Breathing in deeply, Fabia looked up into the face of this man who just yesterday had been unable to speak. Now he had a name, a family, and—from the quick thought Adalbert had shot her—no wife. By tomorrow, his family would take him away, back to where they lived in the United States, and heal him. All Fabia would be left with was her worry about Niall and the worsening problem of Macara, Kallisto, and Quain.

"You're right," she said, tucking her thoughts into a neat package and putting them away. "Let's finish this stew and play cards or something. Gin rummy."

Rufus smiled. "Gin rummy isn't enough of a distraction. Poker. That I remember. My brothers . . ." he began, pausing, his eyes wide. "My brothers and I play small stakes. Nickel, dime, quarter. Felix—Felix always wins."

Fabia looked up into his amazed face, and then, without thinking, hugged him, pressing her face against his shirt. Niall's shirt. Under her cheek, she felt his heartbeat, heard his quiet tears, his amazement at the return of his memories.

"I remember," he whispered.

She nodded against him, and he pulled her tighter and kissed the top of her head. Fabia should be only happy for him, but in the deepest part of her mind that she didn't want to share with him, she wanted him to stay. Not that she would wish a *sortilège du blanc* on anyone. But there was something about Rufus, his voice, his thoughts, that was almost as familiar to her as Niall's, even after only a four days' acquaintance.

"That's brilliant," she said, pushing away from him and wiping her eyes. "I knew the spell would wear off."

Rufus left a hand on her arm, but she backed up, knowing that she needed to start letting him go. Right now before she grew even more attached. He wouldn't be so afraid tonight, and she could sleep on the sofa. Or he could. In the morning, she'd make him breakfast, and then Adalbert would whirl in and take him back home where he could recover with his family. And anyway, she'd have to set out to find Niall, even if Adalbert didn't bring back information. For all intents and purposes, Fabia knew she had to prepare for Rufus's departure now, at this very moment.

"Let's finish here with the vegetables." Fabia

turned back to the counter and the geometric vegetable shapes on the cutting board. "And then I'll get out the cards. You can explain to me what nickel, dime, quarter means. Of course, we don't have any American money here, so you better do some quick thinking."

She knew Rufus was staring at her, and she kept her thoughts to herself, ignoring his gentle push at her mind. Rufus had gone through too much and did not deserve an overwhelming dose of her self-pity and her pathetic yearning for a man she hardly knew.

"Come on!" she said, rousing herself. "The potatoes will brown!"

He cleared his throat and went back to work. Neither of them talked, the only sound in the kitchen the quick slice of metal through vegetables and the *ping* of the gas on the hob as the stock boiled.

"This one is called five-card stud," Rufus said as he shuffled.

"Five-card stud!" Fabia said. "That sounds like some kind of pub creature, a man on the prowl."

Rufus laughed, his face relaxed and happy. "Maybe that's what we should call Liam. The jerk would probably think it was a compliment."

Fabia smiled. "Indeed he would. We best not or I'll have him ringing my bell every night. So tell me how to play."

"Okay. The game is actually quite formal. I'll go slow."

"Don't bother with that," Fabia said. "Didn't I just beat you?"

He opened his mouth to say something and then didn't, shaking his head instead. "I won't go into the weakness of that last game and how it is based on luck, not skill. You were just able to give me the terrible cards you didn't want."

"I liked playing 'screw your neighbor.'" She sipped her Guinness.

Rufus raised his left eyebrow. "We best make sure Liam knows that the name of the game is only a metaphor. Otherwise, he will knock down the door to get dealt in."

Blushing, Fabia took the second card he dealt, leaving the first on the table—the queen of hearts. "And it always *will* be a metaphor," she said, knowing that Liam could only dream his way into her bed, and unfortunately, she'd caught a few of his dreams of her when she scanned his thoughts. She grimaced, shook her head, and glanced at her second card quickly and then pressed the ten of hearts against her chest.

"No mind reading," she warned Rufus.

"I told you earlier that I'd shut down." He looked at his card and then fingered his change. "So, you bet first, having that lovely queen and all."

Fabia looked at her ten and then studied the list of hands Rufus had written down on a piece of paper before they'd begun: royal flush, straight flush, four of a kind, full house, flush. She picked up fivepence and put it in the middle of the table.

"There," she said, smiling.

"Oh my. Be still, my betting heart. Well, I'll see your five-pence and raise you another five." The coins clacked together as he dropped them on the table.

"Now what?" she asked.

"You either see me or you fold. I'm sure my little five of spades has you all in a twist. Best to give up while you're only out tenpence." He smiled at her and pushed his hair away from his face with his free hand. His sable eyes glittered in the warm glow of the dining room light.

Niall, she thought, not knowing if she was talking about cards or Rufus. *I'm in trouble here. I need some advice!*

But there was no response, and she sighed.

"Fine. I'll see your fivepence." Fabia put another coin in the pot.

Rufus nodded and dealt another card to each of them. "Oh, lassie. Without magic, I'm trying to imagine what you have in that little hand of yours. Another heart? If there is, I'll think there is a wee spell being cast here."

"No! I promise!" Fabia said, laughing and clutching her new card—the ace of hearts—tight. "I haven't done a thing."

"What now? You've got to give up. Even if that was another heart, you can't think you're going to get another at this point." Rufus tapped his hidden cards on his cheek.

"Don't blather on. I'll bet tenpence." Fabia picked up the coin and dropped it on the pot. "Now what do you say, Mr. Smartie?"

Rufus looked up, trying to be intimidating. "There's no way this deck will yield up to you another heart. Mathematically impossible."

"You might want to consider folding," Fabia said.

"I never fold."

"That must be why Felix wins every time." Fabia loved saying this, and she could tell Rufus loved hearing his brother's name, sinking into a silence that must be filled with his memories.

"I'll see your tenpence," he said, picking up the deck. "Here comes another."

He slid a card across the table, and she picked it

up by the corner, peeking carefully, and seeing—red! Another heart! The king of hearts!

Trying to keep her face still, she arranged her cards in order, glancing down at her queen.

"Okay, moneybags, what are you going to do now?" Rufus hit the edge of his cards on the table, his eyebrows raised.

"I'll bet—I'll bet fifty pence!" She picked up the coin and smiled, dropping it on the pile.

"Oh, this is turning into a disaster, I can see. You've been reading the chart correctly, I hope. Do you need a little reminder?" He teased her, his voice so soft and lovely sounding, all his American vowels in her ear.

"No, and you better ante up or fold," she said, her voice clear and crisp. "I need to run and get some milk, and this is the money I'll use. So, as you say, put up or shut up!"

"My word, Fabia! What a cutthroat." Rufus stared at his cards and then picked up fifty pence. "It's your loss. Here we go, down and dirty."

Picking up the deck, he threw down their last card. Fabia gasped when she saw the jack of hearts slide next to the ten. "Oh my God!"

Rufus cocked his head and sighed. "That's not the best tactic, Fabs. Not exactly a poker face."

Fabs, she thought. *That's what Niall calls me.*

Niall, she threw out, knowing nothing would come back. *Niall?*

Rufus reached across the table and touched her hand. "He'll turn up. Maybe he's finally found the woman of his dreams."

They looked at each other over the cards and the coins, and Fabia felt her lungs and throat and mouth turn to liquid, to tears. In one day, she'd felt like she'd lost everything. Despite the spell Rufus had helped her weave that had repaired everything in the flat, she'd lost her belongings to someone's anger, her brother's steady, constant presence, and Rufus, who would be leaving tomorrow.

I didn't say I was going anywhere, he thought. *Maybe you're stuck with me, bad memory and all.*

You said you weren't reading my mind! she thought, swallowing down her sadness. *Don't take me for a bawheid.*

Rufus stared at her, shaking his head, seeming to want to tell her she wasn't an idiot. *I wasn't doing anything until just now. I was keen to see that jack sliding in your fingers*, he thought.

"Twit. Cheater," she said, tiredly, putting down her two cards, arranging them all in a royal flush.

"Looking at that hand, I'd be careful who you called a cheater. And I've never been clear on the exact meaning of twit. Not to mention bawheid." Rufus put down his hand, a mishmash of cards from various suits.

"I'm not usually like this," Fabia said, standing up, the table jangling with coins.

"Most people aren't usually in possession of a royal flush," he said. "At least you have your milk money now. Or should I say café latte money?"

"No, I mean—I mean about you. A man." Fabia rubbed her cheek with her palm, scared to look up at him.

But he didn't say anything, and she heard his chair scrape back and his steps as he came to her. Then his hands were on hers, moving them away from her face.

"Fabia," he said as he looked down at her, his dark eyes full of such tenderness she couldn't resist his gaze. "I feel the same way. Even when I didn't know anything, I knew you somehow, as if I'd known you forever. When I couldn't think straight, I kept looking at you, imagining you'd say something I'd remember. Your voice. The sound of you. Your expressions. You're like a dream I once had. And when we are together, like right now, I feel that I am home."

Fabia felt her breath in her throat, unable to pull it down into her lungs. Her head felt fuzzy, her skin tingled. She wanted to talk with Niall, to run all of this past him, but he still wasn't there.

But more than anything, she wanted to kiss Rufus, and so she moved closer to him, stood on her tiptoes, and let her lips touch his lightly at first, giving him a chance to pull back.

But he didn't pull away. He put his arms around her, letting his warm mouth cover hers, opening his lips to her tongue, kissing her back in a way that went beyond memory.

If I'd ever had a kiss like this anywhere from anyone, he thought, pulling her even tighter and cupping her face in his hands, *I'd never have forgotten.*

Fabia tried to answer him, but her thoughts became images, which became feelings, and so did his: *heat, skin, flesh, blood, bone, warm, hot, red.* She breathed in his clean soapy smell, felt his stubble on her cheek, his lips moving over her face and down her neck.

Her eyes closed, her head tilted back to give him her smooth neck, she pushed her hands under his shirt and ran them up his back, stroking the hard muscles she'd dried off with a soft towel after his baths and showers. He was so smooth and strong, and as he held her, she could feel him grow hard against her body. Fabia remembered that particular muscle from the bathroom, and suddenly she felt his laugh under her hands.

I guess it's a good thing you're not Florence

Nightingale, he thought, bringing his mouth back to hers. *There might have been a hospital uprising.*

I'm a Brammer nurse, a fine specimen of care and concern.

Really? he thought, breathing against her neck. *You don't say. And what would you call this excitement? This uprising of sorts?*

Do you mean uprising literally? Fabia thought, letting her hands roam around his waist, her fingers finding his jeans button. *What kind of uprising? I've seen it before, I think.*

Her hand went to his fly, pressing against him, and she heard him take in a sharp breath, his tongue still against hers for a second.

That would be the kind of uprising I was referring to, he thought. He began to walk backward, moving her into the bedroom.

A week ago, a day ago, even this morning, Fabia knew she would have pulled away from Rufus and his soft, wonderful kisses and told him to stop. She'd been hurt before—a fact Niall reminded her of constantly and in detail—and she would have imagined that no good could come of moving this fast into whatever *this* was, especially with a man who was just remembering who he was.

This is us, Rufus thought as they stood by the bed.

You barely know who you are, she thought, bringing her hands to his shirt and pushing it up over his stomach and chest.

You're helping me remember, he thought back, letting her pull his shirt over his head, his skin warm under her palms.

She kissed his throat, his chest, her fingers on his flat nipples, feeling them harden under her touch.

Then his hands were unbuttoning her blouse, his big, strong fingers gentle, quick, ready. Her blouse open, he put his hands softly on her breasts, his fingers pushing aside her bra. She was breathing hard, her body wanting to jump out of her skin into his, when there was a quick crack and flash, and they almost jumped away from each other's mouths and looked up into the living room.

Standing by the table were Adalbert, Fabia's parents, Xanthe and Donoch, and a dark-haired woman and man Fabia didn't recognize. But the woman was tall like Rufus, her graying hair clearly once black, her eyes as dark and sharp as Rufus's, and the handsome man next to her had Rufus's eyes and mouth, his body just as tight and lean if not a bit shorter. He was looking around the room, and Fabia almost smiled, seeing him as a younger version of Rufus, younger, more independent, and—from the line of his brow and the fullness of his lips—cockier.

As soon as they'd all come out of matter, they began searching the room with their eyes and mind, Adalbert eyeing the table with its cards and coins, saying, "Someone clearly won this hand."

The dark-haired man nodded, picking up Fabia's hand. "Royal flush. Some sorcery in play here along with the cards."

Holy mother of God, Rufus thought, letting go of Fabia's bra and helping her button her blouse. She grabbed his shirt and turned it right side out, handing it to him quickly. He shrugged it on, and then looked down at her, his face still warm with desire.

Is that your mother? she thought as she tucked in her blouse.

It must be, he thought. *Who else but a mother would show up at a time like this? She probably forced Adalbert into it.*

And that must be your brother, Fabia thought, looking at the man with Rufus's eyes.

Felix, Rufus thought. *The younger one. The one who wins at cards.*

Come on, Fabia thought, and they sauntered into the living room, trying to appear calm and collected, as if it was a generally accepted principle for a man and a woman to casually walk out of a dark room with quickly buttoned, rumpled clothes, their hair tousled and full of static.

When she saw Rufus, the woman exclaimed—her mouth open in relief and sadness—and ran to him, wrapping her arms around his chest, a hand patting his shoulder.

"Oh, Rufus," she said, trying to control her weeping, and Rufus closed his eyes, putting his cheek on her shoulder.

Fabia stayed in his mind for a moment, feeling his body remember his mother first and then his mind, the spell starting to disintegrate in a whir of particulars and blur.

Mom, Fabia heard him think. *Mom. Zosime. Sariel. How's Sariel?*

Zosime squeezed him tight and pulled back, wiping her face with her hands. "He'll be all right. But if you hadn't gone there to fight for him, he'd be gone. With—with that terrible woman. Working for—him."

"Quain," Rufus whispered. Fabia could tell he was remembering more, all at once, Quain's name bringing forth a flood of misery and anger.

Zosime turned to Fabia, her dark eyes glittering with tears. "Thank you so much for finding him. Without you, I don't know what would have happened."

Fabia blushed and nodded, holding out her hand. "I'm Fabia Fair."

Zosime ignored the outstretched hand and hugged

Fabia hard. "I know your parents. Knew them well before . . . before my husband died. But never mind that. You saved my boy," she whispered. "Thank you."

Adalbert cleared his throat, and Fabia and Zosime turned to him. Fabia smiled briefly at Zosime and then walked over to her parents, hugging them both tight, and then standing next to them as Adalbert took off his glasses, wiping them on the corner of his robe.

"One mystery solved, another beginning," he said finally. "Nala Nagode has uncovered information that indicates you were right, Fabia. Niall has been abducted. I took the liberty of contacting your parents, and they, of course, wanted to come here immediately."

Fabia felt breath and sound meet in her throat and leave her mouth, a push of grief into the air. Xanthe took her hand and pressed it hard. Fabia turned to her mother, leaned into her soft shoulder, breathing in the familiar smell of lavender and green tea. She felt her mother's quickened, worried pulse and could read the color of her concern, dark and gray.

"Who has him?" Fabia blurted. "Where is he?"

Adalbert sighed. "It seems these two stories here," he said, lifting his hands to indicate both Rufus's and Niall's, "are connected. Niall was taken as soon as Kallisto arrived in the U.K. She appears to have joined forces with Macara, and he wants you otherwise occupied, Fabia. Apparently, you've been getting a trifle too close to his center of operations, your taking care of Rufus being the worst offense of all. I would assume that the damage that occurred to your flat today was his calling card."

Donoch put a hand on Fabia's shoulder. Her father was tall—almost as tall as Rufus—but fair, his blond hair turning gray and his eyes the same as Fabia's and Niall's. "So how are we going to find Niall, Adalbert?" he said, trying to cover up his concern with slow, carefully modulated words. "The longer he's away, the worse his situation, I'd imagine."

Fabia felt as though she were moving into matter to travel away, but when she looked down, she was still standing in the dining room. Her head was light, full of stars. The place in her mind where Niall usually sat was pounding. How could she have been a heartbeat away from jumping into bed with Rufus when Niall was captured, maybe hurt, maybe . . . ? She put her hand on her forehead, her knees ready to buckle.

Donoch grabbed her and pulled out a dining room table chair, helping her to sit down. Xanthe stroked Fabia's hair, and for an instant, Fabia imagined that she was a girl again, back home, Niall asleep in the other room, dreaming of flying horses, dragons, and pizza. Xanthe was patting her to sleep, smoothing her hair, reminding her to shut down her ears so she wouldn't pick up the night watchman's curses as he ambled down the street or listen to Effie Donegal's curses from across town when Ian Donegal came home later, his head full of stout.

At that memory, Fabia looked up at Adalbert, who nodded, his face calm.

He wanted her to go listen. He knew where they were holding Niall, but not exactly. So Fabia would go to find the place where Macara and Quain and this horrible woman Kallisto were and listen for them, try to parse her brother's voice out of the stream of sound in the universe and save him.

Only she could hear Niall. Only she could save him.

"Who will come with me?" she asked. Both Donoch and Xanthe made sounds of surprise.

"Adalbert! Not Fabia!" Xanthe said. "She's been—she's too upset. This is too much."

"Who better than she?" Adalbert said. "No one—no *sorcière* or *sorcier* that we know—can hear as she does, and she and Niall have a special path of communication. Nala Nagode has found the area where Kallisto and Macara are hiding but not the exact spot. Quain has placed too many spells around the area for any clear reading."

"I'll go with her," Felix said. "I know what it's like to know your brother's in danger." He put a hand on Rufus's shoulder.

"I'm going, too," Rufus said.

"No," cried Zosime. "You're not healed! You haven't recovered from your fight with Kallisto!"

The air of the room was swirling with confusion, parents on both sides wanting their children to be safe and to be saved. But Niall wasn't saved, not yet, and Fabia knew that she was going to find him, no matter what.

Adalbert lifted his hands and the room fell silent. "Sariel is one of our best healers, but I can send for Justus Kilgour. He can work with Rufus and free his memory. Justus is working with Sariel right now, though Sariel will need much time to recover."

No one said a word, Adalbert truly the armiger of the *Croyant* at this moment, his words not conversation but law. "And then I will ask Nala to come here and confer with Fabia, Rufus, and Felix. Together, they can come up with a plan to find Niall and to stop whatever plan Macara wanted Fabia to stay away from."

Adalbert stroked his chin, nodding. "Our world is in danger and has been since . . ." He paused, and

Fabia heard the name *Hadrian* floating in the air. She turned to Rufus, who winced at the sound, and then she felt the word *father* beat a steady, sad drum in his head. "For almost thirty years, Quain has been trying to find a way to disrupt our way of living. Niall's abduction does not seem like a way toward his final plan, but his recruiting of first Macara and now Kallisto does. Kallisto was one of our finest, a *sorcière* of the best sort. That Quain was able to turn both of them says a great deal about his strength. We need to stop them all before we find ourselves in a battle we cannot win. And maybe then, we can all come together to determine how to be *Croyant* in a world such as this, with all its changes."

They stood around the table, the cards and coins of their earlier play looking ridiculous shining in the overhead light. Fabia had never been able to work this particular kind of magic, but she would like to rewind the world, go back to the minutes earlier where she and Rufus were alone in the apartment, nothing as important as the ace of hearts. They wouldn't have kissed yet, wouldn't have moved into each other's bodies, their imminent sex not yet a betrayal of Niall and Sariel. But they would have had the desire, the hope, the promise of what was to come. The world would be nothing more than the anticipation of the next card and the next, the punishment nothing more than losing fifty pence.

Adalbert buttoned his robe and adjusted his glasses. "I'm going home to contact Nala. I will alert *La Force de Recherché* so they can consult with her and help with the plan to find Niall. Of course, I will have to alert the entire Council. But you need your sleep. We will meet here once again in the morning."

Zosime nodded. "First I'm going back to look in

on Sariel. Then I'm going to stay at Adalbert's tonight and work with the Council on this. I'll be back tomorrow, too."

Putting a hand to the brim of his black velvet cap, Adalbert whirled away, nothing left but an idea of where he'd been, a flutter of matter that stilled instantly.

Zosime took Fabia's free hand. She looked at Fabia for a long moment with her dark brown eyes, eyes the same color as Rufus's. Just staring into them made Fabia want to weep, sensing the intense mother love reflected there. "Thank you again, dear," Zosime said. "You gave me such a gift. I hope I can help do the same for you."

She smiled, turned and kissed Rufus and Felix, and then disappeared, too.

Xanthe gripped Fabia harder, pulling her into a hug. "I know you are the right person to go look for Niall, but I'm worried, Fabia. Quain is a horrible man, a nightmare."

"Mum," Fabia said into her mother's hair, the floral smell so familiar, comforting. "We'll find him. Niall hasn't even been gone but a day. It will be all right. I will be all right."

She said each word, pushed the sounds out of her mouth, but she wasn't sure she believed them herself. Niall had been with her every hour of every day since before she could remember a thing. In a way, she felt like she'd lived two lives, his and hers, and no one else felt his absence as she did. Fabia used to wonder what it would be like when either of them finally found a partner, a wife or husband or true love of some kind. Could that person ever be as close to either of them? Without necessarily wanting to, she'd lived through Niall's triumphs and losses, hurts and joys, felt what his first sex had been like as he had felt hers. Even when they promised not to listen in, some impulse of feeling passed between them.

When she had kissed Rufus, she'd automatically closed her mind, but not fully, leaving a little space open, just enough so Niall would understand. But he hadn't been there. Even if a separation between them was long overdue and absolutely necessary, Fabia was sad he'd missed that important part.

"Well," Donoch said. "Fabia, your mother and I are going to stay with Aunt Nessa tonight."

"Why not stay with me?" she said, pulling away from Xanthe, her hands on her hips. "I can sleep on the floor."

"Rubbish. And you have guests already," Xanthe said, smoothing her robe. "Nessa is only across town, and you know how your aunt always cheers us up, at least when we can find her. But I contacted her earlier, and she's just back from an adventure with . . . with . . ."

Xanthe shrugged, and Donoch took her hand. "It doesn't matter," he said. "You stay here. The walk will help clear our heads. And your aunt will probably get so angry about this, she'll try to come with you. Anyway, we'll meet you here in the morning to see you off."

Donoch pulled her close, kissing Fabia's cheek. "I know how this hurts you. More than even us," he said. "But you'll find him. You'll bring him back. You could recognize his voice if he were in the Arctic or on the moon."

Donoch and Xanthe shook hands with Felix and Rufus and then gave Fabia a wave and walked toward the door. Fabia kept waiting for them to disappear into matter, but they left through the door, their contemplative walk starting right away. She could only imagine how upset they were, Niall really the baby of the family, the one they worried about the most after Fabia had her hearing under control. When she lived at home, she often caught her parents' late-night conversations, full of worry about Niall's breezy manner, the way he never took anything seriously, their hope that school would shape him up. And later, they worried that he wouldn't find a cause, a meaning, a purpose, though lately, as he had grown more involved in Council work, their worries had lessened.

And now he was missing, caught because of the very work they'd imagined he'd never have. Their fear and worry shimmered over them as they walked away. All Fabia wanted to do was stay close to her parents, and as the door clicked behind them, she felt as if she'd lost ten pounds, all of it from her heart.

Rufus started to walk toward Fabia, but then there was a rustle of air, and Justus Kilgour stood in front of them, his red hair jumbled from travel.

"Bloody matter like a roller coaster," he said, winking at Fabia. Justus had been a substitute teacher at Bampton Academy during Fabia's third year there, teaching them *charmes du santé* and *maledictions contre maladies*. Of course, there had been terrible mistakes, the health charms and the curses against sickness getting mixed up, students suffering briefly from mumps and boils and migraines until Justus could right them. After only one year at Bampton, he'd decided he'd do healing work for the Council rather than watch fifteen-year-olds bloom with measles.

"So which one of you lads is my patient?" Justus took off his robe and smoothed his hair.

Rufus shrugged. "It's not necessary. I think the spell is wearing off. I'll be fine."

"Ha!" Justus said, holding out his hands in mock surprise. "Rufus, I take it. With my eyes closed, it would be hard to differentiate you from Sariel. Tall, dark, and huge irritants on the planet. Lord, you are just as stubborn as he is. What is it with you Valasay boys?"

"Will he be all right?" Rufus asked, ignoring Justus's blather.

"Pain in the ass, but fine. Or will be," Justus said. "That Kallisto knows her spells. So I need to take a look at you, no matter what you say. For your own good, lad, and if I don't, Adalbert will have my head."

As Justus went on talking, Fabia breathed in, knowing she had to find a way to move through the hours till morning. She had to stop thinking about Niall. She must. There were things to do; people needed healing; the kitchen was still a mess from dinner.

"Why don't you go into the bedroom?" she said to Justus. "I've got to pick up this mess, and it will be quieter in there."

Rufus looked at her, his dark eyes full, and she turned away, moving toward the kitchen and the dirty dinner dishes. She had no right to him now. Not with Niall out there alone, scared, trapped by the same crazy *Croyant* who'd hurt Rufus as well as his brother Sariel.

"Come along, then," Justus said. He took Rufus by the arm and led him into the bedroom. Fabia heard the door close, and she sighed.

"So what can I do to help?" Felix asked, and Fabia jumped, forgetting that he was even in the room.

"God!" she said.

"No one's called me that yet, but I have aspirations." Felix smiled, his mouth and eyes so much like Rufus's. Even with her worry, she couldn't help but wonder how Zosime dealt with having three boys, all three of them apparently a little wild and a lot good-looking. And Felix had the look of a true troublemaker. He looked like the men Fabia would always avoid at gatherings or meetings, the ones who knew they were creation's gifts to the planet, who knew that despite her protestations otherwise, with some carefully chosen compliments and rakish hands on hips, they'd have Fabia staring at them with wide eyes and zero IQ. They'd move all through her thoughts without her even knowing, find the perfect thing to say (maybe something about her eyes or her hair), and say something complimentary about her brogue, telling her, "You sound like the way green rolling hills look in the mist."

Later, she'd shake her head and wonder how she'd been sucked into their trap, but at the time, she'd fall. Felix and his kind were just plain dangerous.

"Well," she said, trying to cover up her thoughts quickly. "I do have to clean the kitchen. And make up the sofa."

"I don't want to be too nosy, but what are the sleeping arrangements going to be?" Felix asked. "I could find a hotel room. Or I could go home and come back. Not a problem."

Fabia tried to press away her blush, but she could already feel the blood pool in her cheeks. She began to speak, but then shook her head. Finally, she breathed in and said, "Rufus and I can sleep in my room. The sofa isn't bad. You should survive."

"Looks great," Felix said. "Let me help you with the dishes."

Grateful to tear apart this conversation, Fabia walked into the kitchen and turned on the faucet, letting hot water fill the sink. Felix picked up dishes from the counter and brought them to her, leaning against the tile counter as the sink filled.

"So you found Rufus just down the street?"

Fabia nodded, squirting soap into the water. "He was really bad off. For two days, he couldn't speak at all. And if you thought his face looked bad today, you should have seen him then. It was awful."

"Justus will take care of him, inside and out," Felix said. "You wouldn't believe how well Sariel is doing."

"What happened between Kallisto and Sariel?" she asked.

She handed Felix a towel and then began washing a plate.

"My mother and even Rufus thought Kallisto was this wonderful woman. But I knew she was no good from the moment I saw her, despite her act. Sure, she's lovely. Gorgeous. All long dark hair and beautiful eyes. She enchanted Sariel, turned him against us. Slowly at first, and then we just stopped seeing him, hearing from him. I couldn't access his thoughts no matter how I tried. It was like he'd disappeared, and we thought he was just, well, you know. Involved." Felix took the wet plate from Fabia, dried it, and put it in the cupboard. "But all along she was twisting him up. Finally at the very end, Sariel called out to Rufus, and Rufus went to help. The fight was horrible, but I only know part of what Sariel remembers about that night. Images of wrong magic."

Felix slapped the towel on the counter once, the *whap* echoing in the kitchen. Then he sighed.

"By the time Sariel woke up, both Kallisto and Rufus were gone. The problem was that we didn't even know Rufus had been involved until Sariel had been under Justus's care for a while. We tried to contact him to tell him about what had happened, but we didn't know we needed to be taking care of him as well. Rufus has lived in London for a few years, and he must have traveled back as best he could, finding the U.K. in general rather than specifically."

"He lives in London?" Fabia put the cutlery in the water, letting it soak. "Why haven't I ever met him before? I should have seen him at a Council meeting at the very least."

Felix shrugged. "He does Council work all over. He spent a long time in the East. And then he goes off with Sariel."

"And you?" Fabia asked, scrubbing at a bit of hardened carrot.

"I live in Hilo. The Big Island," he said. "It sounds like a vacation, but I do Council work, too. We all do. After what happened to my father . . ."

He stopped speaking and breathed in. For a few minutes, neither of them said anything, washing and drying and stacking the dishes in the cupboard. The repetition of mindless work wasn't helping Fabia, though, her thoughts repeatedly turning to Niall, to Rufus, to Macara, an obsessive loop of pain.

"Listen," Felix said finally. "If we could find Rufus, we can find your brother. I'd about given up hope. My mother was destroyed, and Sariel wanted to jump out of his bed and hunt Kallisto down and kill her with his hands instead of magic. But look—there you were the whole time, taking him in and saving him. You've got to have hope."

Fabia took out the stopper and turned to Felix, trying to smile. She wanted to say something positive, but then the bedroom door opened and Rufus and Justus came out, Rufus walking slowly, heavy with memory.

Justus put on his robe and then put a hand on Rufus's shoulder. He looked at Fabia and Felix, and raised his eyebrows. Fabia caught a thought in the air, *Poor lad*, and then Justus pulled away from the idea and smiled.

"This lad's a fair patient. Much more inclined than that other brother of yours. Certainly, Rufus is a bit recalcitrant, but I had my way with him!" Justus laughed, slapping Rufus on the back. "It's all back now, his memory, you know. Got rid of those bruises and aches and pains as well. He'll be fine after some sleep."

Felix went to Justus, talking quietly. Rufus walked over to Fabia, and she put a hand on his forearm.

"How are you feeling?"

Rufus sighed. "Tired. Worried about Sariel. About Niall. I want to get this over with tomorrow and find Kallisto. Make her pay for what she did to us."

Despite his fatigue, his words were filled with metal, fire, anger that Fabia hadn't felt in him before. Memory had given him back desire, and his desire was for revenge.

My desire is for you, too, he thought, his mind wisping into hers.

She shook her head, her throat tight and painful, her eyes pinched with tears. *Not now. Not yet.*

He watched her, his eyes dark and steady. Fabia couldn't hold his gaze and looked at her hand on his arm, the way she gripped him tight. She took her hand away, crossing her arms across her chest.

"So I'm off," Justus said. "Back to patient number one. Be safe!"

Rufus lifted a hand, and then Justus spun into matter, leaving an empty space that was almost visible. For a moment, Fabia wanted to call him back, ask him to heal her, take away the pain and sorrow that beat in her body like a virus. People sometimes visited healers for just that, to rid them of the worst of sorrows and despair. Later, when they had gone on awhile happily, they might ask for the past back, knowing they could handle it due to the passing of time. But Fabia knew that for her, the only cure was to live through the waiting and the anxiety and then to find Niall and bring him home where he belonged.

Felix moved next to Rufus and put his arm around his brother's shoulders.

"Are you sure you want to do this tomorrow? I know Baris Fraser or Mazi Kakkilya would come. Adalbert mentioned them earlier."

Rufus thought about the two *sorciers*, men he knew from school and knew well still. But then he shook his head and breathed in. "No. I want to do this."

Felix looked at Rufus, and then Fabia could feel Felix watching her, his mind circling her thoughts, but she clamped down, not letting him in.

"I think we should get some sleep." She walked to the hall closet and pulled out blankets and pillows and sheets and took them to the sofa, where she began to make up a bed for Felix. Ignoring the brothers' conversation behind her and Rufus's constant but polite tapping at her thoughts, she tucked the sheet around the corners of the cushions. She knew she would rather sleep out here, but the two men would hardly fit in her double bed, their long arms and legs everywhere. And after all, she was an adult; she could sleep with Rufus one more night, though she would make sure he stayed on his side of the bed.

This had all gone too fast. He hadn't even known who his mother and brothers were when he pulled her into the bedroom, unbuttoning her blouse, holding her breasts.

Fabia stopped moving, remembering his mouth on her skin, the way her body responded to his. If Adalbert and everyone hadn't shown up, Fabia knew they would have ended up on the bed. What was wrong with her? How could she have enjoyed that when Niall was in trouble? She should have felt his pain, his fear. She should have heard him calling her.

"Fabs?" Rufus came over to the sofa, picking up a blanket and handing it to her. "Are you okay?"

"Fine," she said, grabbing the blanket from him and opening it up and laying it on top of the sheet. "Just brilliant."

Turning to the brothers, she put her hands on her hips, then crossed her arms across her chest, and then let them hang at her sides. As her body tried to find comfort, both Rufus and Felix stared at her, their dark eyes so steady and kind that she had to look away, afraid of what their concern meant. Afraid for Niall.

She pulled in a breath and looked toward the hallway. "I'm going to bed. See you in the morning."

Without another word, she went into the bathroom, closed the door behind her, and sat on the toilet. She closed her eyes and moved immediately to the wound in her mind, the empty place where Niall lived inside her.

Niall, she thought. *I'm coming. Nothing will stop me.*

Out of habit, she waited for a reply, but there was no sound at all, nothing but the drip from the bathroom faucet, the *click, click* of the thermostat, the constant lull of conversation from the other side of the door.

Fabia put her head in her hands, feeling sick, and wondered how she would make it to morning.

Chapter Eight

Rufus listened to the bathroom door open and then the bedroom door close. He half expected the lock to click, but it didn't, and he breathed out, sitting down on the sofa Fabia had made up for Felix. His head hurt, pounding with the release of thought and memory and feeling, his life unfurling with Justus's touch in his mind. Everything inside him felt raw, as if he had a body and mind hangover. The night with Sariel and Kallisto pounded in his thoughts, the memories of Kallisto hurling matter at him sharp and acidic. Now he could see Sariel, remember who his brother was, taste the bitter reflux of all that had happened.

"Hey, bro," Felix said, sitting next to him. "How are you doing? Feeling okay?"

Rufus shrugged, pushing his hair back off his face. "Kallisto was so strong. Too strong. It took all I had to get her away from Sariel, and look what she was able to do to me. To him. I don't know what will happen when we try to find Niall. She'll be with Macara and maybe even . . . Quain."

Felix leaned back and put his feet up on the coffee table. "Look, don't get all in a twist over this. It's not going to be easy, but she didn't manage to get rid of you, did she? And we'll have Nala Nagode. You remember her coming in to teach us *charmes de destruction*. I thought she'd rip the roof off the building."

Rufus smiled and rolled his eyes. "I remember Nala."

Felix nodded, breaking into a smile. "Oh yeah. I forgot she had a thing for you. Even back then. I wonder when she'll get the message."

"She's too intense," Rufus said. "I've never been as scared of a woman before or since. But she will be great to have on this mission."

"Don't forget Fabia," Felix said. "Adalbert says when she wants to, she can hear everything for miles. That's pretty flipping amazing."

Rufus nodded, looking at the bedroom door. "She's amazing. She saved my life."

Yeah, she's a great nurse, but she's also hot. So what's going on? Felix thought. *Are you two . . . ?*

Rufus shook his head, breathing in. *No. Almost. She's worried about her brother. She thinks that because I kissed her when I didn't have all of my memory, it wasn't real.*

Women, Felix thought. *That's why I like the revolving door policy of dating. One comes in, stays awhile, leaves just as another spins her way in. The longer they're around, the less I want to know.*

"You are a true shit," Rufus said, smiling for the first time since Justus had arrived. "Please, don't ever change. Just you being you makes me look good in comparison."

"I'll do my best. It's hard work, but someone has to do it," Felix said, looking toward Fabia's closed bedroom door. *So what's going to go on in there tonight?*

I may be sleeping on the floor, Rufus thought. He laughed and looked at Felix, patting his brother's shoulder.

There are some potions du amour, *you know*, Felix thought. *Remember that weird-ass Madame Lakritz? She taught me a few things my final year at Bampton.* His mouth open, Rufus stared at Felix, thinking that if he'd ever thought about it, if Madame Lakritz had ever taken down her hair and worn something other than that stiff-necked robe, she might have been—no, she was pretty. "No wonder I couldn't get a date in school. Between you and Sariel I was only an afterthought. Unbelievable."

"You know what I always say. Mom and Dad saved the best for last," Felix said. "But seriously, you don't have to rely on your sad-sack charms."

"We've got more important things to worry about." Rufus stood up. "Get some sleep. It's going to be a long day tomorrow."

"It looks like it's going to be a long night as well," Felix whispered. "The floor's a pretty hard place."

Picking up a pillow, Rufus threw it at Felix and walked to the bedroom door. His heart was pounding, and he realized he was more afraid of walking into this room to face Fabia than he had been when he'd walked in with Justus, who had been ready to unleash Rufus's painful memories.

He took a deep breath and turned the doorknob, opening the door quietly and slipping in, shutting it behind him. The room was dark—only a yellow slit of light coming from outside slipping from behind the curtain—and Fabia was still in the bed. He could smell her lavender soap and the soft floral smell of body lotion. As his eyes adjusted, he could see that she'd scooted to the edge of the bed and tucked the blankets around her, clearly defining the terms of their sleeping arrangement.

Quietly, Rufus took off his shoes, socks, shirt, and pants, and carefully slid in between the blankets. She might have moved to the edge of the bed, but he could breathe in her warmth, her skin, the garden of her hair in the air under the quilt. Even though he tried not to, he thought back to their kiss, the way her hands moved softly up and down his body, the way she pressed her breasts against him, and despite his best efforts, he began to grow hard. With a flicker, he felt her thoughts circle his, asking for permission. Sighing and closing his eyes, he let her in, allowing her to see what was going on in his mind and his body

"Rufus," Fabia whispered. "I can't."

"Fabs," he said, reaching out with his hand and finding the soft flannel of her nightgown. "I'm having a hard time keeping you and my heart in separate rooms, but it's all right."

Fabs, he heard her think. *Fabs. Oh, Niall.*

"He's gone," she said, turning to him.

"We'll find him, Fabia." Rufus stroked her hair, letting his fingertips graze her forehead.

"It's my fault. He wouldn't be in trouble if I hadn't been so keen to find Macara. I don't know what I was trying to prove. I was offered other jobs, you know. I was offered a job at Bampton. Teaching. Something safe. But I had to take this post. I was selfish. I wanted to catch the bad guys. Be a hero. It was like an obsession." She closed her eyes and bit her lip. Rufus saw she was trying to keep her sobs inside her body.

"You took this job because it was the right thing to do. And if you hadn't been here, Fabia, I don't know what I would have done. It's small consolation, I know, but you saved me."

She brought her hands to her face, and as she did, Rufus pulled her to him, letting her head rest on his chest. As she touched him, he flicked away the desire created by her lovely softness, tried to ignore the way her flesh made his body beat so loud he was sure Felix would hear. Rufus swallowed, relaxed, comforted her. Fabia held him, letting her sobs out, her whole body shaking.

"No one . . . no one knows what it's like with Niall and me," she said after a moment, breath and tears in her voice.

"Show me," Rufus said. "Let me see."

She shook her head. "I've never shown anyone."

"Trust me," he said. "Help me understand."

He felt her indecision in her body, her breathing stopping for a moment, and then she moved away from him slightly, a slit of air between them. Her thoughts stilled and then like a blooming flower, Rufus felt her mind open to him. There she was, little, a baby. Or was it even before? In the womb? In the warm dark stillness, Rufus could feel two heartbeats, two consciousnesses strung together with gold light, the strand of color a conduit of two minds, sharing information, feelings, emotion.

At first, in the light of life, the babies didn't seem to understand that they were individuals, different, unique, but as time passed, so did the space for their own consciousness, their own ideas, feelings, thoughts. But even as they became individuals, the strand of light between them developed, twisting thicker as they grew older, ropy with experience and knowledge. In Fabia's mind, there were images of them as children, miles apart but each involved in what the other was doing. Niall on camping trips with his friends, roasting marshmallows, telling horrible jokes, while Fabia sat at the dinner table with her parents. There was Fabia swimming laps at the Bampton indoor pool, while Niall hunched over his *sortilège de protection* homework in detention, punished for having used magic to lift Marguarite Lipton's skirt. Anything one did or read or said or thought, the other had the experience as well. Life was doubled—one could be learning to move through matter as the other ate a cherry pie. One could be fuming in anger over the latest *Moyenne* election, while the other was laughing at a sitcom on television. When they fell in love or kissed someone or cried late at night, in some measure, both did. They talked through their thoughts all day and even nightlong, a running conversation that had lasted a lifetime.

Still firm in Fabia's mind, Rufus moved into the moment Niall had disappeared today, found the hole in her mind, the ragged surface his absence left in her thoughts. He winced but didn't pull away, wanting to really know how Fabia felt the moment the connection was severed. Her mind swirled with so much loneliness and fear and doubt. *Alone, alone* pounded in her mind like an extra heart.

"He's like your shadow or vice versa," he said. "He's always been right there, like an extra part." He wondered if either of them had ever wanted to shuffle off the other like a stifling coat and run away.

No, she thought. *Never. We fight sometimes and bicker and promise to tune out, but it's like a mirror you can't stop looking in. He's myself.*

Rufus heard her thoughts, shaking his head. Could he ever have stood Felix or Sariel that close to him? Sure, he loved his brothers, but sometimes he wanted to deck them both, mostly Felix. They'd all shared their thoughts enough and liked being together in play and in work, but a connection that strong? Rufus always imagined he would only find a connection that close, that permanent in a lover or a wife.

"It's weird, I know," she said. "I've always wondered what would happen when one of us found our true—found someone."

"No. No, it's not weird. It's different. It's not how most people go about life, not even most *Croyant*. You and he have grown up together, in almost all ways. You've been there for each other. But maybe one day you'll have to let him go into his own life."

She didn't say anything, but he felt her tense. Finally she breathed out, "Why would I do that? Why should I have to?"

Rufus shrugged and then pressed her tight, slowly leaving her mind. "I'm here for you, Fabia. Just like you were for me. Thank you for letting me see how you and Niall think."

She nodded against his chest. He kissed the top of her head and sighed, looking up at the dark ceiling. Rufus closed his thoughts and hoped that tomorrow they would find Niall before Macara and Kallisto could do to Niall anything like what Kallisto had done to him. Rufus had tilted for days through cold and darkness, his mind a swamp of confusion, his body shaky and strung out and ready to break. One more night out on the streets might have done him in. No one could be as lucky, not even Niall. What were the chances that Niall would ever find someone like Fabia to pull him out of the darkness, take him home, and save him? There was only one Fabia, and she was here, in his arms, asleep now, her light breath soft against his neck.

* * *

They awoke when the sky was black except for a thin dove-colored band on the horizon. The city lights were just flickering off when Fabia flung back the covers, and Rufus padded into the living room to wake up Felix, who was sprawled on the sofa, dreaming—Rufus found as he looked into his brother's thoughts—of the ocean and a beautiful woman named Keala.

Rufus shook his head and pushed gently at Felix's shoulder just as the dream really began to pick up steam.

Later, while Rufus, Fabia, and Felix hunched over the counter eating a hurried breakfast of tea and toast, Adalbert, Zosime, and Nala Nagode whirled in. Moments later, Fabia's parents knocked on the door, and they all stood together, waiting for Nala to tell them the plan.

Nala was a tall, beautiful African woman in her early forties, who favored the color yellow, her robes always a twirl of sunflower and sunrise. The minute he spotted her at a Council meeting or at a social function, Rufus shut his mind off from view, scared that he would think something ridiculous or stupid. Whenever she looked at him, he heard his thoughts start to stutter and rev. And for some reason, she always headed straight for him, her dark eyes taking him all in, her hand on his arm, her body just a bit too close.

"She digs you, bro," Felix had said once when they were at Adalbert's seventieth birthday celebration. "Go for it."

For about half a second, Rufus had entertained the idea, wondering what Nala's lips would feel like against his own, what else her hands could do besides casting strong spells. But then as she approached him, he shut down again, unable to find any words that might make him seem even slightly interesting.

Now as Nala faced the group, he saw her eyes linger on him for a second too long, and with a flick of happiness, he felt Fabia start as she noticed Nala's gaze, her mind full of a sensation of protectiveness. No, not protectiveness. Irritation. Jealousy.

"I have consulted with other *chasseurs*, and we have determined that Macara and Kallisto have fled the U.K. altogether," she said, her voice clear and calm. "Where Quain is, we don't know. But those two have taken their hostage to California, not far from the Bay Area. Kallisto is familiar with the territory, and perhaps she's been setting up this location for some time."

Zosime crossed her arms. "She told Sariel she was leaving for Europe."

"An incapacitated man will believe just about anything," Nala said somewhat harshly, and then noticing Zosime's stricken face, she added after a pause, "Maybe she left him with that knowledge to throw him and Rufus off her track. Or maybe she was here briefly before traveling back to the States."

"So," Adalbert began, "we've alerted some of our people in the area. Brennus Broussard and Philomel Holly. They will meet you in Truckee."

Brennus, Felix thought to Rufus. *Not that old fart. At least Philomel keeps him in line,* Rufus thought.

Shhh, thought Zosime, intercepting.

"Do you know if Niall is all right?" Xanthe asked. "Have you heard a thing?"

Nala paused, and when Rufus tried to move into her thoughts, he ran into a block, a place she didn't want Xanthe to go.

"No news," Nala said, "is, as they say, good news."

The room was silent, and Rufus tried not to read the worry in the room. But the feelings coming from Donoch, Xanthe, and Fabia were so strong, it was hard to avoid the terrifying pictures: Niall suffering, Niall crying out, Niall . . . dead.

"Let's not waste any more time," Rufus said, pushing his voice out in order to stop the horrible images floating in the room. "The sooner we leave, the sooner we get Niall back home."

At his words, Fabia leaned into him slightly, and he reached for her hand, holding it tight in between their robes.

"Of course," Nala said, her eyebrows raised. "But first, I want to give the three of you my information before we go."

Adalbert nodded. "I think we can leave you all to your work. You know how to contact me, as do Brennus and Philomel."

Rufus breathed in, but before he could even exhale, Zosime rushed to him, pulling Felix with her. Rufus let go of Fabia's hand and moved into the corner of the room, while Fabia talked with her parents.

"Mom," Felix said. "It's going to be fine."

Zosime bit her lip, and looked in the direction of the kitchen, as if her sons wouldn't notice her tears.

"He's right," Rufus said, kissing her cheek. "They seem to have taken Niall as a warning. An afterthought. The big business is with Quain. More than likely, they've tossed Niall in Truckee, and he's standing in front of Moody's Restaurant wondering how he got there. Probably some ski bunny has found him and taken him to her A-frame to 'heal' him."

Zosime shrugged and wiped her face, pretending to smile a little. "I know. It's just I wish we didn't have this business all the time. We say that *Moyenne* are backward and violent, but look at us. People wanting everything. Hurting each other. Killing . . ."

She stopped, and Rufus glanced at Felix, knowing that because their father had been killed by bad magic, hurt in the most final way by Quain, a *sorcier* gone bad, Zosime would never truly be at peace with her boys doing Council work. The diamond in the family mythology was the day Quain tossed Hadrian Valasay onto the tracks of the Châtelet Metro Station in Paris, leaving him to be crushed by an oncoming train. This was the story that motivated all three of them, urged them forward. This was the story that had defined who they were.

"It's time," Nala said. Rufus kissed Zosime as did Felix, and after some quick advice and worried waves, she, Fabia's parents, and Adalbert left, disappearing into the gray.

"I don't expect this to be too demanding," Nala said. "Niall is not worth enough to Macara or Kallisto to muster much resistance to his rescue."

Fabia almost gasped, her mouth open, her eyes intense. "Niall's been doing Council work for five years. He's been important to *Le Société Pour Intégration des Tous,* the very group Macara worked for. Niall's not insignificant!"

Nala gave her a quick glance, and Rufus could feel her irritated sigh. "What I meant is that Niall is not at the center of their attentions. A young man who recruits *Croyant* for *Moyenne* diplomatic relations is useful but not the crucial component to, let's say, a ransom situation. And while you and he enjoy a superlative amount of telepathic ability, he does not offer them anything Kallisto and Macara do not already have."

She's rude but right, Fabia, Rufus thought. *She's*

actually just trying to tell us the mission shouldn't be too dangerous.

Are you defending her? Fabia thought back. *How can she say that about Niall? Why would you let her?*

Fabia, Rufus thought. *She's just—*

"Enough chatter," Nala said. "Let's join hands, and I will show you what I know about both Macara and Kallisto. Also, Fabia, I'd like you to give Rufus and Felix the information you've already given Adalbert about what you've picked up about Macara thus far. And, Rufus, you need to show us all what Kallisto can do."

Barely hearing Nala's commands, Rufus tried to comfort Fabia, but she'd closed her mind off to him and kept her eyes focused straight ahead, staring, he noticed, at Felix, who smiled at him, seeming to have heard everything, said and otherwise.

They all held hands, and Nala said, "Close your eyes."

Nala squeezed his hand and with a jolt, Rufus found himself, Fabia, and Felix in her memory, swirling together in information and facts.

Like birds, they all came down upon the small Sierra Nevada town of Truckee, gliding along the railroad tracks that ran through the downtown. Speeding past the buildings, past the highway, moving over the mountains, they launched toward the blue eye of Lake Tahoe and then settled into a neighborhood of large wood and stone houses, curving up a hill until they reached one. Nala stopped them there, wending around the house's perimeter, making sure they all saw the doors, the windows.

That's as far as I've gone, she thought to them all. *I don't know if there is anything subterranean or not. But Brennus and Philomel are there now, assessing the lay of the land.*

Within Nala's memory, Rufus scanned the windows of the house, and he turned to Fabia, who was doing the same, her face now devoid of jealousy or irritation. She was focused like a falcon, wanting only to find Niall.

Nala lifted them over the house one more time, and then she turned to Fabia, who closed her eyes and breathed in. In another rocking blast, Rufus found himself in a room, standing at the back like an audience as Macara, tall and redheaded, stood in front of another man who was trapped in a chair, locked there by an *esclavage* spell. He pulled at his arms and legs as if trying to free them from ropes or chains.

"You will give me what you know about the Council's plan," Macara said, raising a hand. As he did, the man in the chair whimpered, blood seeping from a deep cut above his eye.

This is what Cadeyrn Macara does best, Fabia told them through her thoughts. *Abbott Jeffreys, the man in the chair, was working with the* Banque de Croyant. *He was in charge of Council funds for social programs in South America, funds Macara soon got his hands on and gave to Quain.*

He was, Felix thought. *As in the man is dead.*

Was. Fabia nodded. *Dead.* And then like a nightmare movie, she showed the same scene time after time, *sorcièrs* and *sorcières* tortured, weeping, begging, only to be found later, dead.

Fabia's images faded, and then Nala turned to Rufus, and he breathed in raggedly, the newly restored memory of the battle with Kallisto like cut glass in his throat. Nodding, he closed his eyes and pushed the past out for them all to see.

He brought them to Sariel's house in Sausalito, the night fogless and cool, stars and a full moon overhead. The group stood as they had in Fabia's memory, watching as Kallisto chanted softly, holding Sariel's body aloft in the middle of the room, pulling his mind like taffy. She was so calm as she tortured Sariel, her hair slick and still down her back, her eyes calm as Sariel's body recoiled from the pain of her magic. But then Rufus saw himself burst into the room in a flame of matter, whirling to face Kallisto, who was stunned only for a second. He hit her with spell after spell, and she retaliated so easily, too easily. She sent plumes of hot, burning spell at him, throwing him up and against the walls of the room. Nothing he did mattered, her strength amazing, as if she was fueled from another source.

She was, Nala thought. *By Quain*.

During the battle, Sariel fell to the floor unconscious, and Kallisto began to move closer to Rufus, her magic overwhelming him. He let her voice peel into the memory, allowed the group to hear her taunts.

"Come to save your dear brother, have you?" Kallisto had said, her eyes full of laughter. "You want this sad thing?"

Rufus hadn't dared to look, knowing if he really focused on Sariel, his pale skin, his dangling limbs, he would stop. But he caught a glimpse, his tall, strong younger brother a broken doll on the wood floor.

"You never deserved him," Rufus said, pressing forward, and for a long while, he fought back, Kallisto reeling a few times, but then he began to slow, to fade, his body slack and clumsy, and then, in a blip, the memory was gone.

I can't find what happened for the next few days.

We don't really even know how many days it was. Justus couldn't even locate a trace, Rufus thought. *It's all a mystery until Fabia.*

For a brief second, Rufus thought he could hear a snicker in Nala's mind, but he ignored it, letting the past seep back into the gray. He turned to Fabia, who had her eyes closed, still focusing on the scene before her, wanting every clue that Rufus's scene could afford her.

Nala raised her arms and thought, *Here is what I imagine will happen.*

A vision flew before them, a scene in the house, the group whirling in protected by spells, aiming spells bolstered by all their magic at Macara and Kallisto. In Nala's vision, Niall sat trapped in a chair, and then Nala gave them other views: Niall on a table and then unconscious in the corner. Worse, but possible, Niall was not there at all, the chair, the table, the floor empty. When the group appeared, Macara and Kallisto tried to stun them with *sortilèges de ètourdir*. The group's protection spells deflected these attempts, and knowing that they were free from *Croyant* law now, Cadeyrn and Kallisto switched to *sortilèges du mort*, not caring who died, knowing Quain was strong enough to whisk them free of any Council court.

Where is Quain? Felix thought. *Where is he going to fight us from?*

Nala's vision faltered, flicked for a moment, came back in full force. *We don't know. We just have to know he has power there. Kallisto and Macara are conduits, pulling in his strength,* she thought.

So why do you think this is going to be so easy, no problem at all? Fabia thought, her mind whirring with anger and anxiety. *If Quain is giving them power, what do we possibly have that can counter any of it? What can* we *use*?

The scene disappeared and then Nala opened up another, magic, a spell none of them had ever seen. For a second, Rufus's eyes were full of light, electricity, current. Bringing the group back to the vision of the house, they saw Nala raise her hands, creating a bright ball of gold in her hands. The ball lifted from her as if pulled by a string and hovered in the room like a miniature sun. With a crack, the ball exploded, draping the room with shimmering lines of sparkling color. In the middle of the room, trapped in the bars of color, Macara and Kallisto slowed, stopped, froze.

What is it? Rufus thought.

A sortilège du nature morte. *A still life. Something the* comitè de magie *came up with recently. If it works, they won't be able to move for days, enough time for us to transfer them to Council cells.*

Ever been tried out in a true battle? Rufus thought

No. Here's the alternative, Nala thought, showing them Macara and Kallisto chanting counterspells, both of them somehow knowing what to say to attack the aching fatigue and stillness overcoming them. And then, the battle began again, spells arcing into the room, everything chaos, the end unknown, even in Nala's imagination.

Slowly, Nala's scene disappeared, and Rufus again felt her hand and Fabia's in his own. They floated in matter together, and then Nala thought, *Let's go. Brennus and Philomel have found a place for us to stay tonight. They've been keeping a close watch on the house, and we will confer before we enact our plan.*

Why wait? Fabia thought, her mind shrill with feeling. *Why not take them on now, by surprise, while we're ready? You have the bloody magic in your hands. Why let any more time go by?*

Rufus felt Nala's body tense, her fingers stiffening in his palm. *We need Brennus's and Philomel's information. They'll know what spells are surrounding the house.*

And without another word, she brought forth an image of another house in Truckee, smaller than the one she'd shown them before, set back deep in a forest of sugar pines and white firs. But Rufus liked the scene, imagining the sharp clean air, the smell of snow in the wind. And he knew he had to get Fabia away from the images of Niall in pain.

Rufus nodded and turned his mind to Fabia's, cutting his thoughts off from Nala's and Felix's. *It's as good a plan as I can think of*, he thought. *And who knows what else Brennus and Philomel have come up with?*

For the first time since they'd gone into matter, Fabia turned to him, her blue eyes almost black, full of distrust and fear.

My second half, she thought, shaking her head. *I don't know how to act without it. Him. Niall. I'm scared.*

I know, Rufus thought, and he dropped Nala's hand and pulled Fabia to him, holding her tight in his arms. Keeping the vision of the Truckee house in his mind, he brought them both up and into the thick of matter and moved out into the field. The others moved too, rising up behind him, and in an instant, they all were there, breathing in Sierra air, feeling the dappled, chill mountain air on their faces.

"My boy," Brennus Broussard said, walking toward Rufus, the wind of matter still ringing in his ears. Brennus's blue robes billowed behind him, his long gray beard whipping in the wind.

Without letting go of Fabia entirely, Rufus extended a hand to his father's old friend. Brennus grabbed it, shaking it thoroughly, a smile on his lined face. But then he looked at Fabia, and his smile faded.

"You must be Fabia Fair," he said, dropping Rufus's hand. "I'm Brennus Broussard."

Fabia nodded, pulling away from Rufus and extending her hand. Rufus knew how much it took from her to be strong, normal, functioning, when Niall was in trouble.

"That's right. A pleasure to meet you," she said. Then she added, "Thank you for your help."

"I'm sorry about this trouble. I've known your parents for many years, and I know this must be hard on them," Brennus said.

Fabia didn't answer right away, and when he turned to move into her thoughts, all he could get to were her emotions, irritation like barbed wire around her. But then she took a deep breath and nodded.

"They're very worried about my brother," she said, her voice sticking on every word.

As she spoke, Rufus tried to slip into her thoughts undetected, but she'd slammed down her door, his attempts bouncing back. He reached out with his hand to touch her, and she moved away, just enough to avoid his fingers and not enough for Brennus to notice. But Rufus noticed, felt her rejection like a fork in some soft body part.

Brennus shook his head. "This is bad business. I always told Sariel that his woman was no good. No good at all. Something in her face. Too pretty, I always said. Beauty is deceiving. Beauty can be a lie. Your father—"

"What have you found out?" Rufus interrupted.

In another whirl, Felix and Nala appeared from matter. Brennus turned to greet them, and as he did, Rufus saw a small, gray-haired woman in the window of the house. She waved down at them, and Rufus waved back, knowing he would recognize Philomel's aureole of hair anywhere. Following his gaze, Brennus looked up at the window and then turned back to them.

"Let's go inside," he said. "And Philomel and I will tell you everything."

Chapter Nine

Fabia knew she was breathing and walking and making small communicative noises and gestures: a smile, a nod, a *Hmm*. Now she was sitting, her legs crossed, and holding a cup of tea, smiling absently at Philomel Holly, whose amazingly curly hair seemed to be carrying the knit hat she wore. But this pleasant, quiet person wasn't who Fabia was inside. As soon as she and Rufus had touched down in Truckee, she'd been filled with rage. Why were they here, sitting in a comfortable living room, sipping tea and coffee and beer, when Niall was only miles away and probably in great pain? Nothing about this plan made any sense to her. None at all. Of course there were protective spells cast about the house and property where Niall was being held hostage. Of course it would be dangerous to travel by matter and confront Macara and Kallisto. Of course Quain was somewhere directing all the action, sending his terrible magic their way. What were these people telling her that she didn't know already? Didn't they have the new spell? Wasn't it supposed to change everything?

And why wasn't Rufus fighting harder for her? He knew how she felt about Niall. For God's sake, she'd let him into her mind and heart, shown him her entire life, Niall. And now he was sitting in an overstuffed chair drinking a beer, talking to Brennus, who looked more like someone's grandfather than a warrior. But there Rufus was, relaxing as if he were here at Lake Tahoe on holiday. As if this were a social visit instead of a rescue. As if tomorrow's event were a hike into the hills rather than the rescue of Fabia's most important person in the world.

"There are layers of spells around their house," Philomel said. "The first is a *sortilège du fil de fer*—like a fence, basically. Barbed wire. That's nothing. But there is something else just after that. We've sent down our thoughts to a friend of ours in The City. Pico DeSanchez. He's going to let us know as soon as he can."

"Nullify it," Fabia said flatly. "Surround it with *disparaître*."

Philomel smiled kindly, her face warm and soft, her hat bobbing on top of her hair. "We don't think that will work, dear. And that spell takes time. By the time the protections were gone, Kallisto and Macara would be alerted to our presence. That wouldn't be good for your brother."

Fabia breathed in, tapped her foot on the hardwood floor, and then looked out the window. Dark gray clouds were blowing in over Outlook Mountain from the lake, the fall sky filled with an early snow. The wind pushed through the sugar pines, needles tapping on the large front windows.

"So what's your plan?" Rufus asked. Fabia could feel him watching her, and she stared into the fireplace, ignoring his constant questions circling in her mind. Brennus had piled the wood high, and the fire cracked and hissed as the wood split from the heat, pine oil filling the room. Flames leaped up and around the logs, tongues of orange and red flicking and hissing, the sound lulling Fabia. She stared into the burn, felt her gaze go soft, the colors merging, melding, becoming one red lick, one long sound, one full smell of wood and smoke. *Shhh,* the fire said. *Wheesht. Hush. Hush. Listen to me. Never mind the rest. Hush, hush. Listen, listen to me. I know what's going on. Hush, hush, hush. Close your mind. Listen, my dear, listen. No, don't open to him. No. Only me. Listen only to me.*

Her eyes drifted, and she saw the fire through clouds, her ears filled with the crackle of heat and her mouth with the thick air full of ember and scent. The rest of the group talked on about spells and plans, but all Fabia paid attention to was the low, persistent voice licking at her from the fireplace, slipping into her mind, filling her with warmth, the only warmth she'd felt since Adalbert told them Niall was missing. As the Sierra afternoon turned into evening, the group's conversation constant, she realized she was the only one in the room who understood what had to be done.

Cold. Her feet were cold. What was it? Something hard, crisp, frosty on her feet and her cheeks. Her forehead. Her hands. It didn't matter whatever the biting feeling was, because she needed to move away from the house, from those people who didn't care. But why? Why was she walking? Where was she going?

Don't worry, said the voice from the fire. *You'll know when you get there. Just a little bit farther.*

But why was the fire still talking to her? She remembered moving away from the fireplace, sitting at the dining room table and eating a meal, talking to Rufus and Felix and the rest, and then falling asleep in a twin bed in one of the bedrooms on the second floor, Nala asleep in the other.

Trust me, the voice said. *I know what has to be done. I can help you. I can show you the way.*

Fabia nodded. The fire had been right. She should leave the house and find Niall. She shouldn't tell the others. No one cared about Niall as much as she did. Her parents weren't even here. Adalbert didn't bother to come. She was the only one who could save him. That's what the fire said, and the fire would show her where to go and what to do.

But the fire was dead. She'd walked past it on her way out, hadn't she? Out where? Where was she? Fabia tried to clear her mind, shaking her head as if she could fling away her confusion.

Just a little bit more, the fire said, its voice as smooth as flame. *Just beyond those aspen trees. Hear them? I know you can hear the leaves singing in the wind.* She stopped, listened, opening her ears to the sounds. Of course she could hear them. They were calling to her, saying her name, whispering in a soft slip of leaf, *Fabia, Fabia. Come to us. Here. Now.*

Fabia took another step. The fire knew what she could hear. The fire knew everything. She moved forward, following the sound of the wind in the aspens, stars guiding her.

Right there. Almost there, the fire said. *Good girl. That's right. That's the way.*

If she reached out a hand, she could almost touch the first aspen, its bark ghostly white even in the darkness. A strong wind whisked a sudden snow flurry through the tops of the trees, yellow leaves the size of silver dollars falling at her feet.

Here. You are here, the fire said, but then there was another sound, a *thump, thump*, and then something grabbed her from behind and pulled her back and yanked her away from the trees.

No! said the fire. *Fight him. Fight the man and come to the trees. What about Niall? Don't you want to see your brother again? You can save his life. You can make the difference.*

Fabia twisted in the strong arms that held her, needing to follow the fire's voice. "Let me go," she said. "You're keeping me from Niall. Let me go."

The man connected to the arms—who was it?—ignored her, pulled her farther back, squeezing her ribs too tightly as he did. She tried to think of magic she could use to stop him, but her head ached with confusion.

"You're putting my brother in danger!" she said, beginning to weep. "The fire's voice promised!"

"No, Fabia. I'm not doing anything to Niall," the man said. But he didn't say any more until they were back in front of the house, far from the aspen trees, far, far away from Niall. Fabia blinked, began to breathe, and turned in the man's grip to look at him. She stared at him, her mind clearing as she saw his intense dark eyes and felt his hand on her face. It was Rufus. Rufus.

"Fabs, that voice isn't going to do anything but lead you into danger. Look at me. Look at me!" Rufus cupped her face in his palms, and she brought her eyes to his.

"*Lâcher prise*," he said slowly, and as he said the words, Fabia felt her mind wriggle free from the fire's tight grip, the evening suddenly as clear as her knowledge that it wasn't the fire who had spoken to her but Cadeyrn Macara.

For the first time since Nala had shown them her plan, Fabia felt her anger release and float up into the cold air. What had she been doing? What had she almost done? If not for Rufus, in another second, she would have been as trapped as Niall was.

"Oh, Rufus," she said, laying her cheek on his chest, listening to the strong beat of his heart. "How did I let that happen? I should know better, I should."

Rufus didn't speak, but simply held her close. A great horned owl *hoo-hooed* in a sugar pine and then took off, beating its strong wings. In the distance, she could still hear the whipping tinkle of the aspen leaves, could almost feel the fire's lick of promise.

Kissing the top of her head, Rufus pulled away so she could see his face as he spoke. "He knew you'd be vulnerable, and somehow he managed to use the fire as a conduit, despite our protections. He almost had you—the aspens were at the edge of Brennus's defense spell."

"I'm endangering the mission," she said. "I'm endangering Niall. I shouldn't be here. I was so rude to everyone, so sure about hurrying the rescue. I almost ruined everything."

Shaking his head, Rufus held her close again. "It's all your feeling that worries Macara. The reason that he has Niall in the first place is to get to you. He's playing on your worry and love for Niall, and he was trying to get you the easy way. He'd rather not fight you and us, Fabs. He'd rather have you with him, on his side. He knows how you used to admire him. You were the obvious one to go after.

He probably used Niall's mind to get to you, finding the path that connects the two of you and sending his message through it."

"But what if I let him in like that again?" she said. "How can I fight him?"

Rufus caressed her head, pulled her even closer, close enough so that she could hear his heart. "We need your help. We need your hearing. We can't do it without you."

Niall, he's right, Fabia thought as Rufus held her. *This time, I won't make mistakes. I'm coming to get you.*

She almost winced at Niall's silence.

"You must be cold," Rufus said. "Let's go back to the house. I'm sure you've been missing your roommate Nala." He didn't say anything for a moment and then sighed. "I'd gotten used to sleeping with you, and I was a bit surprised that Nala could steal you away from me."

For the first time since leaving Edinburgh, Fabia felt like she could smile. "Aye. Nala really likes me. And I have only you to blame."

Rufus ran his hand down her hair. "What does that mean?"

"Well," she said as they started walking toward the front steps. "Did you go out with her or what?"

He laughed quietly. "What are you implying?"

"Don't give me that. I see how she looks at you. I can read her thoughts even if she tries to cover them up."

"Are you jealous?"

Fabia was glad for the darkness, her face a sudden red. "No, I am not jealous of Nala Nagode," she lied.

I heard that lie, Rufus thought.

Conceited, Fabia thought back.

Just before the first step, Rufus held her still, turning her to him. As she looked up, Fabia felt her body stop, shimmer with anticipation, all her worry about Niall and the mission slipping away for just a second. *Just for a moment*, she thought to Niall. *I need this. I haven't forgotten you. I promise. I'll tell you about it later.*

For the briefest slice of a second, she waited for Niall to say, *Scutter off with you both, then. Don't keep the man waiting.*

But, of course, there was no answer.

With his eyes open, Rufus leaned down and kissed her, his mouth soft on hers. Fabia opened her mouth to his, their tongues pressing softly, softly, his hands on her face, smoothing her hair. Circling his neck with her arms, she moved even closer, harder, wanting his strength tight against her. He pressed her close, so close she could feel his pulse, his heart against her ribs.

Thank you for saving me, she thought as she reached a hand behind his neck, pulling him even tighter.

Who is saving whom? he thought back, picking her up, their mouths still pressed close, and walking up the stairs and into the house.

Fabia had seen Rufus naked, soaped his body with her own hands, run her fingers through his long dark hair. She'd rubbed his chest, kissed his neck, felt his erection under her palm, and almost fallen with him onto her bed. But as he stood in front of her in his darkened bedroom, slowly taking off his shirt, she thought she might blow a blood vessel. In the moonlight, his body gleamed, the shadow and light playing off his muscles, his hardened pectorals, the flare of his lats. Her breath was everywhere but in her lungs, and she felt that she might float away.

Moving closer to him, she placed a splayed hand on his chest, feeling his heat, his small, hard nipples under her palm. She bent to him, placing her mouth on his sternum, breathing in his warm skin smell. Slowly, she licked him, savoring his slightly salty taste as she ran her tongue up to his collarbone. Rufus breathed in quickly, and then lifted her head up, a palm on either side of her face, and leaned down to kiss her.

His mouth felt just like he was—safe, warm, exciting. It reminded her of magic, of places she'd gone in spells where she forgot the real world, the make-believe worlds she'd concocted with Niall, lands with only warm beaches, yellow sun, the lapping of soft, lulling waves. Or places with only deep, temperate forests, the air soft on every part of her skin, the voices of the ferns and redwoods a constant, pleasant hiss of sound.

Rufus's kiss was like a journey through matter. She was aloft, sailing forward, able to go anywhere with just a thought. Any destination was possible.

I know where I want this journey to end, Rufus thought, bringing his hands to the bottom of her shirt and pulling it up.

With some regret, Fabia moved away from his mouth and allowed him to pull her shirt off. She'd closed her eyes when the fabric went over her face, and kept them closed until she realized Rufus wasn't moving. Opening them, she saw that he was staring at her, his eyes glittering, his breathing ragged.

"You are amazing," he whispered. "So beautiful."

She smiled. "I think I'm fairly run-of-the-mill."

"Like hell you are. Let me just show you what I

think of you." Rufus shook his head, throwing her shirt on a chair. He moved to her, and leaned down to her breasts, cupping them in his hands, and taking one hard nipple in his mouth. Fabia arched back, closed her eyes. His suckle dragged something from the bottom of her, from her core.

She put her arms around him, stroking his back. With a nipple still in his mouth, he dropped his hands to her pants, unbuttoning them, pushing at the waistband and sliding it over her hips, taking her panties along with it. His fingers seemed to politely skirt the very place she wanted him to touch the most, so she put a hand on his, moving his fingers over her, letting him see how her body responded to his.

Oh God, Fabia, he thought, sliding his hand farther, slipping through her slickness. *You're so wet.* Then his thoughts became sensation and image instead of language, his mind full of the shape of her body, the feel of her wetness on his fingers, the need for his body to be inside hers. His breath was full of want. His skin, heat. His arms, need.

As he touched her, she pushed her pants down, kicking them off and away. Fabia pushed herself closer to him, thrusting against his hand and the two fingers he'd slid inside her. She brought her hands to his jeans, unbuttoning the fly and peeling open the waist. Fully erect, he was just as large as she'd imagined he'd be that night when she'd brought on a reaction by simply rubbing lotion on him. She took him in her hand, squeezing him in her palm. Under her fingers, he pulsed, growing even bigger.

Bad Florence Nightingale, he thought. *Checking out your patients. Doing nasty things to them with body lotion.*

If all of Flo's patients had lovely packages like this, you know she would have done more than tend fevers, she thought back. *You know she gave up tending patients to live a life of a recluse. All those missed opportunities.*

Poor Flo, Rufus thought.

Take off your pants, Fabia thought.

That means I have to take my hand off you, he thought. *I don't want to move. I want to move, but I want to stay in you forever.*

You can stay inside me forever, but let's trade body parts, Fabia thought, turning around quickly and leaning over the bed. *You can leave your pants on this way.*

Slowly, he pulled his fingers out and then leaned over her, his chest hair light on her back, his mouth on a shoulder blade, a hand on each cheek of her rear, pressing his erection against her and then sliding inside her with a quick, sudden intake of breath. Fabia closed her eyes, stretching out on the bed, letting herself feel all of him, the way he filled her up completely. And not just her sex. But her heart. And her thoughts. As he moved slowly at first, she felt her body clench him, but she also knew that her pleasure came from more than his full thrusts. Together, Rufus and she were two pieces of something that had once been whole, and now they were back together, connected, fixed.

I love the way you hold me, he thought.

I feel like I should have always been holding you.

Yes, Rufus thought, kissing and then biting her shoulder blade, his warm breath on her neck. *You've come back to me.*

Where was I?

I don't know. And I don't care. You're here now. I

can touch you and feel you, he thought, bringing his hands down along her spine, resting them in the dip at the small of her back.

Fabia pressed against him, arching, her rear high, letting him fill her even further, gasping at his long, sure strokes. He took her hips in his hands and almost lifted her off the bed, fitting himself into her harder, harder, and then slower, and longer, his strokes firm and sure.

For a few long minutes, they moved together, Fabia feeling her body pull all her blood to her center. She noticed nothing but the heat of her body, nothing but Rufus moving inside her, moving on top of her, his thoughts holding her tight.

Thank you, he thought, running his hands along her ribs. *Thank you.*

Fabia tried to turn to face him, wanting to see him, but she knew she couldn't bear to be separated from him for a second. But somehow, he'd kicked off his pants, and now he brought his hands under her, pulling out of her for a moment as he turned her over gently. *I need to see you, too.*

She pushed his hair away from his face, and stared at him as he moved back inside her. He was breathing hard, his body covered in a light sweat, his arms shaking. She brought her hand down to where they joined, circling him, and then she touched herself.

Keep your hand there, Rufus thought, as she started to pull away. *Touch yourself. Come. Come with me. I can barely hold myself off.*

Smiling, she touched herself, touched him, and the place where they joined, and rubbed gently. She didn't need more than that, her body so full of him, his body so hard inside her, his mouth clenching her nipple, her fingers pressing, pressing, and then she felt it. Her breath stopped, circles of pleasure radiating out, until her whole body was flush, her head back, her moans loud in the dark room. In quick, hard pulses, her muscles clamped over him, and she felt him grow to bursting and then he pushed into her harder, his head thrown back. He moaned once, twice, his eyes closed, and then he shook, his breath trapped in his body.

Oh, my beauty, he thought, finding his breath. *Oh, my lovely girl.*

He leaned down and kissed her gently, and then he rested his head on her shoulder, and she could feel his heart pounding against her. Slowly, though, they both calmed, and their thoughts merged together, flowed apart, came back together, wrapping themselves into sentences of contentment. In the quiet room, she stroked his hair, loving the pressure of his weight on her body, loving the body she'd admired finally revealed to her at last. He ran a hand down her chest and stomach and took her hand from between her legs where they were still joined, bringing it up to his face. He kissed her fingertips, tasting their combined juices.

Do we taste good together? she thought, leaning back on the pillow, her body rich with him. She felt wide and full, her body both calmed and wide awake from her orgasm.

Best vintage ever. I didn't have a chance to taste you before. Next time.

Cocky one, aren't you? Planning ahead? she thought, reaching down to grab him as he slipped out of her. *A braw idea though.*

"You know, I don't know half of what you're saying sometimes." Rufus kissed her temple, running a hand along her collarbone, sternum, and rib cage. "It's like your English and my English are from other planets."

"That's not it at all! It's because you're a stubborn, thrawn lad. But at least you didn't give me the swallie reel just then. Didn't swick me out of my pleasure," Fabia said, trying not to laugh as she brought forth all her father's favorite expressions.

"I would never swick you out of your pleasure," Rufus said, leaning down to pull her nipple into his mouth. "Whatever swick is." In her hand, he began to harden.

Fabia reached her arms around him, smiling into his neck. *You have a lot of stamina. A great deal of capacity,* she thought, as he lay down on top of her, his erection easily finding its way home.

As she moved with him, pressing against his slow thrusts, Fabia could hear Rufus's replies in her mind. Quips about his virility and his need and his hunger. But in the swirl of his thoughts, full of ideas and sensations, she finally heard him reach out to her, thinking, *It's you, love. You. You I adore. You are what I hunger for. You are what I need.*

It was late, the sky outside the large bedroom window turning to slate. Fabia had fallen asleep—Rufus's head on her chest—after the third time Rufus and she made love, but now she blinked and looked out the window, only Venus in the lightening sky, the planet brilliant against the gunmetal sky.

In only a few hours, she and Rufus and the group would break through the protections at the other house, jump through matter, find Niall, let loose the *sortilege du nature morte*, and escape. Or maybe they would have to stay and fight Macara and Kallisto, bringing one or both of them back to the Council to face trial. Macara had a string of crimes that went back five years. And not only had they both kidnapped Niall, but Kallisto had broken all the rules of magic when she'd enchanted Rufus's brother Sariel. The slew of charges would keep them imprisoned for years. So, of course, they would fight back. The battle wouldn't be easy.

And maybe she was simply dreaming that this could end well. Quain could show up, deciding that his power was best delivered in person. What then? What would happen if they failed? What would happen to Niall then? To all of them?

She sighed, shaking her head. She couldn't go there. She had to stay positive. She couldn't let the fire's destructive negativity take her over again. All Fabia cared about was finding Niall. She wanted him back in his flat in Paris and back in her head, where he belonged. Actually, she wanted to bring him back home to Edinburgh and keep him where she could see him. Maybe he'd want to come work at the clinic.

Maybe you could turn him into a ten-year-old, Rufus thought, stretching against her body. *Instead of his sister, you could be his babysitter.*

Fabia stiffened and had the urge to shake Rufus off her body. How could he kid her about Niall?

"Fabs," he whispered. "Niall's a man. At some point, you're going to have to let him have his own life without you in the corner of his mind like a referee. And the same goes for him. I've been in your mind, and I can see how much space he takes there."

"But—" she began.

"Maybe you have relied on each other too much," Rufus said. "Of course it's easier to go through life with another person giving you advice. I can completely see the appeal. But someday, you and he are going to need to split your experiences into two. Yours and his."

"He . . ." Fabia didn't know what to say, because in the instant of the word leaving her lips, she knew that she wouldn't have wanted Niall in her mind the past few hours. Not at all. Nothing she'd had with Timo or Fletcher had even come close to what had happened here in this bed with Rufus. Would she want Niall to be in the corner of her mind as she ran her mouth down Rufus's belly, taking him in her mouth? Would she even want to tell him about it? No. It was her business, her life, her love. Finally. But there had been such a lack of passion in her for other men, that she liked to let Niall in sometimes to show him how silly, how ridiculous, and, she had to admit, how sad it all was. She'd loved his laugh ringing through her mind as she let him see Timo trying to kiss her without his glasses on, pressing his tongue against her cheek. Or the time Fletcher had sat down at the table and missed the chair. Showing Niall these moments hadn't been fair or kind, and she was more interested in hearing Niall laugh than helping the men in front of her.

And if Fabia thought about it, maybe it was her connection with her brother that kept him from really getting serious with a woman. He often saved up some of his dates' comments, sending them then to Fabia like a gift.

"You're so handsome," the one woman said. "You remind me of Brad Gibson."

"Brad Gibson?"

"Yeah." She'd nodded. "The actor."

"You mean Brad Pitt or Mel Gibson?"

"Both," she'd said, shrugging.

How they'd laughed over that one, time and time again.

It was more fun to tease and share and laugh than to get serious. Why would either of them form a stronger relationship elsewhere when they had each other? Wasn't it easier to turn to someone known for advice or affection or help? What else could they have accomplished if they weren't so busy talking to each other all day long? Maybe by being so close, the two of them had overlooked some wonderful experiences and wonderful people.

I'm wonderful people, Rufus thought, kissing her behind her ear.

Fabia turned to him, holding him to her. "You are *brilliant* people. Ripping people. But did my brother have to be kidnapped for me to notice?"

"You noticed when he was still there," Rufus said, his mouth on her neck. "In fact, you were noticing plenty when Niall was around."

"What do you mean?"

"Justus gave me back all my memories, remember? I distinctly recall sitting in the bathtub and hearing you think about my body. And then there was the morning we woke up together. I—"

Fabia pushed him away. "That's quite enough."

He grabbed her, pushed her down on the mattress, his long, thick hair hanging down and around them both. "It will never be enough. And when we get Niall back, he and I are going to have a little talk. Maybe I can give him a shave or two and give him some pointers on thought concealment."

"We *are* going to find him," Fabia said quietly, seeing her brother standing in her bathroom, laughing as he shaved the then very scruffy Rufus.

"Yes, we are," Rufus said. "So let's sleep now. There will be so much more of where this came from later. I'll be hard to get rid of. You might wish you'd never found me in the first place." He kissed her chin, her cheek, her nose, her lips, letting his mouth move down to her neck.

"I'll never wish that. From now on, I'll want to know exactly where you are." Fabia pulled him down to her, nodding, and closed her eyes. She hoped that by the time night came again—by the time she could fall into bed with Rufus again—Niall would be home.

Only two hours later, the group stood in the living room, quiet, robes on, all of them listening to Brennus describe the mission. When Fabia and Rufus had come downstairs, Nala had watched them both carefully, an eyebrow raised. Fabia had felt the woman's mind circling hers, and Fabia quickly shut down her thoughts, realizing so clearly now that she didn't want to share Rufus with anyone.

As he'd poured a cup of coffee, Felix had winked at Rufus, thinking, *It's about time, man. One of these days, you might be as good with women as I am.*

Fabia felt Rufus's irritation at and fondness for his youngest brother, his quick, *We'll talk about it later.*

But now all coffee drinking and mind reading had stopped. Brennus was reminding them of the plan, laying it out in words once more before they left. Fabia's stomach seemed to be filled with stones, her throat constricted and aching.

"We'll appear one at a time at the specific points on the periphery of the house," Brennus said, his voice quiet and clear. "Remember, as we move toward the house with our minds linked, we will be chanting the counterspells, taking down the protections one by one. Keep your *grande cape du deguisement* in force the entire time—we can't let them see you until the last minute. Once we are in the house, we will move through matter, into all the rooms until we find Niall. And then Nala will conjure the *sortilege du nature morte*."

"That's not our only purpose," Rufus said, his voice flat. In his mind, Fabia could see the night with Kallisto again, her eyes black and glittering, her arms slim and white held over her head as she threw a scorching spell at him, flipping him in the air, now ready to unleash the spell that landed him confused and alone and cold in Edinburgh. His thoughts were full of the black blank hole she'd ripped in his mind and of Sariel's pain and loss.

"It's our main purpose," Brennus said. "Only after we've gotten Niall out of the house can we turn to Macara. Or Kallisto. Keep that in mind."

Niall first, Ru, Fabia heard Felix think even as he listened to Brennus.

I know, Rufus thought to both Felix and Fabia, nodding. *I'm thinking of Sariel, too.*

Catching Kallisto won't make Sariel better, Felix thought. *Only time and healing will do that. And if he can ever get over Kallisto, perhaps a decent woman.*

Knowing Kallisto was imprisoned might do wonders for his recovery, Rufus thought.

Enough! Nala broke in.

Fabia grabbed Rufus's hand, and his conversation with Felix whisked out of his head. She could see that he wanted to help find Niall, and she could also tell that he loved his brother as much as she loved hers. Together, they would save them both.

It was snowing when Fabia opened up matter and stepped onto the property around the house. The sky was cracked pewter, jagged with dark clouds that were just holding off their force. Swirls of storm rustled the tops of the pine trees and howled down onto the Martis Valley. Quickly, she muttered a *sortilège du chaleur*, rubbing her hands together as her body flushed with warmth. She'd been the first to arrive, and as she waited for the signal from Brennus, she surveyed the property. From where she stood, Fabia could barely see the house in the early morning darkness—all it was now was an indistinct black square in the distance, almost completely surrounded by a stand of pines.

As she warmed, she opened her ears to the waves of sound around her, ignoring the wind, the tree branches scratching against each other, the grass pressing down in pale sheets against the breeze, dirt and empty seed pods and small cones bumping across the forest floor. Far away, she could hear the rumble of the 80 Highway, the chug of semis pulling loads toward Reno, the ache of small car engines whining up the incline. Somewhere miles away, campers woke up, stretching in their sleeping bags, sitting up in their tents. Dogs barked in yards; people flicked on lights and turned on televisions.

She brought her attention back to the landscape in front of her, wanting human sounds, footsteps, curses, sighs, and whispers. She wanted plans and specifics and commands. But the house was silent, nothing moving inside or out, looking like nothing more than what it was: a cabin waiting for its owners to come back, cart in skis and snowboards, light fires in the stone fireplaces, and live.

Despite the silence, Niall was somewhere in there, and it took all she had to avoid contacting him. Brennus had warned her that Macara would probably set a trap for such communication so close to the house. Her thoughts and her body were concealed, and she had to keep them that way until Niall was back with her, until she could touch him and say to herself he was safe.

Prêt, Brennus shouted into her mind, and she knew that the entire group was ready to move forward. That was the last word she would hear from them, the group keeping all their thoughts contained until they were in the house.

Closing her eyes, seeing with her other senses, opening up to her full hearing range, Fabia began to walk forward slowly, her arms held out at her sides. She mouthed the words *Enlever les sortilèges a charmes du protection. Maintenant.*

Through her fingertips, she felt the energy from the entire group passing through her body, all their words and heat cracking one by one through the protections Macara had conjured. Though the energy was combined, she could feel and almost see a different pulse for each person: Nala was saffron, Philomel tea rose, Felix teal, Brennus pumpkin, and Rufus a deep vermillion. Together mixed with her energy, which she had always seen as emerald, Fabia could feel their power. With the whip and strength of all of them fused together, Fabia forced her way through the bad magic, as if the spells were wire she was cutting through or a window she was breaking.

For a brief flick, Fabia thought she heard the fire's voice—Macara's voice—touch her mind with hot stroking fingers, but then it was gone. Fabia almost spoke the counterspell aloud, her heart pounding, her mind desperate to stay on task.

Enlever les sortilèges a charmes du protection. Maintenant, she whispered, feeling another spell crack wide and allow them to close the circle between them.

Was the fire there? What else did she hear? Rustling? The struggle of someone pressed down hard on a chair? She could almost hear the ache of bones and muscle as a body was twisted and bound. Then the whispers: *They come. They advance*. A chipmunk on the top branches of an aspen. The group's quiet footsteps through the fallen pine needles, shuffling in the soft loamy forest earth. The wind blowing over the dry, dead grasslands.

Enlever les sortilèges a charmes du protection. Maintenant.

Another whisper, the air near someone in the house heating up to a roaring crackle, full of bad spell. *He knows. Macara knows*, Fabia thought. *I should tell Brennus or Nala.*

But she couldn't think or speak the words lest she break their combined magic, so she concentrated on her energy, turning her color from emerald to pitch, telling them all through darkness that they'd been detected.

Enlever les sortilèges a charmes du protection. Maintenant.

Another protection broke loose, drifted up to the gray sky. Fabia walked closer, feeling the twist of rainbow energy in the circle connecting the group. They'd understood. Nala flamed to crimson, Rufus shuddered to sable, Brennus flumed to sunflower, Philomel turned scarlet. But Felix stayed teal, his energy unwavering. Why? What was going on with him? Fabia turned her ears toward his part of the circle, hearing only his feet crunching small twigs, kicking away pine needles.

The fire laughed, quietly. *I have him*, it said. *He's such a sweet one. Like candy.* But the fire had a different voice, cloying, full of calm honey, lulling, almost enough to take Fabia with it and pull her away from the circle.

Enlever les sortilèges a charmes du protection. Maintenant.

The fire's voice disappeared. Fabia pulsed darkness into the group again and heard their connection twang as the circle clamped down upon the house. Felix was still teal, still unresponsive, still moving forward.

They were two-hundred yards away, the protections almost all destroyed. *Enlever les sortilèges a charmes du protection. Maintenant.*

Inside the house, she heard laughter, someone grinding his teeth, the drip of water from a faucet.

Enlever les sortilèges a charmes du protection. Maintenant. Crack! The last protection spell was dislodged, falling in a wisp to the earth. The energy of the group tightened, and she could see Philomel and Nala to her right and left, but she didn't allow her thoughts to open to them, knowing that the fire already had access to her mind, had sensed too much. Inside the house, she heard another laugh, the scraping of furniture on the hardwood floor, a stifled moan. From the noises, Fabia could almost see that Macara, Kallisto, and Niall were in a large room, the one probably right in front of her, calm in the darkness, more ready for them than the group expected. With her ears, she searched out for any indication that Quain might be there, listening for words of deference, for commands, for blasts of powerful magic. But the energy in the house stayed the same, the people in the house excited, ready; the air around them fairly burned with giddy anticipation, hot and red and happy.

Something was very wrong. But it was too late. Even if she told the rest of the group, they had no choice but to try to save Niall. They had no choice.

The band of energy connecting the group was

strung tight like a violin bow, and together, they began to lift off the earth slightly, opening up matter, finding the entrance to travel, and pushing forward into the gray, and then with a burst, they were in the large dark room.

Fending off immediate and constant whorls of hot, red spell—*flèche du morte*—Fabia opened her ears as wide as she could, finding Macara's location by sound: his quick breaths, his rapid heartbeat, his sure stance on the floor. She could almost see his red hair, his impassioned face. Oh, how she'd admired him once, believing that he believed, that he cared. And now here she was, wanting nothing more than to track him down and force him to stillness, to compliance. And, if she was honest, to hurt him. To make him pay for what he had done to Niall.

With her attention entirely on Macara, she walked closer to his sounds, knowing that he would hold Niall—the prize—close.

As she approached Macara, her protection spells woven tightly around her, Fabia glanced around for Nala. Where was she? Where was her golden orb of spell? Why hadn't she unleashed it, making the room stop still and stiff, Kallisto and Macara frozen long enough so that the group could subdue them?

She heard a scream, saw Philomel fall to the ground, her stream of pink energy collapsing on top of her and dissipating into the air.

Without wanting to, without being able to stop it, Fabia opened her mind, and called out *Niall!* even as she fought off spells, even as she saw that Felix stood still in the room, his face blank, caught in the heat of the fire's wicked magic.

Her mind filled with something familiar, something warm, something just right. It was Niall, though he seemed drugged, struggling, weak. Finally, she heard Niall's voice, Niall's thoughts, and she wanted to weep from relief that he was alive, that he was back with her, but as she turned her attention to what her brother was saying, she froze.

Get out of here, Fabia. Now! It's too late. It's over. It's a trap.

Chapter Ten

Rufus knew something was wrong from the moment they appeared by the house, the gray letting them out lightly and rolling away. Of course, it shouldn't seem wrong—they were hidden by the *grande capes du deguisement,* they had the proper countercurses that would crack and splinter the protections keeping them from Niall, and Fabia was here, able to hear everything going on in the house.

But as they walked, Rufus felt Fabia's message, her darkened energy filling his body, cutting away at his confidence. Something had happened. Something was off, but because Macara could so easily reach them, they all shut off their minds. Fabia's darkly colored message was their only warning. And worse yet, the energy of their circle was marred, one of them not responding with the others. Who was it? He closed his eyes, picking through the streams of energy coming from the rest, and knew with a jolt that it was Felix. His brother's blue stream was constant, steady, unconcerned, as if Felix were on autopilot, drawn forward as if in a dream, pulled toward the house by Macara or Kallisto—or Quain.

As they closed upon the house, Rufus was between Nala and Brennus but too far away to signal them with an expression. But what good would that do? How could they stop now? They needed to get to Niall. And if Fabia and now he realized something was wrong, so must Brennus and Philomel. Maybe together, they could take what was headed toward them.

With a whoosh and a crack, they were inside the dark house, immediately blasted by spells. Rufus sent up a protection spell, looking quickly for Fabia. In the red glow of a *flèche du morte,* he saw her advancing toward Macara, Brennus, Philomel, and Nala behind her.

After all the stories about Macara's lawbreaking, Rufus had expected the *sorcier* to be a larger man, tall and full of muscle and energy. But he was slight, whip thin, his cheeks almost hollow, his large dark eyes seeming to take up most of his small face. As he cast his magic, his long red hair was flung wide behind him, revealing his small shoulders and chest. Rufus and Felix alone could have knocked him to the floor, but just as Rufus thought that, he felt the flexed current of a spell thrust from Macara's palm, the jagged, lighting quickness of it burning through Rufus's protection.

Rufus tucked, fell to the floor, and rolled, catching a glimpse of Felix as he did, his brother motionless, vulnerable to attack. Where was Nala? Why hadn't she opened up the magic that would stop this? Rufus wiped the sweat away from his eyes and breathed in. His brother stood still in the center of the room, blank and adrift. Rufus pushed up and ran to him, pulling Felix to the floor.

Stay here. He pushed inside his brother's mind, breaking through the liquid commands someone had planted there. *Don't move.*

He wrapped a protection spell around his brother's prone body and then stood and hurled his own spells toward Macara, who was slowly backing up. Rufus felt a flick of joy in his chest. They were advancing! Macara was weakening, and Nala would work her magic now. Now! His body flushed with energy, he conjured forth another protection spell. *Hurry*, he thought, trying to find Nala. *Do it!* But then he heard Kallisto calling to him.

You must have missed me a great deal, she thought, her voice like cold black ink. *To come all this way. And after such a short parting. I suppose you are wanting a little more of my special treatment. You want what I gave Sariel, don't you? You were always a little jealous.*

Kallisto, Rufus hissed. *Where are you?*

Oh, I'm here. I can tell how much you want to see me, Kallisto thought. *How lovely. But I'm just putting the finishing touches on a special place for you and your true love over there. Look at her! Look at how she thinks she's going to get Macara.*

Rufus tried to close his mind to her slick voice, and he banged out a thought to Brennus. *It's a trap. They got to Felix.* But he couldn't reach Brennus, much less Nala, Philomel, or Fabia. It was as if Macara and Kallisto had put a lead box over his head, cutting him off from everything except for Kallisto's horrible words.

Lonely, isn't it? Just like you must have felt in Edinburgh. Touching how your love saved you. But don't worry. I'll put you in a place where she will always be with you, but the good news is, you won't get sick of each other. And you'll stay away from

Macara and me. It will be much more enjoyable than killing you.

Rufus ignored her and began to move through the spinning spells around him to Brennus, closing his eyes against the explosions of air and furniture. He had to tell them what was happening, but as he was walking forward, almost near enough to Brennus to touch the man's shoulder, he felt himself begin to pull away from the scene. Oh, he was still there, but he began to see himself as if from above, standing slightly behind himself. Then his body slammed into the self behind and the process repeated itself, his spirit and then his body one-stepping back until he was at the far end of the room.

Finding his breath, Rufus thought to yell out, but his voice had moved behind him along with his spirit, his body slamming back and knocking away his words. Blinking, he noticed that the same thing was happening to Fabia, and though he could not read her mind, he saw her words.

Niall!

Fabia turned to Rufus, her eyes wide and afraid, and Rufus tried again to speak, to call out to her, to grab her, but suddenly he was outside, alone, lifting off the ground, rising as high as the tallest sugar pine.

Enjoy yourself, Kallisto thought. *Don't forget to write! And don't worry, I'll take special care of Felix. You know how I can hardly resist a Valasay.*

Rufus felt a gust of energy grind into his gut, pushing him far above the trees, into the gray, matter swirling all around him, and then everything was spun air and matter and silence.

* * *

He awakened with a start, sitting up, his anxious heart pounding in its cage. Blinking against the bright light, he strained to determine where he'd landed this time. At first, all he could see was sun, then sky, and then water, the sound of which he finally recognized as it swushed against the shore. The shore? What shore? Rufus shook his head, found his breath, and stood up, dusting sand—sand?—off his jeans.

As his eyes adjusted, he realized he was on an island or a peninsula or a stretch of isolated coast, somewhere—somewhere warm, tropical, slightly humid. The Caribbean? Far away from land, the water was azure, but as it neared shore, it rippled to aquamarine and then to almost white as it gently waved in and curled on crystalline sand. The indigo sky was still and cloudless, the only movement a swoop of gulls and terns above. He was reminded of Bora Bora or St. Barts or Nevis, the exotic places Felix found on the map when they were teenagers and stuck at home for the summer.

"Come on!" he'd said, annoying Rufus and Sariel so much that the three of them sneaked off into matter as Zosime slept. Felix had liked their tropical travels so much that as an adult, he'd moved to the big island in Hilo, vowing never to live where he had to use a forced air furnace again. Felix's house was—Felix. Felix was in trouble.

Closing his eyes, he tried to bring forth matter, straining to find the gray that should be right now rolling up in front of him. But it didn't. He needed to get back, to help his brother, Fabia, and Niall. He tried again but with the same empty results. With his eyes still closed, he tried to conjure a spell, something easy, a *charme du disparaître*. But when Rufus opened his eyes, he was not camouflaged, did not blend into the scenery, his legs and torso like sand, his body green like the foliage, his head full of blue. Sighing, he looked up into the wild blue sky and yelled out in thought, *Adalbert! We're in trouble. It's gone wrong.*

For a few hopeful moments, he waited, hanging breathless for a reply from the armiger. But there was nothing.

Fabia! Mom! he tried. *Sariel. Justus. Fabia!*

Nothing. Not a word, the world blocked to his magic.

Turning to face inland, Rufus saw coconut palms, wax plants, creeping fig, and sago rimming the edge of the slim beach, the jungle beyond dense and the deepest green. From the trees, brightly colored birds called out and then flew from branch to branch in wild darts of color. At the far end of the beach was a thatched hut of some kind, and as he walked toward it, he began to differentiate the sound of the ocean from a stream set back behind the dense green of hibiscus, cibotium, and the red rush of jade vine flowers. Beach, beauty, warmth, fresh water, food.

As Rufus stood taking in all the beauty, the soft, warm air held him in slightly salty arms.

This was paradise.

He sighed, smoothing his hair and looking around. Why would Kallisto send him here? Why would she use this beautiful place as punishment? How could this be worse than death? What had she thought just before flinging him out of the room? Oh yes. *It will be much more enjoyable than killing you.*

Rufus sighed and then started walking along the beach until he neared the hut, which was built of wood planks and fronds. Looking in, he noticed a wooden pallet and a shelf that held a bowl and a knife. He ducked and walked in, unable to stand completely straight, his head touching the underside of the palm frond thatching. Rufus picked up the knife and stared at it, seeing that despite a freckling of rust, it was a good blade.

Pointing it toward the open space in front of him, he murmured, "*Couper*," hoping that the spell that would allow him to cut into another world and out of this one would work. But even as he said the word, he knew it wouldn't. There was no electricity in him, no current, no magic at all.

Maybe she put it here for me to kill myself with, he thought, shaking his head. *Bleed myself right into the bowl.* But if Kallisto had wanted him to kill himself, why wouldn't she have worked that magic weeks earlier? She'd had the chance. And, really, she'd almost succeeded. One more day lost in his own chaotic thoughts would have made him jump into the Forth River, even if he couldn't remember what a river was. If Fabia hadn't found him that morning as he sat on the stoop, he couldn't have stood his brain, the random, dark, staticky thoughts that pushed against his forehead all at once.

Rufus put down the knife and picked up the metal bowl, tinging the edge with his finger. A knife, a bowl, a bed. He shook his head and looked around the sandy floor of the hut. He was going to have to stay here, at least until he could figure a way off the island, either by magic or by his own two legs. And if he was here on the island, Fabia might be, too. After all, Kallisto seemed to have been working the same bad magic on Fabia.

Walking back outside, Rufus breathed in, pushed his hair back off his face. He would clean up the hut, figure out how to open a coconut (he had watched that movie about the FedEx man who was stranded.

That poor guy with the volleyball friend Wilson), and start a fire. After that, he'd keep trying to conjure matter. He'd try all the spells that might work. Eventually, he'd figure out why Kallisto put him here—eventually, he'd escape. It was only a question of when.

By the time Rufus was done with all his tasks, the sky had turned navy, a glimmer of turquoise fading fast at the horizon. The moon was full, white and large as it slipped up the sky, and he absently poked the fire he'd managed to start with the rusty blade and a piece of dried frond he'd ripped off the roof of the hut. The blaze crackled and hissed as it burned the weathered but slightly wet driftwood he'd collected at the edge of the beach, and Rufus stared at the flames. Actually, he was hoping it would begin to talk to him, just as the fire had talked to Fabia the night before. Any voice—even an enchanted one—would be reassuring. Here, on this island, it was easy to imagine he was the only person in the world and that all he had known before this moment was a dream.

But no voices talked to him, no wicked hiss lulled him into doing anything other than what he was doing—sitting on the sand and poking a fire. All afternoon as he'd worked, he'd tried to conjure matter. He'd tried to do magic. He'd called out to Fabia and his family and Adalbert. Once, as he'd fallen from a palm tree, two coconuts in his hands, he'd even cried out to Kallisto, daring her to tell him what was going on. To come to the island and have a fair fight. But she hadn't answered him either. Rufus felt as though he were caught in one of those snow globes. There was the pretty scene—water, beach, sky, happy tourist—and there was the plastic dome that enclosed it, trapping the scene and the tourist in a dense bubble of water. Nothing came in and nothing came out, no noise, no magic, no help.

A hot patch of wood cracked and poofed, sending writhing embers up into the dark sky. Rufus threw another piece of driftwood on the fire and realized that this helpless feeling was what *Moyenne* must carry with them all the time. They had to use what was available in the environment, unable to conjure what they needed. Eating, moving, living, and working must be so hard he was exhausted just contemplating their daily lives. It was so much harder to exist without magic than Rufus had ever imagined. Whenever he wanted to start a fire, he simply said, "*Incendie*," and there was a fire. Of course, he wasn't as good at it as his former classmate Sayblee Safipour, who could set whole buildings ablaze, but he'd always been able to come up with a brisk campfire on his fishing trips with Felix and Sariel.

A night seabird whisked overhead, calling to its mate in the black distance. Rufus put down his fire-stirring stick and lay down on the sand. He had to try to stop thinking about what was going on back in Truckee. There was no point. He was stuck. But whenever he closed his eyes, he saw Felix on the ground, Nala unable to let loose her magic, Brennus casting magic about wildly, Philomel being knocked over, Fabia being yanked backward. Fabia.

Oh God, what had happened between Fabia and him last night seemed as magic as anything Rufus had ever experienced, more amazing than all the times he'd whisked his teenaged self into a dozen tropical climes. She'd wanted him, needed him, taken his body into her, and liked it. The way she'd looked at him as he held himself over her! The way she'd taken him in her hand. Rufus swallowed, feeling himself grow hard at the memory.

But it was more than the sex. He knew that. He knew that she knew it, too. As Fabia had said, it was as if they'd been separated for years and then been brought back together. They'd recognized each other's bodies and minds, as if at some time in another life, they'd planned this one out. *Come to me in Edinburgh,* he imagined the past-life Fabia saying. *And I'll find you.*

Sounds good, he'd have said. *But about that memory loss part?*

Has to be like that, Fabia would have said, her face stern. *Deal with it. And don't worry. I'll find you.*

Even in another life, Fabia would have had a plan.

Rufus turned on his side, his face resting on his arm. He'd had lovers in the past, girlfriends, dates. When he was twenty-six, he almost proposed to Beena Singh, a *sorcière* he'd met on a Council mission in Bangalore. They'd had a whirlwind romance, but something had stopped him at the moment he'd almost spoken the words to Beena. Something had kept his voice from changing both of their lives. And later after they'd broken up over a minor squabble about the amount of time they spent together, he realized that he didn't really miss Beena and was glad he had never proposed. He was glad now, even though he didn't know if he'd ever see Fabia again. He was grateful he'd been able to meet her, to be with her, to hold her body in his arms the times he had.

The night spun on, the stars rising in a glitter show of light. Rufus sat up to throw more wood on the fire and then lay down again, closing his eyes, falling asleep to the sound of fire, sky, sea, the water lulling him into dream.

* * *

In his dream, the little voice was talking to him again, asking him questions about his life, just as it had always done.

"Where are you? What are you doing? Where have you been? I was waiting and waiting for you."

He had so many answers, he couldn't speak.

"Are you sad?" it asked. "Are you crying? Who are you looking for?"

Rufus wanted to tell the voice that he wanted to cry now. He wanted to tell the voice about Felix and Fabia. But his voice was stuck deep somewhere inside his dream. He mumbled, his tongue paralyzed with sleep.

"You are there!" the voice said. "I knew you wouldn't leave me. Even after all this time. But what's wrong? Why can't you talk to me? Why are you so sad?"

The voice was right. He was sad, right now, in his sleep, in his dream. He wanted to talk about it all, but his body pulled him down, his mind pushed the voice away, and sleep hugged him tight. He turned on his other side on the sand and forgot everything.

Licks of a cool, onshore breeze woke him. Rufus blinked, feeling sand in his eyes, hair, mouth. Something scuttled across his shins and ankles and he sat up and kicked away two tiny white crabs that recovered from their instant flight quickly, holding up their tiny mitts of claw at him in battle stance.

"Oh my. I'm scared," Rufus said. "Go ahead, do your best."

The crabs waved at him, then shuttled away sideways, keeping their strange black eyes on him until they disappeared behind a rise of sand.

The fire had died, but there was still a live ember or two, and he stirred at them with his stick. The embers brightened, cracked, and Rufus put the last of the driftwood on top of them, knowing that he was not as smart as the FedEx man in the movie. Without magic, fire was a miracle.

Putting down the stick, he rubbed the sand off his face and then was about to spit out the sand in his mouth, when he saw it. At first, he wondered if somehow the tide had come in at a strange angle, missing the fire and him, curling up beside him to make a depression. It seemed that a water body had slept next to him at night. A nymph. Really. There was its head, the curve of its fluid spine, the triangle of its legs. And feet, even. Tiny triangles of feet.

Rufus looked around him, searching for evidence of this strange night tide, but this was the only smoothed portion besides the place in which he'd lain. He shook his head, and pressed his hand on the slightly damp, flat sand, wondering if he was really in a myth or fairy tale: a nymph slipping out of the sea to escape her evil father, a selkie surging forward from the tide first as a seal and then as a beautiful woman, a goddess running from a too-eager lover, finding safety against Rufus's sleeping form.

His stomach growled, and Rufus laughed, knowing that this stretch of the imagination was clearly a sign of island fever. Maybe dengue. It was only a matter of time before he was writhing with fever. Or maybe he somehow managed to get tetanus from the rusty blade. He was hallucinating, near death, a victim of *Moyenne* disease and no *Croyant* healing.

So he steadied his mind, focused on what was in front of him. Sand, waves, sky. No monsters lurked from the corners of the scenery. The trees didn't whisper to him. The sand didn't rise to smother him.

He was fine. Wherever the nymph had come from, it hadn't come from his brain.

He stood up and brushed off his clothes, thinking that though he was starving, he needed to bathe before he did anything else. And then he saw it happen. A handprint bloomed in the place he'd just been sitting. Right there, in the spot his heart had been, was a handprint.

Falling to his knees, he watched it, seeing the invisible hand pressing down until the print was very clear and firm. Smaller than his hand, the finger marks thin and fine. But a hand all the same. Rufus placed his own hand just over it, wondering if it was some sort of action memory, his print showing up again and again, a smaller, shadow version. But this hand was different, clearly a woman's hand.

Or maybe this was one of many traps Kallisto had planted on the island, just one of many ways to drive him insane.

So for a moment, he stared at it, and then pressed his hand into the sand just next to this new print. Rufus pulled away, sitting back on his heels, when another handprint began to form, the same small hand. His heart began to jump, his breath quickened, and he was about to press down again, when something else began to happen. Lines began to form just under the hand. Was it a T? No. An F. And A. As the next letter rounded into shape, his skin began to flush. B. And then an I. Finally, an A.

It was Fabia, her name in full shape under her little print.

Shaking, he wrote his name under his hand and then the question *Where are you?*

He waited for a moment, and then came the answer. *On an island somewhere.*

I'm on an island, he wrote. *How,* he started and

then didn't know what else to write. Rufus looked around him, putting out his hands as if he could find her invisible body, pull her close. But his hands touched nothing but the warming air.

I don't know, she wrote back.

They were both on an island—this very island, it would seem—and though they were together in time, they weren't together in space. But somehow, even with this strange rent in the world, they'd slept in the same spot, warmed the same patch of sand.

Are you okay? he asked. *Are you hurt?*

A little sandy. I'm useless without magic. Thank God for dates.

Dates?

The fruit. Behind the hut.

Rufus turned and saw the slightly smaller palm, and laughed, thinking about his hard climb and then stupid fall from the coconut palm.

I don't recommend the coconuts.

Show-off, she wrote back. And then after a pause, *What are we going to do?*

Rufus scanned the beach for a moment, wishing he had an answer. For a second, he was reminded of his dream, heard the little voice in his head asking him questions. He didn't have an answer for the voice or for Fabia, and more than anything, he wished he could push through this strange barrier and grab Fabia, hold her close, take them both back to Truckee to find that Niall, Felix, and the rest of the group were safe and whole. *Yes*, he wanted to tell the voice that had come to him last night, *I am sad.*

We'll figure something out, he wrote back finally. *Let's eat something and clean up. Meet me back here in an hour.*

Rufus stood up and watched as Fabia-sized footprints made a path to the hut. He followed them, watching how they grew deeper in the drier sand and then disappeared. She must have gone into the hut—her hut on her island. He put a hand out and steadied himself against the hut's roof, shaking his head. Here she was, right next to him, but not really. This beautiful island, this gorgeous wide ocean, this soft air, and he couldn't touch her. Couldn't reach her. Couldn't really even talk to her except through scrawls in the sand.

He breathed in, but then awareness almost doubled him over. This was what Kallisto had been talking about. This was the punishment. This was the price. Pain in paradise. Everything he could want except the one thing he really needed. Fabia.

Wind blew up against his face, and he looked out toward the faraway horizon. Even from here, he could hear Kallisto laughing.

The stream beyond the beach fell into three clear shallow pools, the water tinted blue from the brilliant sky, shadowed dark by the overhanging ferns. Rufus took off his clothes and stepped into one of the pools, looking around for some kind of dangerous creature—a snake, a water bug with fangs, a piranha, an alligator. Tiny silver fish slipped and flickered away from his feet, but there was nothing else alive but him in the pool, and he reached down to cup water with his hands, spilling it over himself, rinsing off sand and the smell of the beach fire. The water was cool and soft and he sighed, finally feeling awake. Maybe all of the sand writing had been a dream—maybe the island was a dream he would awake from in a second, finding himself on the floor of the Truckee house. All he'd have to do is find a way to shake himself awake and this would be over.

As he washed himself, though, he realized he felt too much for this to be a dream. His skin prickled with cold from the water, his long damp hair pressed against his back, his nose was filled with the salt from the ocean and the crisp, clear water on his body, and then he saw them. Fabia's footprints in the bottom of the pool, walking right toward his. He held his breath, watching as she came toward him, stopping right at his toes. For a silly second, he looked up, expecting to see her blue eyes holding his, but, of course, she wasn't there. But in a way, she was. Rufus flicked water from his eyes, knowing that in another dimension, Fabia stood before him, naked, beautiful, her hair wet, her arms wanting his body.

He swallowed, feeling himself harden and rise. Below him the footprints moved, walking around his body counterclockwise, and Rufus could almost feel her smooth fingers running down his spine and cupping his buttocks, just as she had done in Truckee. As the footprints came back to face him, he looked down at his cock. If they were in the same world, she would slip down and put her warm mouth on him, tasting his skin and the cool pool water, sucking him until he could stand it no longer and he picked her up and laid her down on the soft sand.

Rufus closed his eyes, put his hand around his cock, and imagined her body and what she was doing now. There she was, just behind his eyelids. Her long blond hair thrown back, her eyes dark, lapis with desire. Desire for him. Her lips wet, waiting, smiling. Her chest rising, her heartbeat and blood just below the surface of her moon-pale skin.

Maybe she was touching her nipples until they hardened or she was moving her fingers slowly down to her tight curls, slipping them through her slickness, teasing him, wanting him to see what she could offer. In his mind, Fabia was doing both. Rufus moved his hand up and down, imagining he was inside her, moving slowly, feeling her body push up against his. She was so wet, so slick, so tight. Her mouth was on his, her tongue against his, her flesh against everything his. His head dropped back, the sun hot against his closed eyes, and he moaned, letting himself feel it all, moving his hand harder and faster, and then he came, his cry the only sound on the beach except the waves against the shore.

Slowly, he opened his eyes, his heart pounding, and he looked down. Fabia's footprints were still there, but her stance was wider, as if she'd really been here, allowing him into her. Had she been doing the same thing he had? Had she been able to tell he was pleasuring himself because of the way his feet had moved in the sand under the water? For a second, he flushed, wondering if she'd think he was truly a maniac. Some kind of pervert. Probably, he was.

Rufus laughed and looked around. Thank God no one else was here. Not even a ball named Wilson. Even a volleyball would think having sex with an invisible woman was a bit strange.

Rufus backed up and the footprints advanced once and then backed away. On her island, Fabia turned and walked out of the pool, her footsteps leading in the direction of the hut.

He washed himself off and then followed Fabia to the hut. Both of them needed to eat because they had a lot of work to do. Somehow, they needed to figure out how to get out of here so they could help the group and save Niall. And, Rufus knew, he needed her, with him, in the flesh.

How was your bath? she wrote later.

Not bad. Very invigorating. Yours?

Enlivening. Like yours.

Rufus blushed. *Maybe we can do that again tomorrow.*

I don't want to be here tomorrow. I want to be with you. I don't want to do anything else alone.

He sighed. As he'd eaten his breakfast of coconut and dates and fresh water from the stream, he'd stared out at the ocean, trying to imagine how to escape. Kallisto had cut off all their magic. No telepathy. No way to alter the environment. No charms, spells, or curses. She'd taken every known kind of magic from them, leaving them nothing but their bodies. And an ordinary body without magic couldn't move through matter, cut through place, cross over space.

Their only hope was that Nala, Brennus, Philomel, and Felix would escape Macara or that Adalbert would figure out where they were. But that could take weeks or months, even, depending on what shape the group was in. Rufus shook his head. He couldn't even think about that, because when he did, he always saw Felix on the floor.

Rufus?

I'm here. I'm with you.

I don't have a plan.

Neither do I.

He could see where she was sitting, the sand smooth and flat under her lovely rear. How long would he be able to imagine her as he had done in the pool? How long would he remember how she felt? A month or so after his father had died, Rufus, only six, realized he couldn't remember Hadrian's voice. A little later, he had to go to his father's closet and lean into the long velvet robes to remember his smell. One night, Zosime found him in there, asleep next to his father's shoes. The way she'd cried as she'd carried him to his bed made him never try that again.

So instead, he would sneak into his father's study after everyone else in the house was asleep and touch the artifacts of his father's life—the leather-bound books on the shelves, the pens, the Council medallions for exemplary service, a coffee mug Zosime hadn't been able to clear away from the desk. When Rufus picked up the mug, for a second some childhood magical skill would bring forth his father, a word sounding in the room, a flickering glimpse of his father's face, a waft of wood-spice soap and shaving cream. Once, he'd been able to conjure his father sitting in the chair, leaning back, laughing. But even that magic faded. Finally, he could bring forth nothing but a wisp of memory.

But here, on this island and with no magic, Fabia would soon be a dream. All Rufus had was the smooth sand depression of her body, the particulars of which he would soon forget. It was a terrible magic—brilliant, but terrible.

What's wrong? she wrote.

Rufus wanted to write *Nothing.* But he'd be lying. He wanted to write pages, tell her that he didn't know how he could handle seeing the weight of her on his island but not her. He wanted to be able to see how his weight looked on her island. Was it exactly the same? Was he only footprints and depressions? There had to be a place between the islands where his resistance—his weight on her island—and her resistance—her weight on his—could combine, could come together and push them both into the same place. There had to be something that would crack the seam open and let everything spill out. Even without magic, he knew enough about physics to know that it was possible.

I have an idea, he wrote back. Then he wiped away all his other words and started to write down his plan from the beginning.

Rufus had drawn a line at one end of the beach with a stick, and now he saw Fabia's footprints just behind it. As he walked away from the line, he dragged his stick, marking the course they would take. When he was twenty yards away from Fabia's prints, he drew a wide, deep line, stood behind it, and counted to ten, just as he had written.

On her island, Fabia was doing the same, and when Rufus reached ten, he began to run toward Fabia's line. As he did, he saw her footprints coming toward him. They were headed right at each other, and in his mind, Rufus knew what he wanted. A scream of worlds parting, the slap of flesh on flesh, Fabia in his arms, the wind knocked out of her, but in his arms, together on one beach, one island, one world. His or hers, he didn't care.

They were almost at each other, and Rufus held his breath, ready to feel it, her, the connection, the hit, but before he knew it, he was past her, at her line, slowing down. Turning, he saw her footprints slow and stop as well, her toes facing him.

He'd felt nothing. No difference in air or temperature or place. Kallisto had made sure they would never feel each other's skin or hair or breath. The footprints, the depressions in the sand, were all they would ever have.

He walked to Fabia's stilled feet and crouched down, writing with his finger in the sand.

We'll figure it out. Just maybe not today.

Soon, she wrote back. *Please.*

That night, he dreamed of the voice again. In his old dreams, the voice seemed younger, but now he could tell she was older, a woman maybe. But she called him by a name he thought he recognized, a name he used to answer to—but as he tried to think the name, roll it on his tongue, to say it aloud in his dreamscape, he couldn't remember it.

"What are you doing?" she asked him. "I can't hear you anymore."

"Why not?"

"I don't know where I am," she said, her voice hitching as if she was crying. "I thought I lost you."

Rufus shook his head, looking into the darkness of his dream. "I never left you. You just stopped calling me. You didn't need me anymore."

"I'm sorry," she said, her voice quiet. "I learned how not to need you. I learned how not to hear."

"So why are you talking to me now?"

"I'm scared again. And now I can't hear anything. She took it away, like everything else."

"Who took it away?"

She seemed to be crying, little pauses and sniffles as she tried to tell him. "I don't know. I think I'm dreaming. Or imagining everything. But I know I can't hear."

"Stop trying to listen," Rufus said, his dream beginning to splinter, fissures of consciousness busting open the darkness, the ocean awakening his mind.

"Where are you going?" she cried. "Oh, Tilly. Please come back."

What did she call him? What did that name mean? When had he heard it before? And what did she mean about hearing? But before he could answer the questions, Rufus was awake, the voice fading into the surf, the wind, the growl in his stomach, the dark sadness in his chest.

Chapter Eleven

Time was moving strangely, the heat and sun and water lapping at Fabia for what seemed at times like hours and then like days, maybe weeks. Her skin felt taut from salt, dry from wind. Her hair felt crunchy, even though every day, she and Rufus would follow each other's footsteps to the clear freshwater pool and bathe. Though the baths were sort of fun, without soap or shampoo, she never felt right or clean, her body full of nerves, her body full of sand.

At night, neither of them chose to sleep in the hut, but instead, slept out on the beach under the stars. She would find the depression Rufus's body made in the sand and roll onto it, hoping that suddenly she would feel his arms around her, his mouth on hers, his body pressed close. As she turned, she would fill with hope, but then she'd land back on the cool, soft sand, clutching nothing but air. Sighing, Fabia would lie flat on her back, trying not to completely lose it. But what would it matter if she went stark raving bonkers? Who would notice? And really, she was feeling horrible all the time. Panic and sadness pulsed under her skin like a sound track, a constant reminder that she was really, truly, one hundred percent alone in a way she'd never been her entire life. No Rufus. No Niall. No one but a ghost imprint in the sand, almost as make-believe as her friend Tilly had been those many years ago.

Because there were no hills or mountains to shield it, the sun emerged all at once from the ocean, the day sudden and bright. How many times had she awakened like this? Fabia wondered, looking around at the sand for Rufus's shape. Another day. Another day again. And it proved to be like the ones that preceded it, but this time, Fabia didn't want to bathe at the same time Rufus did, the idea of touching herself without really being able to see him too depressing. But then, like all the other days, they ate, gathered food, and then wrote in the sand, trying to figure out another plan. The strange run they'd tried had failed, as had their two other attempts.

The next plan was something that Fabia had scrawled one evening as the sun sent slanted red rays onto the sand.

What if there is another connection?

What do you mean?

Through something else. Something Kallisto didn't know about. Fabia became so excited, her stick broke and she had to run to the edge of the beach and search for another before she could finish her thought.

Tell me more, Rufus had scrawled, his letter messy with excitement.

Like this writing. Did she know we'd find out how to communicate?

All she said was that we wouldn't get sick of each other.

Fabia rubbed away her previous writing and started

fresh. *Try this. Find the tip of my T. No. Here. Let's write together. The word together. Think about me the whole time.*

Then she saw the depression Rufus made in the sand, and they followed each other's strokes, the smooth O, the curving g, the slide of the e. As she pressed into the sand, she thought of Rufus, his smile, his taste, his breath against her neck. His long dark hair in her hands, the slick rope of braid down his back.

By the time they got to r, she was tingling, sure that the minute they were finished, she'd look up and see him sitting next to her, a stick in his hands, surprise on his face. But r came and went, and nothing happened but the sunset.

Their final plan had come just as darkness took over the sky, the sand hard to read.

Dream about me, he had written. *Try hard to dream about me.*

Then what?

Maybe we'll wake up together.

Fabia had never been much of a lucid dreamer, the ability to control and direct her dreams not one of her gifts, but that night before she fell asleep curled next to her dialogue with Rufus, she incanted his name, *Rufus, Rufus, Rufus*. She asked very politely, *Let me dream of Rufus.* She didn't let another thought creep into her thoughts but those that were about him. She remembered seeing him for the first time on Mrs. Macatee's step. She thought of him looking up at her as he sat in the bathtub. She recalled the poker game, the look in his eyes as he dealt her cards, his face when he realized that his mother had just appeared in Fabia's flat. On and on she thought until she finally fell asleep.

But that night—despite all her pleas and focused thoughts—she didn't dream of Rufus at all.

Instead, she found herself in a strange dream dialogue, listening in to a little girl and boy talking about being lost. But the dream was fleeting, and she actually slept more soundly that night than she ever had in her life.

I didn't dream, she wrote when she woke up. *Or, I didn't dream of you.*

Neither did I, Rufus wrote back. *Kallisto thought about this. She thought of all the things that could connect us.*

After that try, they gave up. What had they been thinking? Without magic, they were as weak and helpless as fish without fins, birds without wings, snails without shells. They were simply *Moyenne*. Running at each other? Even if, as Rufus said, atoms flowed into other atoms, worlds flowed into other worlds, the whole plan had been ridiculous, like a scene in a movie she once saw, the lovers running at each other across a flower-strewn field, missing each other's embrace by inches, running on toward nothing. And what about the other tries? Writing in the sand? Dreaming?

So today after their bath, they tried to talk, to write to each other again, but after a while, they gave up of words, nothing hopeful left to write. So they played tick-tack-toe and a couple of games of hangman before the image of the man on the scaffold made Fabia too sad. The poor guy had it just as bad as they did. The hangman, Rufus, and she were in a right fankle.

When she thought the Scottish word, she looked up, hoping to see Rufus's confused look, his eyebrows raised, his eyes bright. But all she saw were palm trees, white beach, the green and twist of creeping jungle vines.

Finally, in the afternoon, they decided to explore

their island a bit, but they would have to do it on their own. The beach turned into a dense jungle of plumeria, silk trees, and bird-of-paradise, the sandy floor covered with leaves and dropped flowers, making it hard to track each other. Fabia and Rufus had discovered that the only clue they had of each other was the sand. It didn't matter if they pulled on branches or splashed water or banged coconut shells together loudly. It didn't matter if they jumped on the creaky floorboards of the hut or threw sand in white arcs. The only way they could reach each other, the only way they could connect, was through the soft porous surface of the beach.

We'll walk to the edge of the sand together, Rufus wrote. *And walk for about a half hour. That's it.*

But how will I know? I don't have a watch, Fabia wrote back.

Walk for what seems like fifteen minutes.

What's fifteen minutes?

Half a sitcom. Does that help? Rufus thought.

No, it would only help Niall. He watches too much TV.

Then think of that. Think of the spaces of time he was absent in your mind. Does that help?

Aye.

Then we turn around and come right back here.

Start now, Fabia wrote. *And don't be late.*

Rufus drew a smile, and then she saw his feet turn and walk toward the edge of the sand. She followed him, imagining for a second that she could see him, his strong, straight back, his long dark hair, his lean legs. She hadn't told Rufus this, but two days ago, she'd decided not to wear any clothes. The fabric constrained her in the island weather, making her itch and sweat, her skin chafing under the outfit she'd had on in Truckee, so she'd folded everything up and stowed it in the hut. As she followed him now, she wondered if he'd done the same, his cute tight bum just ahead of her. If he were here, she could reach out and squeeze.

She breathed in and shook her head. She had to stop wishing. She had to just try to think up a plan to get them back together and off this island so they could save Niall. For a second before she could stop herself, she imagined the dark room in the Truckee house, the spells, the group falling one by one, Niall's cry, *Get out of here, Fabia. Now! It's too late. It's over. It's a trap.*

What was happening to Niall now? Had the days gone by as they had here? Had they hurt him? Had they tortured him for information?

Fabia gasped, hypnotized by the fear her thoughts had sent through her body. She blinked and noticed that they had reached the edge of the beach. Rufus's footsteps disappeared into the carpet of green. Fabia stepped into his last steps and closed her eyes, trying to pull a bit of his energy into her. But all she felt was the dry grains of sand on her soles and a wisp of evaporating water. Sighing, she looked up into the sway of ferns and palms, the moist air pulsing from the body of plants in front of her.

Stepping into the jungle, Fabia cleared her mind. *No more thinking*, she promised herself. *Not until we are off this island. Not until I have Macara and Kallisto in my view and I can give back what they've given us. By the cartful. In spades.*

After about ten yards, Fabia felt she was in another world. The air was humid, moist, still, the plants humming their heat into the air by her ankles.

Overhead, magnolias and candle nut trees moved to a high breeze, their limbs full of swallows and zebra finches. In the tumble of growth on either side of the thin path, she swore she heard small, unseen animals twining through vines and over roots. Actually, she hoped what she heard were animals and not snakes or alligators or some other kind of toothed creature with scales. Dinosaur. Dragon. Demon. And who knew? The plants here didn't seem quite right, everything a jumble of all things tropical, images from movies and botanical garden tours and romance novels.

This island could be an island solely from Kallisto's magic imagination, and she probably wasn't a pro at tropical islands. The entire landscape could simply be a *sortilège du scenario,* unreal except through spell, filled with whatever creature Kallisto saw fit to put into it.

Fabia tripped and righted herself, grabbing on to a branch. An orange lizard glided across her hand, and she screamed, her sound muffled and quieted by the jungle. What were they doing in here? There was no hill to provide a view, no tribe with ancient *Croyant* magic to unite her and Rufus, no exit booth at the other end of the shore where they could check out of this spell.

Both she and Rufus had to face facts. They were stuck here, and there was nothing on this island that could save them. Certainly, there was nothing in this donsie dreich jungle that would help them escape.

Fabia stood up straight, imaging Rufus a few hundred feet in front of her. "I'm going back," she said to him, her eyes suddenly filled with tears. She hadn't spoken a word aloud for so long, her voice was raspy and cracked as if her words were filled with sand. "I'm going to the beach to wait for you. Be careful."

Still pretending, she saw Rufus look over his shoulder and give her the smile she'd already grown used to. He raised a hand and waved, turning back into the jungle, turning away from her and walking on.

The orange lizard scuttled away, and Fabia walked back along the path, following the turns and twists until she could finally breathe the sea air again, until she could see Rufus's footprints as well as her own.

The sun had arced to its middle and was now falling back into the ocean, heat fluming up from the sand. Fabia scooted beneath a coconut palm, leaning against its smooth grayish trunk. She'd been back for well over a half hour (what would have been a full sitcom), and now she was so nervous, it felt like her heart was beating in her mouth.

What if something happened to Rufus out in that jungle, with its vines and potentially hidden bogs and great scaly long-toothed creatures? What if Kallisto had laid traps and land mines and dangers, knowing that Rufus would want to explore and find his way out? How would Fabia be able to help him? She couldn't hear, couldn't connect with his mind, couldn't pull him out of a snag of plants with her magic. And what if he was beyond hurt? What if she were too late to do anything? She would be stuck here alone forever on this island that probably wasn't even real, without even his shape in the sand for company.

Why had she agreed to the adventure? They never should have gone into the jungle. Kallisto was too smart to have allowed for an escape hatch. After all, hadn't they proved to each other that Kallisto had thought of every way they could find each other and escape?

Fabia shook her head and sighed. Now she knew what the knife in the hut was for. If Rufus never came back from this walk, she would have to end her misery herself, trying to find a vein with the rusted blade. She'd probably die of tetanus or blood poisoning before blood loss.

You're late, she wrote in the sand. *If you aren't hurt, I'm going to kill you.*

But he didn't answer, and so she stared at the sand, waiting for his footprints to come toward her, circle her, and his handwriting to flow. *I am so sorry. I found something amazing. We're going to get out of here.*

But that didn't happen either. Fabia closed her eyes and rested her head against the trunk, hearing the fronds flick in the breeze. The water lapped at the shore, the sky buzzed with insects and heat, the sand warmed her body.

In her dream, she was back in her parents' house in Edinburgh, in her twin bed. As always, it was late, too late. Her ears wide open to the sounds of the world, the sounds of breathing and sleeping like cymbals in her head. Everywhere, all around her, was the cacophony of night living—toilet lids falling shut, bedsprings, whispered murmurs under blankets, night delivery vans, water in the tap, the clink of glasses on counters.

Niall was already asleep, and Fabia wanted to run into her parents' room, but she had done that too often and she wasn't a baby anymore. She was a big girl. She was five years old, a smart girl, and she knew it was just the sound of the world, but she hated it, hated it, and there wasn't anyone who could make it better except for . . . Tilly.

"Tilly," she cried. "Are you awake? It's me, Princess Sofia. I can hear too much. I need you. I'm scared."

In her dream, Tilly didn't answer right away, but when he did, it seemed to come from much farther away, his voice somehow different from how it used to be, deeper, older. And his breath was short and quick as if he'd been running.

"Sofia? Is that really you? Princess Sofia?"

"Aye, it's me, Tilly. I'm alone. It's scary. And I can hear everything," Fabia said, but then she realized that all the noises she had heard in her childhood—the toilets and water and glasses—were gone. There were other noises, though, softer and farther away, something like water sifting over soft sand. Above her, she heard wind blowing through fronds, the call of gulls along the shore, the twitter and squeak of running sandpipers. Yes, of course. *Duh!* A beach. She heard a beach.

"Am I really talking to you, Sofia? I thought I heard you last night. It's been a long time."

"No, it hasn't," Fabia said, but then she knew that it had been a long time. Years. She wasn't just a big girl, she was a woman. She wasn't Sofia anymore, hadn't been since she'd gone to Adalbert, who helped her adjust her hearing.

"Yes," Tilly said. "It's been a long time. You used to be a little girl. And now you sound like a woman." His voice was getting louder, closer, nearer.

"Tilly," Fabia said, suddenly embarrassed. "I'm sorry I called you. I'm not really scared of all the sounds. I used to be, though, and you helped me. You're right. It was a long time ago."

"Why did you call me now?"

Why had she called out to Tilly? Because Niall wasn't available? That's why she'd found Tilly in the first place, needing a voice when Niall was asleep. Fabia breathed in, her dream starting to crack open, the smell of salt in her nose.

"I don't know. I should go, I guess."

"Stay, Sofia! Don't go. Don't let me go for a second. It's very important that we keep talking. Listen to me. Don't go away." He was even closer, his voice wide in her head. "So tell me why you called."

"Because you always made me feel better. And I am scared right now. I'm all alone, and someone I love might be in danger. I needed you to tell a story so it would all go away and I could wake up in the morning and everything would be all right."

"Someone you love? Who is it?"

"His name is Rufus, and he's alone in a jungle. I can't find him. I can't even hear him, Tilly. I'm so worried. He could be hurt. I love him so."

"Should I tell you a story so you don't worry?" he asked, his voice almost on top of her now. Fabia knew that if she shook herself out of dreaming, she would see her imaginary friend right there, standing in front of her.

"Yes, Tilly. Tell me a story. A good one."

There was a pause, and Fabia slipped deeper into her own mind, the world around her fading.

"Don't leave, Sofia. Stay with me. Listen. You promise?"

"Aye, I promise." Fabia focused, found his words, clung to them.

"All right. Once," Tilly started, "there was a man who fell in love with a beautiful woman. She saved him. Took him into the light. Fed him. And eventually, he thought she seemed so familiar. What he didn't know was that he'd met her years and years before, long before he first saw her."

"When did he first see her?"

"He saw her when she saved him from the cold and the wet. She saved him from his own demons and some bad magic," Tilly said, his voice near her ear, so close she thought she felt his lips.

"Then what happened?"

"She took him inside her castle and fixed him. Warmed him, fed him, loved him. Took care of him like a mother would. But then they fell in love. They were happy, but they had to travel to a faraway place to fight the bad witch, who punished them by separating them. They couldn't see each other or touch each other. All they could do was write notes to each other in the sand."

Fabia's mind jumped with recognition, but her dream kept her stuck in sleep. She knew this story. She remembered it.

"But what the witch didn't know was that the man and the woman knew each other from long before, when they were children. The woman was once a scared little girl who cried out in the night for a friend and the boy answered. He was so happy to find her because he was lonely and sad. He was away from his mother and brothers for the first time and could never sleep. When he first heard the girl, he thought she was an angel. He imagined she was all light hair and blue eyes with wondrous wings. The girl thought he was pretend, imaginary. They talked for many months, forging a connection that even they forgot about. And one day, the angel disappeared and then the boy grew up and forgot about ever knowing her at all."

"So what happened?" Fabia asked, feeling light beat against her eyelids.

"In the place where the witch sent the man and the woman, the woman fell into a deep sleep. In her dreams, she called out to the boy because she was scared. The man heard the cry as he was walking back from an adventure and remembered the angel. Knew that the angel was really the woman he loved. Once he realized that the woman was his angel, he understood."

"Understood what?" Fabia said, blinking against the light, her eyes catching a shadow that hung over her.

"That the old path they talked on was a kind of magic the witch never knew about. She couldn't have taken it away because the man and the woman had forgotten about it themselves. They thought it was pretend, so even if the witch had found it, she would have believed it to be child's play. But it was that connection that would bring the man and woman back to each other. All he had to do was ride it, pull it, push himself back into the space where the woman was. So the man thought about the name she used to call him."

"What did she call him?"

"You remember, Fabia. You called me Tilly. And I called you Sofia."

"What do I call you now?" Fabia knew the answer as she asked the question, opening her eyes wide into the sunlight, seeing her lover's face appear within the shadow above her.

"You call me Rufus, if I'm lucky," he said. Fabia breathed in as the shadow over her turned into Rufus, all of him, and he leaned down to her, kissing her. "You love me, and I'm very lucky."

"Are you really here?" Fabia asked, even though she held him tight against her body, clinging to him with her arms and legs, even though he was still inside her. Their lovemaking had been swift, as if they were both trying to prove the answer to the question Fabia had just asked.

"I would say that yes, I'm really here." Rufus kissed her neck. "I suppose I could prove it to you again."

Fabia laughed, and then pushed him over so his back was on the sand. "I think we better try to see if we can make some other kind of magic now. Maybe if we're both together, we can conjure up matter."

Rufus nodded, running a finger along her jaw. "I suggest we get dressed, first. Naked might not be the best way to travel."

"What? You don't want me to fight showing my bumbaleerie?" Fabia kissed him on the chin and then stood up, holding her hand out to him. He took it, stood, dusting sand off his thighs and knees, and then together, they walked toward the hut.

"How did you really do it?" Fabia asked as they grabbed their clothes from the shelf in the hut (strangely, both sets were folded and sitting next to each other) and began to dress. "How did you use the path our voices used to travel on?"

Rufus buttoned his shirt and shook his head. "I knew I was late, so I was rushing back. I could almost hear you in my head, telling me that you were going to kill me unless I was dead. Maybe I was really reading your thoughts, and I knew I was in trouble. But then your voice changed. I didn't realize at first it was you, but then I started to figure it out. You were Sofia. That's why you'd always seemed so familiar."

"I started dreaming," she said, slipping on her pants. "I dreamed about Tilly."

"And I followed your dream, hearing you in that old way, just like when I was a little boy and you came to me at night. I just kept talking and walking toward the connection. I was so scared that you'd fall back into a deeper sleep, and we'd lose each other. The minute that we both understood our old connection, I knew it would be lost. But you didn't go away, and then I saw you." Rufus stopped dressing and brought his hands to her face. "I felt so . . . I couldn't believe it was really you, naked and asleep against the tree. At first I thought I was hallucinating. Or that Kallisto was trying to trick me."

He kissed her. "But you were talking to me, so I went with it, walking closer and closer, and you didn't disappear. Maybe Adalbert can explain it to us later, but it was as if our old story cleared away the spell, brought us together."

Fabia kissed him back and then they finished dressing. "So now what?"

"If we broke through that spell, we can break through the others. We just have to try it together. Use our connection." He took her hand and they walked away from the hut, standing on the clear open beach, looking out toward the smooth sea.

"So we head right back to the house," Fabia said, not needing an answer.

Rufus nodded. "We won't know if we've lost any time until we get there. This . . ." He waved his hand, scanning the beach. "This may have all been an illusion, a moment, maybe even less. Or, we could get there, and the place will be deserted. We won't know until we arrive."

"We have to go, then. Now."

Rufus stroked her face. "We have to focus. We have to be calm. Otherwise, what magic we can conjure might not work."

"Aye. All right." She gripped his hand tight, and they both closed their eyes. At first, Fabia wanted to stop, feeling that same blankness she'd felt since arriving on the island, her head filled with nothing but what she'd forgotten how to do. But then, she felt the pulse of Rufus's energy, his hand hot in hers, and in a spot on the dark horizon behind her eyes, she saw the gray glimmer, rise, and roll forward. Matter. It was coming for them.

Concentrate, Rufus thought, and she welcomed his mind into hers, relieved to have him back with her in all ways. So she thought hard, urged the matter forward, feeling her energy and Rufus's act like a magnet pulling the matter close. And then, it was there, opening up to them, available, and they stepped together into its fluid, mattery waves, and left the beach, the water, the sun, the island that had once been two islands, two prisons, two paradises.

Truckee, Fabia thought, feeling her body rise and move. *Niall.*

Felix, Rufus thought. *The group.*

And in seconds, they were there.

When they appeared, no one noticed because there was no one in the room, not even the fallen that Fabia and Rufus had been torn away from. All that was in the room was the smell of burn, the sulfur from expended spells.

Fabia realized she'd held her breath during the travel, and she exhaled into the quiet room, her eyes wide, her mind and ears alert for any noise. They both looked around, quietly moving between the piles of broken furniture and torn curtains. But there were no clues left as to where the group had gone or where they'd been taken.

"Where in the hell—" Rufus began, and Fabia shot out a thought.

Wait!

Her ears opening into the silence, she heard a laugh, a swish of robes, the tiny articulate sounds of someone shaking her head, neck bones clicking, the metal and jewels set into earrings moving in quiet ticks against each other.

"You were always expendable," the woman—Kallisto—said.

She's outside, Fabia thought. *With someone.*

Holding Rufus still, Fabia waited for more.

"He was waiting for me because you hadn't been able to do a thing in Edinburgh," Kallisto went on. Instead of a response, Fabia heard moans.

"Please. Don't try to explain. In one day, I managed to get rid of the delightful Miss Fair and two Valasay brothers, while all you could do was find a stand-in, the twin. Niall. Pathetic."

There were more moans, and Kallisto laughed. "If you don't stop thinking such insulting things, I can take away that from you, too. Now, give me access to the twin, and I'll be on my way. He may prove to be useful to us. And if I were you, I'd clean up that mess in the house. And then find some place to hide. Adalbert will be looking for you. Maybe he'll send you to Siberia? Or some place in Kansas? South Dakota? That's probably the worst punishment of all."

There was a pause, and Fabia almost heard Kallisto smile, could hear her lips moving upward along her slick white teeth.

"That's right," Kallisto said. "Let's keep him there, next to you. Partners in crime, shall we say?"

Fabia froze, not wanting to believe what she'd heard. Kallisto had gotten rid of two Valasay brothers? The mess in the house—did Kallisto mean more than the broken piles they'd stepped around? And what was she going to do with Niall now?

We need to go out there, she thought.

What's going on?

She couldn't bear to say the words, so she flooded his mind with what she'd just picked up. As he listened to her memory, he stood straight, his face pale. For a quick second, she could see that he was trying to reach Felix with his thoughts, and she closed her eyes, hoping that Niall could hear her. But there was no reply, not a sound, not a whisper.

She can't take Niall, Fabia thought.

She's not going to take anyone, Rufus thought back. *Use the* sortilège du étourdir. *We are going to need her later to find Quain. To end this, once and for all.*

Fabia nodded, and he grabbed her hand. Together, they plunged into matter and then broke out, stepped into the windy yard, and pressed out the magic they'd prepared for.

Her eyes on Kallisto, Fabia held up her hand, whispered, "*Étourdir*," but nothing happened. Rufus's spell had failed, too, and he glanced at Fabia, thinking to take her hand again, combining their energies.

When they'd first appeared in the yard, Kallisto had gasped, her dark eyes wide with surprise, but now she took advantage of their magical glitch, throwing them far apart, and trapping them with one quickly whispered word, "*Contenir*."

Fabia flew back and fell onto the earth, contact with the cold, hard soil knocking out her breath. Above her, she watched the pines moving with the wind, brown needles dropping like broken wings to the ground, landing all around her. A jay flapped in fright from a branch, its screech bouncing off the eddies of air twirling between the trees.

For a moment, she struggled to find her breath and was ready to stand up and fling herself back into the fight, but she was stuck, forced to the ground, paralyzed except, it seemed, for her neck.

"She's a proper bitch," a voice said next to her. "Just figured that one out myself."

Fabia turned her head to the right, and there was Cadeyrn Macara, held tight to the ground just as she was. All these years of looking for him, and there he was next to her, trapped by the same spell as she, looking pale and tired, his red hair dirty and full of leaves, pine needles, and dirt.

"She's been tossing me about all afternoon," he whispered. "Once I woke up from the enchantment, she wouldn't do less than treat me like a rag doll."

Fabia strained to see what Kallisto was doing to Rufus, but she and Macara were lying flat between two fallen trees that blocked her view. She tried to push her hearing up and out and over where they lay, but Kallisto's spell had blocked her ears as well.

"So what do you mean, enchantment?" Fabia said, her flesh creepy crawling from the idea of finally being so close to him after all this time. But she turned her neck so she could look in his eyes, which were such a pale blue they seemed almost white.

"I know you've been looking for me, Fabia. All your career was spent on me, so you'll likely not believe this, lass," he said. "But who will? It's my word against whose? Quain's? Adalbert will have my ballocks, not to mention my magic."

"How could you—why didn't you?" Fabia began, not knowing how to articulate the rest: *How could you let go of your work? How could you kill for him? How could you let this happen? For Quain?*

Fabia had always imagined that if she were enchanted, forced to do magic for others—*Moyenne* or *Croyant*—she'd do anything to stop it. Turn her own magic on herself. Destroy her power and her life.

But Macara had stayed at Quain's side for five years. Five long years.

He seemed to understand her thoughts and turned to face the canopy above them, closing his eyes. "Aye, good questions. There were times when the magic would ebb, and I would awaken at night, a slice of freedom right before me. It didn't happen often, but it happened, and I think I was scared to grab for it. I'd become the easy one to hate, the one more accessible than Quain. Quain . . ." He trailed off, exhaling deeply. "I just couldn't pull myself out. Until now."

"So you're going to run? Like Kallisto said? Go to South Dakota or Siberia?"

Macara nodded. "I thought you might have heard that."

"You knew we were here? Why didn't you warn her?" Fabia asked.

"Queer as it may sound, I'm no longer on her team. Neither she nor Quain can save me now," he said. "But it's too late for me, I think. You know what I've done. It doesn't matter that I was enchanted by Quain. I've stolen and killed and—and worse—and if I was honest, some whole, intact part of my mind knew what I was doing. But no one ever tried to save me, find me, and unless I come up with something brilliant—"

"Then help us. That will save you. That will make them all believe. And then you can tell everyone what you know about Quain." Fabia knew she was begging for her life, for Niall's, for all of their lives, even Macara's.

She took in a deep breath, knowing she had to convince him. "It's not too late. They're all right, aren't they? Where is the rest of the group?" Fabia wished she could move, wanting her hands to help her words. She needed to lean closer to this man she'd long wanted to imprison and beg him to save her brother, Felix, the rest of the group. She wanted him to allow her into his mind, so she could understand what had happened to him. But she couldn't move, couldn't do magic, and he had long stopped trusting *Croyant*.

Macara turned back to her, his clear eyes full of sadness. Fabia remembered Rufus's terrified face that night she'd brought him in from the cold. Magic could be so wrong, so bad, turning good men into murderers and thieves or carving out their memories and feelings and lives. Even if Niall and Felix and the rest of the group weren't in danger, Fabia wanted to capture Kallisto and Quain for that reason alone. Before his enchantment, Macara had wanted nothing but the best for *Croyant* and *Moyenne* alike. Like the Valasay brothers, he hadn't ignored the world around him. *Les Croyants* didn't number enough that they could lose a Cadeyrn Macara or a Rufus Valasay without a tremendous loss.

"I'm not strong enough to do everything," he said. "I can untangle us from this spell, but I can't get the rest—"

"Where are they? Are they alive?"

He nodded. "Aye. In the garage of the house. Tied up and knocked out with a *charme du sommeil*. For now. Kallisto is going to take them to Quain for ransom. Barter. Trade. Quain kept mumbling something about Hadrian Valasay. An obsession of his, I guess. He wants Rufus and Felix, especially. Tried, I guess, to capture Sariel, too. Anyway, he won't rest until he snatches up their weight in gold from the Council before, well, not handing them over."

"And Niall?" Fabia felt her heart beating against the containment spell.

"He's here. He did his part well. He brought you all to Truckee."

"Where is he?" Fabia turned her head, looking in the V that lay in between the fallen trees.

"Next to you, but she's knocked him out and covered him with an *incantation de transparence.*"

Fabia stared at Macara, her mouth wide open. "Where?"

He sighed. "I can make him visible for a second. But I don't want Kallisto to know I've broken through her spells. So I'll count to three. Turn your head to the right. Okay. One, two, three."

Fabia turned, listened to him count, and then, at three, there was Niall, next to her. His hair was stringy, his face pale, his breath so slight she had to concentrate to see it, but he was breathing. He was alive. Tension she'd forgotten she carried in her shoulders pulsed down her body and disappeared. He was alive. The place in her mind where she carried him tingled, ready for his thoughts. But she couldn't reach him. Not yet. Not in the middle of Kallisto's magic.

But for a second, she tried to reach him anyway, feeling him next to her like a shadow, there, yes, but his mind was sluggish, almost still, as quiet as his breath.

"This isn't just a spell. What else happened to him?" Fabia said, her voice full of tears. "What did she do to him?"

"I did most of it," Macara said softly, and as he

spoke Niall's form shimmered and disappeared, turning back to leaves, wood chips, air. But now that Fabia knew where her brother was, she could see the depression his body made in the ground cover.

"What did you do?" Fabia whispered, wishing she could go in and feel Niall's pain so she could know.

Macara shook his head. "Horrible things."

"Why?"

"Because I was told to," he said slowly, his lips barely moving.

"So now do something different," Fabia hissed. "You can fix the past. Redeem yourself."

"The past is a hard stone."

Fabia stopped talking and closed her eyes, trying to swallow her sadness, trying not to think about each and every breath Niall managed to take next to her. "Never mind," she said finally. "What I mean is you can make up for the past. You can do it."

"Do what?"

"Take us out of here. Take us back to Rabley Heath and the Council, and I'll explain everything. You can let Adalbert read your thoughts and see the enchantment." Fabia kept her eyes on his. "It might not explain everything, but you will have saved us all. That will count for so much. I'll tell them the whole story."

Macara bit his lip, and she could see his jaw working under his fair skin. "It wouldn't explain the deaths. The torture. Nothing will. No matter what, I'll end up in the *palissade* with the rest of the *criminels Croyant*."

There wasn't much time, and Fabia felt her stomach twist. Somewhere beyond her, Rufus was fighting for his life. Maybe the fight was already over, Rufus on the ground, Kallisto heading toward them.

Next to her, Niall was barely breathing. "Aye. But you'll help us first. You'll explain how they enchanted you. Then you'll help us find Quain. And all of that will take time off. It won't be long. And part of you—like you said—needs to be punished, Macara. Cadeyrn. You know that."

Fabia watched him, seeing his eyes fill with tears that fell down the side of his face. "This isn't what I planned for my life. This isn't how I started."

She wanted to tell him that no one can plan a life. Even if you tried, it didn't ever turn out the way you imagined it would. It could come close, but somehow, plans skirted or flew from the edges of what life brought. Life had its own plans. She wanted to tell him that if his life hadn't taken its course, she would never have found Rufus. But she imagined that her joy would bring him little solace now.

"Is it ever how we planned it?" she said after a moment.

He shook his head. "Maybe you're right. But I can't save you all. I don't have that much magic left in me. Maybe I can take two. Probably just one. But I have to take you. You're my only witness."

Fabia tried to swallow, her mouth suddenly seeming to fill with sand. Take her? Only her? How could she leave here with only one other? How could she leave without Niall, without Rufus, without the rest? She couldn't abandon them, leaving them to face whatever it was Kallisto would dole out. Quain could show up himself, tiring of waiting for Kallisto to find the opportunity to do what he could achieve in an instant, with a simple flick of his wrist and the exact, deadly word. Maybe he was here already.

And if Fabia had to pick, who would she take? She remembered what Rufus had said to her about Niall that night in bed. "But someday, you and he are going to need to split your experiences into two, yours and his."

Was that moment now? Fabia turned back to where Niall lay unconscious and invisible, trapped for so many days. How ill he'd seemed, so tired, his face pallid and glowing from fever, his body still. How she'd wanted to break out of the spell, hold him to her, pull the leaves from his hair, beg him to wake up, wake up.

And what about Rufus? A week ago, she hadn't even known who he was, and truly, neither had he. As she lay on the cool ground, her shoulder blades aching, her heart pounding from the decision she had to make, Fabia remembered the curve of the beach under her body as Rufus lay on top of her, kissing her collarbone, pushing himself into her.

"Solomon," Cadeyrn said.

"Pardon me?" she said.

"Solomon. His decision. Split the baby in two. But of course, the real mother wanted the baby to live."

"I want them both to live," she whispered. "They have to. How can I decide that?"

"You make a decision. I'm telling you, lass, I haven't more magic left over. I'm not lying this time. If it would explain what I'd been doing these past five years, I'd take the whole town and lay it in front of the Council's feet like a right good bone. But I need you for certain, and you have to decide whom we should take. And you better hurry. I can sense that Kallisto's getting ready to do something."

For an instant, Fabia almost reached out to Tilly, needing her imaginary friend to tell her what to do. All along, Tilly had been Rufus, an older boy sent away to boarding school for his first year, alone without his little brothers, awake as his dorm mates slept. Together, he and Fabia had managed to keep each other from thinking about what scared them most. And this, right here, was scaring her more than anything ever had before.

She couldn't reach out to Tilly now—couldn't get into Rufus's mind through the bubble of Kallisto's magic. Turning again to look at her invisible brother, Fabia wondered what Solomon would do now if he had to pick between two deep loves. Would he cut his own heart in two so he could save one and not the other?

"Fabia," Cadeyrn whispered. "Make it quick, lass. She's coming."

At his command, Fabia knew what she had to do, and she turned to Cadeyrn and whispered a name.

As he promised, Macara's magic was jumpy, jerky, matter stuttering and lurching around them. The matter didn't seem round and smooth as it usually did, but sharp and grainy as broken glass, biting into Fabia's flesh and making her wince.

Because of the layers of spells Kallisto had put on her, Fabia was no help to him, unable to join her energy with his. All she was able to do was cling to him as well as to the man she held tight against her, who was barely breathing now, the crackly matter seeming to take away what little strength he'd had left. Under her arm, his body seemed to be fading, falling away into the gray around them.

"We have to stop!" she cried, leaning into Caderyn's ear. "We need to emerge."

The matter seemed to explode black, then white, and then black again, as he brought his attention to her.

"It's not too much longer," he yelled. "We can make it. I can do it."

"No!" Fabia gripped his shoulder tight. "We can't. He's dying. He can't take the travel."

Cadeyrn glanced down at the man she held so tightly and then nodded. He closed his eyes and in seconds the matter screeched into reality that opened wide around them, the world cracking bright into desert, blue sky, a house. A woman stood next to the front door holding a pailful of what looked like roses, her face first full of confusion and fear and then, surprisingly, understanding.

Fabia felt her nerves and heart and blood in her ears. She found her breath and sucked in a large gulp of hot, dry air. Her arms trembled, and then the man she held against her body sagged and fell to the dry, dusty ground.

Chapter Twelve

Rufus turned to watch Fabia fly up and back, landing somewhere behind two fallen trees. His body filled with energy, with magic, but when he looked at Kallisto, he knew he couldn't tap into it, not with her paying him so much attention. Still depleted from the island spell, he was powerless, unable to help Fabia, his brother, or anyone else.

Kallisto grinned, her sharp, strong features softened by cruelty. "Oh, Rufus. We meet again. I guess the little island retreat I planned for you and your girl just didn't go as intended. Truly, I can't help but think you have a thing for me. Look how you keep coming back, like a trained dog. Did you ever tell Sariel about your secret desires?"

He closed his eyes, trying to erase the gleam of her bright face from his mind. But even behind his lids, Rufus could feel the power of her energy, tendrils of her mind roaming around in his thoughts. Since she was there, he pushed out a memory of a dinner with Sariel and Kallisto at Sariel's Sausalito home, let her see how he looked at her with disgust from across the table as she twisted Sariel into a pretzel of dependency. He let her feel how she revolted him despite her beautiful eyes, her long shiny dark hair, her lean body.

Kallisto's eyes narrowed, her grin flattening into anger. "So judgmental. Just like Sariel. Neither of you is smart enough to understand. Oh, I thought he was the one, of course. For a while. Thought he'd see what I was offering. Together, we could have done everything."

Rufus shook his head, trying to keep his thoughts away from Fabia, not wanting Kallisto to tire of him and start in on her. "Even with your enchantment, he wouldn't have gone. He chose to stay. That's why you tortured him. It seems you don't take rejection very well, and you've faced quite a bit of it lately. Lost your latest boyfriend, too."

Kallisto stared at him and then laughed, throwing her head back, her long neck arching in happiness. "Oh, Rufus. You are so transparent. I haven't forgotten about Fabia Fair, pain in the ass though she is. Quain will be so happy I've managed to get rid of her and her abnormal ears. Her brother, Niall, too. All of his work trying to bring *Moyenne* and *Croyant* together. Bringing them together! Why? So they can learn more about us and then decide to kill us all? Drug us and then burn us at stakes or drown us in rivers to see if we'd float? Blame us for the plague, or what would it be now—AIDS? Send the religious right into our homes to purge the world of the devil? We need a world where we control them, not join with them. Where we get rid of them altogether. Quain will bring us that world. And without this group bothering us." She waved her hand toward the house, distracted for a moment, seeming to be stuck in the middle of her fantasy of a *Moyenne*-less world.

Finally, she breathed in, turning back to Rufus. "Well, all in a good day's work. So, say good-bye. I do feel for your mother, though. But she had her chances to join Quain, a long time ago. Now she will suffer for her wrong decision."

As she spoke, Rufus searched his body, trying to find the energy he'd need to counteract her attack. He and Fabia had managed to get off the island, but they'd joined their energies, the current strong between them. Still, he had to have something left within himself, enough to fight Kallisto off for a little while.

He concentrated, finding a pocket of heat in his chest, when he heard Fabia cry to him, warning him, saying good-bye.

I had to. Be careful. Rufus . . . And as if he could see her rushing through matter, Fabia was gone, Macara and Niall with her.

"No!" Kallisto screamed, throwing out loops of spell into the sky. "Traitor!" For a second, it seemed that she'd snagged something, great chunks of matter rending the sky, flashing white and black, but then the blue repaired itself, the sky smooth and cool. They'd escaped. Fabia had left him.

Using the magic he'd found and taking advantage of the distraction, Rufus threw a spell at Kallisto, yelling, "*Contenir*."

Even though for a minute, Kallisto seemed contained, trapped, he knew his spell was no more effective than those he'd practiced his first year at school. She'd be free in a matter of seconds. With his last bit of strength, he closed his eyes and thought hard, conjured from memory Adalbert's home, saw him sitting in a wing-backed chair by the fire, his shaggy old Hungarian Kuvasz at his feet, whining a canine dream.

It's as good a time as any to come help, Rufus thought, bearing down on his image of Adalbert, seeing the older man's face, flaring robes, seeing him lift his hand in recognition of the call. *Now would be very nice.*

All around him, Rufus heard the whir of Kallisto's magic, felt her anger and desire seep into his body through his pores and mouth and nose and ears. And even though he detested her for what she'd done to his brothers and to him, Rufus finally understood how Sariel had fallen into her trap. Her magic was like a drug, thick and honey-colored and warm, wrapping around him like the tastiest sweet. Hadn't she really always been a sweet woman? A wonderful woman?

Rufus remembered the first time he'd seen her, she and Sariel appearing in Zosime's living room, Kallisto's face flushed from excitement, her lips so red, her voice as smooth as a wind chime. She'd sat down at the oak table, holding Sariel's hand, talking about her work for the Council, how she was going to change things. Make everything better. She'd been so strong! So clear. So right after all.

He'd been attracted to her body, her energy, her voice, her eyes, just as Sariel had. He'd kept himself from looking at her too often, not wanting to piss off Sariel. Not that Rufus ever had posed competition for his two younger brothers.

But he could have Kallisto now. She could be his. Only his. All he'd have to do is open his eyes and walk to her, and he'd be lost. And why shouldn't he go to her? Fabia had left him here alone, flying off with Macara, picking Niall over him. Yes, she'd chosen Niall over him. Her brother, her true love. Rufus was nothing to Fabia. Nothing.

Quain can give you more than you imagine, Kallisto thought, her voice low and soft in his mind. *Soon, very soon, we won't have to worry about the Council again. We will make the rules. We will decide how the* Moyenne *live.*

Yes, Rufus thought. *Yes. Why do we allow them so much rein? Why aren't we making all the decisions? Why do we have to hide from them and not the other way around?*

Right, Kallisto hissed. *Exactly.*

Rufus felt himself nodding, thinking about all the times he'd covered up who he was from neighbors and friends, never able to show himself truly except to other *Croyant.* Why should he have to hide his true self every time he wanted to shop or see a movie, using the world as was his right? Why did he have to worry where he appeared out of matter? Why did he have to hide behind what looked normal? It was the *Moyenne* who should be hiding. Not him. Not *Croyant.* Quain was the only answer, his cure, his salvation.

Opening his eyes, he looked at Kallisto, her long, sleek hair blowing behind her shoulders, her arms stretched out wide, and all he'd have to do is walk toward her and it would be done. His life would change. He could have—

No. The voice rocked against his new feelings, his true, righteous ideas about the world.

But—

No, the voice came again. *She's not the answer. Stand back.*

Rufus blinked, breathed in sharply, and stared at Kallisto. In a flash, Adalbert Baird spun in a whirl between Kallisto and Rufus, and something snapped like a dead pine bough. Rufus's chest ached, and then he felt Kallisto's magic release his heart.

Heat spilled and spun in the place Kallisto's spell had been, rejuvenating Rufus, and he knew Adalbert had healed him, giving him back his magic. Without saying a word, he joined with Adalbert, creating a spell, ready to throw it over her, when the ground shook, rocking them both.

Adalbert fell into him, and their magic missed the mark. Kallisto laughed, and then she was gone, nothing but a red-winged blackbird circling overhead, flying fast, arcing higher and higher until it was gone.

Rufus held on to Adalbert, both of them breathing heavily into the cool morning air.

"It seems to me," Adalbert said, "that Kallisto will be a battle for another day."

Rufus let him go and nodded. "They have plans."

"I heard what she has in mind," Adalbert said, straightening his robe. "And we will all have to focus on it, but now I think we should see about our friends."

"Where are they?" Rufus asked. "No one was in the house."

"Just about the time you called me, I received a faint message from Brennus. Faint, but quite clear in forceful intent, as you might imagine," Adalbert said as they began walking toward the house. "We'll find them in the garage. Can you conjure matter?"

Rufus nodded, and together they rushed into matter and then were falling out of it, standing over Brennus, Philomel, Nala, and Felix, who were bound and gagged by a *sortilège du emprisonnement*, flat on their backs on the cold garage floor.

It appeared that Nala had not succumbed completely to her bonds. She was struggling, her voice a low, deep, incomprehensible grumble in her throat. When she saw Adalbert and Rufus, Rufus heard her thought, *It's about bloody time.*

Brennus looked up at them both, his dark eyes just as full of opinions and comments that Rufus knew he wasn't ready to hear, but Adalbert waved a hand, and the spell evaporated. Nala, Brennus, and Philomel slowly sat up and rubbed their aching mouths and sore wrists. Brennus shook his head and cleared his throat, taking the glass of water Adalbert had conjured. But Felix was still, trapped in Kallisto's spell, unconscious and limp.

Rufus was just leaning down over his brother, when there was a flash, and he looked up to find Sariel standing next to him. His brother was still pale, his face drawn, but his light brown eyes were focused, intent. They glanced at each other quickly, and Rufus's mind knocked hard with everything that had happened since that night with Kallisto in Sariel's house. So much loss and pain and trouble, Rufus didn't know how to pull the narrative together.

I know, Sariel thought. *Later.*

They both bent down to Felix, Sariel closing his eyes and putting a hand on Felix's chest.

"Is he all right?" Rufus asked after a moment. Sariel opened his eyes.

"I want to take him to my house. It's close, and we can take care of him there."

Adalbert adjusted his glasses. "Are you ready to heal someone? You are just fresh from that process yourself, my boy."

Rufus could feel all the blame in Sariel's mind. *It's all my fault, my fault, my fault.*

"Yes."

"I'll go, too," Rufus said, but he felt pulled in two

directions. *But what about Fabia?* he wanted to say. *How will I find her again? And will she want me to find her?*

"That will be my job for now," Adalbert said, reading Rufus's mind. "I have long wanted to talk with Cadeyrn Macara about his sudden career change five years ago. And it would seem, he's made another impetuous shift once again. But first I will take Brennus and Philomel home."

"I am ready for anything," Brennus said, standing up and smoothing his dirty robe. His face was puckered and reddened from the bonds, his gray hair tangled in a wild mop on his head. Philomel rolled her eyes and tried to contain her hair under her hood.

"Your loyalty is appreciated," Adalbert said. "But we need to reconsider many things, one of them being the way we approached this situation. Our world has changed. Quain has changed it. We are, at this point, broken into factions, splintered in our approach to the world and to the *Moyenne*. It's a dangerous time. I need to gather the Council. Nala, I want you to go to them and alert them to the situation. But as I said to Rufus earlier, this will be a battle for another day."

Shaking her head and breathing in quickly, full of irritation and what looked to Rufus like embarrassment, Nala adjusted her yellow robe and then disappeared.

Brennus nodded and held out a hand for Philomel, who took it and stood up. "I'm sorry about Fabia and Niall," she said to Rufus, and Rufus felt his body twist in response, his stomach and head pounding. Fabia was gone. She'd left him. No. That wasn't right. But even though he knew Kallisto had been pulling his mind like taffy, he couldn't let go of the idea that Fabia had picked Niall, made some kind of choice he couldn't alter.

But what would he have done in her place? Left Felix for Fabia? In his head, he knew Fabia had made the right choice, the only choice she could have made. Niall was likely injured and in need of immediate healing, just like Felix now. But Kallisto's taunts had left a dark, sticky residue inside Rufus, a wicked red acid of blame and resentment and anger that he kept having to swallow down.

Sariel put a hand on his arm, looking at him, sharing some of Rufus's sadness. "Let's take Felix home."

Breathing out, Rufus pulled Felix up into his arms, and he and Sariel stood close to each other, ready to go into matter.

"I'll be in touch shortly," Adalbert said. "Once I find Macara and Fabia." He reached out a hand, patting Rufus's shoulder. For an instant, Rufus recalled his own father, leaning over him, moving in the same compassionate way Adalbert did now. In a brief flicker of magic, Hadrian was before all three of his sons, smiling. But just as suddenly as the image appeared to Rufus, it left, leaving only Adalbert's open, honest face.

"These have been weeks of mysteries," Adalbert said to Rufus right before they left. "Don't make an answer out of a question."

And then Rufus and Sariel stepped into the gray, taking their unconscious brother home.

It was late. The sun had set beyond the Farallon Islands, the sky a smoky haze of dark gray and black, starless, with only a sickle of moon hovering over

Mt. Tamalpais. Felix lay in Sariel's bed, in a deep sleep but no longer enchanted, and Zosime sat at his side, watching him. As she always had done, Rufus thought, remembering her vigils by his bedside before a healer would arrive. When he closed his eyes sometimes before bed, he could hear his mother's voice telling him a fairy tale in French, maybe *Les Trois Garçons Magiques et Le Bateau Argent* or *Le Canard et La Reine Magique*, stories where good magic always prevailed over the bad.

Rufus and Sariel sat at the dining room table drinking Bordeaux. After healing Felix, Sariel had been quiet, the silence punctuated by his deep sighs. At first, Rufus had tried to engage him, but it was clear that Sariel wasn't ready to talk yet, so Rufus was happy to sit here in quiet, sipping his wine, looking out to the glow of the moon. There was too much to talk about and no words, no way, as Adalbert had suggested, to make answers out of all the questions.

But it was hard to sit here in this room without thinking of the last time he'd been here. Everywhere Rufus looked, he remembered that night, Kallisto dangling Sariel in her net of spell. Now that he had his memory back, he could almost feel her spells pushing at his flesh, throwing him around the room. The very floorboards reminded him of his bruises, his fear, the cold of the Edinburgh sidewalks. He wondered how long it would take before Sariel's house became just that—a house, not a place of pain.

"How do you think I feel?" Sariel asked.

Another question, Rufus thought. *No answers out there for anyone.*

Sariel took a sip of wine and then put his glass down, pushing his long hair back from his face.

"When I think about the last two years, I realize I have no other thoughts but those of her. Why didn't I see what she was doing? Why couldn't I feel how she was pulling me away from all that I believed and all that I loved? I failed. I don't deserve to be forgiven. When I think what she did to you—"

"Don't." Rufus put down his glass next to Sariel's and leaned forward. "It's fine. We're all safe. It worked out."

Sariel threw himself back into his seat, crossing his arms, turning his head to look out the window. "Then why aren't you out there looking for Fabia?"

Turning back to him, Sariel stared at him with his sad gold eyes. Rufus picked up his wine and looked down into the glass. "I don't know."

"There's no excuse."

"I know."

"You've showered and eaten. You could leave right now. Go to Adalbert. Felix will be fine, and I'll tell Mom what you're up to."

"I know what you're doing," Rufus said, shaking his head.

"Do you? I'm glad someone does," Sariel said, his eyes tearing as he spoke. "I don't know what in the hell I'm doing. I don't think I ever will again. I have no idea what anything means anymore. Who I should be fighting for or with or against. But, Ru—I saw in your mind what happened with you and Fabia. That's real. That's no spell. You have now what I never had with Kallisto."

"You're wrong. It wasn't real with Fabia," Rufus blurted. "It was a Florence Nightingale thing. She had to do everything for me. I can't even think about it without cringing. And then there was that thing she and I had when we were kids, playing imaginary friends together over miles of silence. I made up stories for her and she listened. She doesn't know me, Sariel. She's never seen me for one minute in my real life. I've either been helpless, crazed, lying, amnesiac, invisible, or fighting."

Neither of them spoke for a moment. A light wind beat at the large glass window, the salty smell of the ocean curled under the door and into the room. Rufus sighed and rubbed his forehead.

"I've never been good with women. Not like you. Nothing like Felix."

Sariel shook his head. "You just never noticed how they looked at you. You weren't paying attention."

"But it's not how it is for you and Felix. You have all the luck."

Sariel wiped his face and raised an eyebrow. "You're saying I've had good luck? Me with my insane *sorcière*? The one who almost just killed the three of us? I'll never find what you have found with Fabia. I don't think I'll be as lucky as that."

Rufus shrugged. "Forget Kallisto. Think about before. Think of all that luck. You have quite the reputation, my brother. Don't even get me started. What is that rhyme the girls sang in school? *Sariel Valasay only goes all the way*."

For the first time that day, Sariel grinned. "I think I made that up so that Vita Mackenzie would leave me alone. I bet she still hasn't gone all the way."

"But you know what I mean."

Sariel nodded. "I know what you mean."

"So, I guess. Well," Rufus said. "It boils down to—it means that I don't know what to do now."

"You find her and you take her home."

"There's her brother. They're joined at the brain."

"So there's her brother. If you want her in your life bad enough, you can figure anything out."

Sariel refilled both their glasses and then sat back, watching Rufus. Finally, he raised his goblet. Rufus did the same.

"What are we toasting to?" Rufus asked.

"Whatever will make us happy. Me, I'm thinking quiet. Gardening. Working alone. Being alone. No women. None. You, the opposite. I'm toasting to what you haven't had, Ru. To what you want. I'm toasting to Fabia."

Rufus sipped from his glass, watching his brother. *Whatever will make us happy.* He hoped there was something out there in the world that would make Sariel happy, but it would have to wait for the sharp edge of Sariel's sorrow to fade. But for himself, he knew Sariel was right. He was scared, but he wanted Fabia, in his real and unreal lives, the enchanted and the ordinary, the night and day. The now and now and now.

And when he found her, he would make some real life time for them, ordinary days that would seem like magic.

"Go," Sariel said. "Find her."

Rufus stood over Felix, his hand on his mother's shoulder. Felix would be fine, Rufus knew that—but he was still pale and still. Zosime patted his hand.

"He's just trying to get attention, as always," she said. "Like when he was a little boy, following you and Sariel around, lighting little fires on your heels with his new magic."

Zosime laughed, but Rufus could hear the worry under the happy sound. She wouldn't leave Sariel's house until Felix was up and talking and cracking jokes; she might not leave until Sariel's heart had healed, and that could take years.

Rufus took his mother's hand and kissed it. "I'm going to Adalbert."

"Adalbert?" Zosime looked up at him, smiling. "I don't think you're going to that old man."

He shook his head and then scratched his cheek. "No, I'm not going just to see Adalbert. Though, from his message an hour ago, it looks like he might need my help. They're in Arizona by some petrified forest. On a reservation. It was confusing. There's some man who has news or information—I don't know. But it's . . ."

"It's Fabia." Zosime nodded. "She's the one, Rufus. I could tell when I saw her."

"I think you said that exact same thing to Sariel about Kallisto," Rufus teased, and then wished he hadn't, seeing his mother's face close down in disgust.

"Maybe I did. Maybe I was as enchanted as Sariel," she said. "But I wasn't enchanted when I met Fabia. She's pure and whole and loves you, Ru. That I could see. That any mother would have seen."

Rufus sighed, hoping his mother was right. "When he wakes up, tell Felix I'll be back to visit."

"Bring Fabia," Zosime said, and she stood up and kissed him on the cheek. She pulled away and smiled. "Or don't bother coming home at all."

He laughed, and then stepped away from his mother, closed his eyes, and brought forth matter, thinking about the dry desert, wood turned to stone, and Fabia, her eyes as blue as the Arizona sky.

It was dark when he arrived, the large sprawling ranch house lit like a pumpkin in a field of darkness. Somewhere close by, a horse nickered, calling to him for carrots or sugar. Others stomped their hooves, anxious in their corral. Farther away, he heard animals in the bracken, the call of something big—a coyote, he supposed. Stars he had never seen before were thick and glowing in the sky overhead, the light so bright his eyes quickly began to adjust.

Walking along a stone path that led to the house, he was glad he'd decided to appear outside. There was at least one *Moyenne* in the house. Of course, now that this man had four *Croyant* as guests, he might have figured a few things out. One being that people could just show up at any time or place out of seemingly nowhere. But as was usually the case, Adalbert or someone would have to take the *Moyenne*'s thoughts, leaving him or her with a strange hole in the narrative of days. It wasn't safe to leave traces of *Croyant* life anywhere, especially now when Quain was on the loose.

Adjusting his robe and smoothing his hair, Rufus knocked softly at the front door, his breath caught up somewhere in his throat. After a moment, the door opened, fanning yellow light across him. Blinking, he saw a dark-haired woman standing before him wearing a white dress embroidered with wild red flowers and twisting green vines, an outfit that strangely seemed appropriate for the island he'd just left.

"*Mí'jo*," she said. "You're here."

Rufus almost shrugged, but then nodded instead. "Hi. Hello. I'm Ru—"

"Rufus," she said. "*Claro*. Come in."

Puzzled, Rufus walked into the house. Maybe these folks weren't *Moyenne*. She must be reading his mind, but he hadn't felt her touch.

"No, no," she said, winking at him.

Rufus stopped walking, ready to go back outside and try again. Who was this woman?

But just as he was about to turn and leave, Adalbert came into the hall. He was wearing the strangest outfit Rufus had ever seen him in. Usually, Adalbert was regal, his robes purple or dark blue or deep red, keeping in line with his position as *Armiger des Les Croyants.* But now he was wearing jeans? A plaid shirt? Boots?

"Rufus, my boy." Adalbert patted his shoulder, ignoring Rufus's confusion. "You've met Maritza, I see."

"Who . . ." Rufus stopped, not knowing what else to say.

"Maritza graciously took Fabia, Niall, and Cadeyrn in when they arrived." Adalbert smiled at Maritza. "Showing up rather suddenly, I would think."

"That was the most *muy loco* thing I ever saw," Maritza said, whirling her hand above her head as if to display what coming out of matter looked like. "*Y pensé que una vida con Reynaldo era estraño.*"

Rufus picked up most of what she said, wondering who Reynaldo was and how living with him could in any way be as strange as seeing three people appear out of nothing.

"Thank you for taking them in," Rufus said to her, turning to Adalbert. *She's not Croyant?* he thought.

No, but come see for yourself. Reynaldo is with the others.

"They're okay? Niall?" He swallowed, barely able to say her name without his bottom lip quivering. "Fabia?"

Adalbert nodded. "Really. Come and see for yourself. And come and meet Reynaldo."

Rufus followed Adalbert, Maritza behind them. They walked down the hall and then turned into a room full of warm light. The walls were paneled with a blond wood that reflected the lamplight, and sitting in a number of mismatched but comfortable-looking chairs were Justus, Fabia, Niall, and Macara. The man who must be Reynaldo sat at the top of the room in an overstuffed but beat-up leather chair. He was a solid man, thick in the waist, but with strong arms, the muscles pushing against the sleeves of his white button-down shirt. His eyes were almost black and looked even darker because of his thick, curly shock of completely white hair. His dark face was unlined, though, the skin smooth except for a small clipped mustache. To Rufus, he looked like a prince of some kind, someone holding forth, given the respect he deserved. Compared to the way Adalbert was currently dressed, anyone walking into the room would assume Reynaldo was the armiger.

Rufus tried to take in the scene—Macara sitting sipping a drink instead of being in the *palissade*, Niall laughing, and Fabia staring at Rufus—but he suddenly felt ridiculous, like he used to back in school. He'd come into his room to find his dorm mates having a forbidden party, and he wouldn't know what to say to the girls sitting in a row on his bed, going off to the library to study until the librarian Marva Villepreux kicked him out.

"There he is," Niall said, standing up slowly and then holding out his hand. "Don't worry. I won't give you a shave tonight. Just my thanks."

Rufus nodded, shaking Niall's hand, trying not to notice how much Niall looked like Fabia, blond and blue and fair. They were so connected in everything, Rufus wasn't sure how anyone could really come between them.

"I'm glad you're okay," Rufus said, letting go of Niall's hand and stepping back. "All of you." He realized that *all* would, of course, include Macara, and he wasn't sure he meant to include the man Fabia and the *Croyant* world had been hunting for years. A man who worked with Quain. Quain who killed Hadrian. But it seemed that in the time it took to heal Felix and Niall, everything had changed. He looked at Fabia, who stood up, her hands behind her back.

What is it? she thought. *What's wrong?*

Nothing.

Where were you?

With Felix, he thought back, turning to Niall, who took his arm.

"Rufus, this is Reynaldo Arroyo." Niall brought Rufus forward, stopping in front of the man, who stood up from his leather chair.

"*Mucho gusto*," Reynaldo said. "Your friends, they showed up suddenly and in a way I have never seen before, but I am glad. My house is, of course, your house."

Rufus glanced at Niall and then extended his hand to Reynaldo. "Thank you, sir."

Why are we letting him know who we are? Rufus thought to Niall, but Adalbert picked up the question as did, it appeared, Reynaldo.

"Sit, sit," Reynaldo said, and Rufus looked back, noticing that Maritza had brought him a chair that she placed next to Fabia's. Rufus sat down, his gaze on Reynaldo, though he felt Fabia next to him, could smell her skin, a tinge of some new spicy soap wrapping around her. What he wanted was to get up, take her with him outside, and forget about the rest of this, whatever it was. Let Adalbert take care of Macara—let Justus take Reynaldo's and Maritza's memories. All Rufus wanted now was to surge into matter with Fabia and take her to his flat in London and find out there and then what they really had together.

He glanced at Fabia, who was now avoiding his gaze. Great.

Everyone was settled again, and Adalbert cleared his throat and patted Rufus's knee. "My boy, many years ago, I came to the realization that the world is not split solely into *Croyant* and *Moyenne*. It could not possibly be that easy. Duality is a concept foreign to life. Look around at the world with all its variations. When we formed *Les Croyants des Trois*, we were extreme, cutting ourselves off from those who would hurt us. But in the process, we ignored the in-between."

Rufus listened to Adalbert and looked across at Niall, who nodded at Adalbert's every word. In fact, they all were, even Macara, who up until a few hours ago wanted nothing more than to destroy all those not specifically and totally *Croyant*.

Adalbert took off his glasses and rubbed them on his plaid shirt before putting them back on. "The problem we have with Quain is a problem of perception."

"I'd hardly say that murders are problems of perception," Rufus blurted, the image of his father in front of him. "Death is real, a cold, hard fact, sir."

Adalbert lifted his hands. "Maybe. We don't know that, either. Rufus, we think we know it all. We acknowledge that we are the believers. The ones who know. Unlike 99.5 percent of the population, we aren't average, ordinary. But these are definitions we've given to ourselves to explain what we don't know. On this planet, among people we've excluded and ignored, are answers to questions we've given up on."

"I can't believe you're listening to this," Rufus said to the room, not letting his eyes fall on any one person. "After what we've been through with Quain. And with him."

As he said the words, he looked at Macara, who paled and looked down into his glass of tequila.

"But that's just it," Adalbert said. "Quain wants to destroy *Moyenne*, and by doing so, he could banish forever the knowledge that would truly bring us all together. He will stop at nothing, as you know, to get what he wants. Turning our best and brightest, leveling any and all who stand in his way."

At the front of the room, Reynaldo sat placidly, his eyes taking in Rufus's reaction. In a different, strange way, an un-*Croyant* way, Rufus felt the man approaching his mind, asking for admittance. His request came sideways, almost under, when *Croyant* requests seemed more direct. But regardless of the method, this man was clearly magic. *Moyenne*, but magic. Rufus turned away, slamming his wall hard against Reynaldo's almost shy touch.

"*Mí'jo*," Reynaldo began, his voice soft, and when Rufus looked up, he saw that Reynaldo was not speaking aloud. But his words were in the room, everywhere, everyone hearing them just as Rufus did.

"I have long known of your people, even out here, in the desert where the summer is long and the winter is one short afternoon in January."

Fabia laughed aloud, and Rufus wished he could take her hand. But he was angry. Angry at her for stopping the fight. For changing midstream. For sitting here in this room when Kallisto was still out there. For leaving with Cadeyrn Macara. For leaving him alone.

Reynaldo went on. "In the world of the people, my people, magic is not unexpected. It comes to us at night in our dreams, in the shape of our ancestors, riding the Spanish horses of the conquistadors. We understand all the worlds on this one world, but we go to the market like anyone else. We line up at the unemployment line. We wait for rain. We haven't learned how not to learn, and that seems average to you."

Rufus sighed, thinking of how he'd felt that day on Grassmarket Street when Fabia explained to him the meaning of the word *Moyenne*. Without his memories, average seemed totally wrong, a word that nothing really ever was. As he'd stood there listening to the traffic, watching the elms sway overhead, the world had seemed a bright and impossible mystery, way too complex for him to understand. And truly, anything examined could become amazing. A rock. A pencil. A blade of grass, nothing as simple as it seemed.

"So," Rufus asked quietly. "Are you skilled?"

"I make a mean dish of *nopalitos*," Reynaldo said.

At the back of the room, Maritza laughed, saying, *"Nopalitos? El ni puede calientar agua."*

Rufus didn't know what *nopalitos* was, so he waited, knowing that some truth was just on the man's lips. "Perhaps I cannot boil water, but I am talking without talking. I can move through the air when I want. But more than anything, I listen to the earth. I do not like to leave it. There are secrets stored within her bones that I want to know. But, like anything *precioso*, digging them up takes time."

Rufus breathed in, noticing that even though everyone else must have heard this explanation before, they seemed to hang on his words as if they were brand-new. Why? Had Reynaldo enchanted them all? For a quick minute, Rufus had almost felt himself fall into the man's words, the ideas so completely right, but then he was jerked out of the lull of Reynaldo's thoughts. Was Reynaldo really just Quain in disguise, enthralling them with some lame-ass theories of earth worship? What he said was like some terrible self-help book in a *Moyenne* bookstore: *Listen to the Planet and Save Your Life*. And was any of this revolutionary? Didn't the three *Plaques de la Pensee*—the symbols and holders of *Croyant* belief—represent earth, fire, water, the very marrow of the earth?

Why was Adalbert sitting here in jeans and a T-shirt, hanging on every word this little man said? Adalbert, who should know better. Adalbert, Hadrian's friend.

Rufus stood up, ignoring the minds trying to reach his, pushing them all away. His body felt hot and aching, a sorrow building deep in his chest, and without looking at anyone, not even Fabia, he walked out of the room, down the hall, and into the dark night of the Arizona desert. In seconds, he would be home, where things made sense.

Chapter Thirteen

Fabia watched Rufus leave the room, felt his anger and regret spread behind him like a cape. She turned to Adalbert and then Niall, both of whom said to her at the same time, "Go to him."

She stood up and walked quickly after Rufus, hoping to catch him before he opened matter and flung himself home to London. His reaction to Reynaldo was exactly what Adalbert had feared others' would be, the entire *Croyant* Council in an uproar over this newly found world of magic. But Fabia understood Rufus's reaction, having experienced it herself only hours before.

Pulling open the front door, she ran out into the front yard, conjuring a tiny light with the word "*Allumer*," holding a tiny white ball of fire in her palm.

"Rufus," she called aloud. *Rufus*, she thought with all her heart.

She stopped walking, her feet still on the dry ground, she listened, opening up her ears, and then heard him standing still, only a few feet away, just outside the light.

Rufus, she thought again. *Talk to me.*

He didn't move, but she felt his thoughts open to her a crack, a slip of anger pulsing into the night.

I didn't believe him either at first, she thought.

So why do you now? Do you even know who he is?

Not really, Fabia thought back. *But he's not out to hurt us. Or control us.*

She paused, and then looked toward him, his body a darker shape against the night. *I didn't know you either. But I was right. At least I thought I was.*

"But I didn't immediately make you change your beliefs," Rufus said, walking into the white globe of light. "How can you tell Reynaldo isn't like *Moyenne* from our past? The kind who enslaved and tortured and burned? We don't know anything about him. He could be working with Quain."

As he walked to her, Fabia felt her heart beat like a fist against her ribs, an awkward, painful rhythm she had to breathe into. Since she'd left Truckee with Cadeyrn, she'd felt half, felt uneven, as if she were riding a bicycle with only one training wheel. Now, staring at him in the glow of her magic light, she wanted nothing more than to go to him, kill the light, hold him in the darkness, and feel him under her hands. She needed to make sure he was real, now that the trouble was over, now that their lives could go back to—

"Average? Ordinary?" Rufus said, picking up the last of her thoughts. "You don't even know how to be with me in ordinary time. All I've been to you is something damaged or in danger."

Fabia stopped breathing, staring at his face. "That's a right paukit idea," she said finally. "How do you manage to come by it?"

He turned from her, shaking his head. "And now

there's this. This new thing. These new people. More trouble. You could stay here with Reynaldo and Macara, for Christ's sake. Cadeyrn Macara! Learn new magic. Fight new battles."

His thoughts slammed shut, and Fabia stood with her mouth open. Rufus was reminding her of—of Niall. Of Niall having a big boy tantrum. She was about to respond to Rufus as she would her brother, telling him that he was acting like a baby. Like a right shit. But she caught herself up, remembered how it had been with Fletcher. All the fights they'd ever had mirrored their very first fight. No matter if they were fighting about work or who did the dishes last or Fletcher's angry "Why can't I go out tonight with my mates?" Their first fight, their real issue, lay at the bottom of everything.

Even though Niall had always asserted that Fletcher had been nothing but a complete humpty, totally useless, the core of all Fabia's troubles was Fletcher's belief that Fabia really couldn't commit to him. And he'd been right. She'd never been able to tell him the truth about her life, keeping her *Croyant* work a secret, hidden, when that was, to her mind, her best part. He'd sensed she was holding so much back, and he fought around her omissions, battling closer and closer until she would finally shut down. Everything else just grew up around that terrible soil like poison ivy, until the night she finally told him to leave her life. But what was it with Rufus? What had he just said? *All I've been to you is something damaged or in danger.*

She started slowly. Going back over all the time they'd spent together, Fabia plucked memories from her mind like grapes. Rufus holding her tight in bed, his arms encircling her completely. Rufus at the clinic with Ewan Addison reading him *Beauty and the Beast*; Rufus cleaning up her apartment, playing poker, comforting her, tearing her away from the fire's voice, finding her on the island. She brought forth Tilly, who saved her a hundred nights or more. She held her last image of him battling Kallisto as she was flung backward on the forest floor. All strong, all true, all Rufus. And then she pushed her memories to him, held them up for him to look at. For a moment, it seemed he wouldn't take her offering, but then she felt him soften, open, taste each one. He remembered how she saw him.

This would be the soil they grew on. Not anger. Not distrust. They wouldn't make up over an argument they could never heal. They would heal first and start again. Now. On this magic land in the middle of a mystery Fabia couldn't even begin to understand yet. But she knew she would. And she would understand with Rufus, both of them going into their lives together.

She moved closer to him, speaking so as not to jar her thoughts lined up in his mind like gems. "You did make me change my beliefs, Rufus. Maybe it's not like admitting that *Croyant* aren't the only magic people in the world. But you made me see that I could connect to someone else wholly. In the time we've been together, I've shared more with you than I've ever shared with anyone."

Rufus didn't say anything, but she heard him anyway. *Niall.*

She sighed, a ruffle of irritation swirling around her. *He's my brother.*

I know. And I love my brothers, too, Rufus thought. *But I don't take them everywhere with me. And I could. We are that connected. Have been since my father died. I let them have their privacy. Their own lives. I've been inside your mind, Fabia. He's like a response to a question you haven't even asked yet. Something you have before you even want it.*

A long-eared owl *hooed* once overhead and then was silent. Fabia listened, hearing his wings beating fast toward the end of the sky. Rufus's heart thudded against his bones, the rhythm quick and hard. Inside, Reynaldo was telling stories about his mother, who would conjure the past from an iron pot. Adalbert was drawing a draft on his pipe, Niall was cracking walnuts with a metal cracker, and Justus sat back in the creaking leather chair.

Breathing in, Fabia turned off her ears, concentrating on the part of her mind that was Niall. Rufus was right. She could almost see his spot inside her like a long sofa he would hold forth on, waving his hand, telling her what to do, answering her questions, conferring with her about problems. Why had she always needed him? Needed a Tilly? Someone to bounce her life off, as if she were a rubber ball without any self-direction.

"You're right," Fabia said. "We're a habit to each other."

Rufus walked closer, his body only inches from hers. In her light, his eyes were the color of the pot Reynaldo had been talking about, burned black from fire and use, shining in the orange lick of flame.

"I want to be your habit, Fabia. I want to be with you and not just in the ways you've seen me these past weeks."

She smiled, her body flooding with flesh memory, feeling his hands again, his mouth. "How I've seen you has been pretty spectacular."

Then he smiled, his face losing the tenseness he'd carried into Reynaldo's house. "And I want to fight against Quain. I don't know if Reynaldo and his people can help us. Maybe so. Maybe they will be the answer. But I have work to do that I believe in. I can't forget what Quain did to my father. And I certainly will never forgive anyone who has ever worked with him. Seeing Macara sitting in there like that was . . . unbearable."

His face closed down a bit, and she saw his sigh fill his chest.

"Cadeyrn was enchanted," Fabia said. "Just like Sariel was. But by Quain, not Kallisto. The spell was strong, Rufus. Stronger than anything I've ever heard of. He's been coming out of it for a while, and it was only today that he could escape. He didn't let Niall get hurt. He made sure of it. And Nala, Brennus, and Philomel are alive because of him, too."

Rufus blinked, watching her, and slowly, quietly, she felt his mind turn a bit, allowing her words a space in his thoughts. Finally, he shook his head.

"This is why we have to fight." He bit his lip and turned toward the house. "If Quain can do what he did to Macara, then we have to continue on. To make sure this never happens again."

He reached out to her, touching her sleeve gently. Fabia felt his warmth, and then felt his thoughts want her. Dropping her spell of light, she moved inside his arms, laying her cheek against his chest, taking in the whoosh of his heart and blood, listening to the sound of him loving her. The world was soft and gray around them, and she breathed in his smell, his hair full of ocean and herbs.

"I didn't know what I would do when you escaped with Macara." His voice was deep in his body, a sound she heard with her mind and ears.

"I didn't know, either. I would have stayed, but he knew if I weren't there, he'd never be able to explain to Adalbert. And Cadeyrn was so weak, Rufus. He could only take me and one other."

Rufus swallowed and then pushed her from him gently, taking her face in his hands. His hands were warm and smelled like lavender. She moved her mouth so she could kiss an index finger, tasting him, herb, salt, skin.

"I know," he said, taking his finger and running it across her lower lip. "I would have done exactly what you did. Niall was failing. I wasn't. I'm sorry I ever thought otherwise."

Looking down at her, his dark hair loose and long around his face, Rufus smiled and then pulled her close, his lips touching hers so softly. He kissed her once, pulled back, kissed her again, and then again, each time with a little more pressure.

You're really here, he thought.

I'm not going anywhere, she thought back, opening her lips and letting her tongue press against his.

Oh yes, you are, he thought, and then, in a whirl of wind and magic, they were moving into matter and then falling out of it. Fabia pulled away from him and gasped, breathing in the push of warm, salty air and ocean she'd just left that morning. The island. But it was the island at night, the time when she'd felt most alone. The time she'd missed Rufus the most, running her hand on the depression his body made on another island in a different world. But here they were together, breathing the same air, standing on the same beach, knowing that when they wanted to, they could leave.

"The whole time we were here," Rufus said, "I kept thinking that this would be a perfect honeymoon spot. It was paradise except, of course, you weren't with me."

"Is it real?" Fabia asked, amazed that he could bring them back. "Isn't it a spell?"

"You're the spell, Fabia. A true piece of magic."

For a fraction of time, Fabia was going to send a quick thought to Niall, flooding him with images of the island, her feelings, asking him a hundred hurried questions. She hovered in her old habit, and then breathed in and looked up at Rufus. Here was her answer, right here, a question Niall would never understand. And shouldn't.

As Fabia had thought, she'd felt Rufus waiting for her decision, and when she closed her mind to Niall, he hugged her tight and then began pulling up her shirt, fumbling with buttons. Finally, he gave up and whispered, "*Disparaître*," and their clothes and shoes vanished into matter. The warm island air wrapped around them, and he pressed her tight, kissing her again, this time not as softly, needing her mouth hard against his, craving her tongue, even her teeth.

Fabia opened her eyes and at the same time, so did Rufus, and she saw his desire flame in his irises that were black, full, taking her in. And for a quick second, she saw herself as he saw her, her eyes holding his image, pressing all of him into memory.

A light wind rustled the palms overhead, sand skittering lightly across their feet. Somewhere at the edge of the beach, a creature wound through ferns and vines, chattering in animal language.

Rufus closed his eyes, and so did she, the beach and sand and sea disappearing. Fabia wanted nothing more than to feel his body tight against hers, his hair in her hands, wrapped in her fingers. It seemed to her that she'd never felt a man before Rufus. No one had felt this good, so soft, and so hard. She let go of his hair and ran her palms down his back, fingers following his spine, both her hands pressing him toward her as she held him above the tender curve of his bum. He sighed against her mouth, his hardness between them.

They were all hands and arms, skin against skin. Slowly, he bent them down to the beach, taking his mouth away from hers in order to kiss her jaw, her neck, her collarbone. He inched his lips down to her breasts, cupping them with his hands, sucking her nipples slowly. His mouth was warm, wet, his hair was soft, falling across her chest.

Rufus seemed to want to kiss every part of her, following the arc of her ribs down to her stomach, circling her belly button with his mouth and tongue, his stubble a harsh, sexy rasp against her flesh. Then he was biting at her abdomen gently, and then, his hands moving under her, his tongue and mouth found her.

Fabia arched back, smiling up into the sky, the stars a white swirl above her in the moonless sky.

"Rufus," she moaned. *Rufus*, she thought, letting herself fall into his thoughts as he gripped her. She was swamped with his desire that seemed to become her own. She felt his breath quick in his lungs, his need for her in his mind, his tongue on her even as her own body ached and filled from his mouth.

My love, he thought, the words rippling with adrenaline. *My love*.

Fabia took handfuls of his hair, and let go of his thoughts and her own, becoming nothing but her body, circles of pleasure beating out of her in waves until she sighed, pressing hard against him, and then falling back against the sand, her heart punching a wild rhythm in her chest.

Rufus kissed her inner thighs and then laid his head on her abdomen.

"Come back," Fabia said, pulling him up to her

and opening wide under him, feeling her wetness pressed against his belly. She reached down and grabbed him in her hand, loving the way his desire was visible. "It feels like forever since we've done this."

"I hope it's forever that we do this," Rufus said, sliding up, his erection finding her, sliding in, so full, so hard.

"Is that what you want?" Fabia asked, realizing she didn't know if she meant forever or the way his body was now, moving inside her.

Yes and yes, he thought, kissing her as he held her face between his palms. *Is that what* you *want?*

Yes and yes, she thought back, as she rolled him over, straddling him, feeling him stiff inside her as she rocked slowly. *Yes and yes and yes*.

As the island held them in her warm darkness, Rufus held her hips, rocking back. And this time, Fabia knew, her breath quickening, her body humming with the friction between them, their combined weight was pressed into the sand, a mark that would remain, something they could both touch together later before they left, evidence of what was starting now and what would last.

They stayed on the island for what seemed like hours, holding each other until the horizon gleamed pewter, a slit of silver against the water. In the half-day, half-night light, the beach glowed like a moonscape.

Finally, Fabia sat up, brushing the soft pale sand off her arms, looking down at Rufus and smiling.

"So what did you say earlier? That I've only known you as damaged or in danger?"

Rufus shook his head. "I was upset. I shouldn't have said that."

"Well, you can see how it's not even remotely true, can't you?" Fabia breathed in, following a frigate bird that swooped along the quiet sea, dipping a wing and then flashing white as it disappeared. "Even when you didn't know who you were, you knew what you wanted. That morning in my bed—"

"Okay, all right," Rufus said. "The body is often smarter than the mind."

"I like what your body thinks. In fact, I think it's brilliant. A genius."

Rufus turned on his side, tracing the outline of her bum in the sand. "My heart and my body are in total agreement. No debate there."

"Thank God for the consensus," Fabia said. "You know, I never thought I'd thank Kallisto for anything. Especially during that first day when I thought I'd never see you again. And not after what she did to Niall and Felix. But this island . . ." She stroked his chest with her hand. "This was wonderful. A honeymoon with no moon. Only stars and sand."

Rufus took her hand in his and kissed her palm. Then he sat up, their shoulders touching as they watched the water gleam with the beginnings of sunrise.

"We can have a moon," he said. "This is my spell, you know. Not Kallisto's."

Fabia smiled, thinking of a children's book she read once, something about saying good night to a moon that hung just outside a window. She was about to tell the story to Rufus when their island's moon was rising up into the morning sky, its face round and white, its light reflecting on the calm water.

"A moon for you, honey," he said, his mouth against her ear. "You taste like honey. Better than honey." He licked her neck, and Fabia smiled, holding him against her. He started to push her gently against the sand, when she laughed.

"I know we said forever, but don't you think we should get going?" As soon as she said the words, she felt the sand against her back. Rufus leaned over her, smoothing her hair off her face.

Fabia pulled him to her, her hands against his shoulder blades, and then whispered into his mouth, "As they say, one more for the road."

What had been hours on the island must have been only minutes in Arizona. Free of sand, their hair smoothed, their clothes back on, Fabia and Rufus appeared where they had left. Immediately, Fabia opened her ears, and to her amazement, Reynaldo was still telling the story about his mother and her pot, answering questions Cadeyrn asked about the healing techniques of *curanderas*, the evil power of the *brujos*. Adalbert tamped down another bowl of tobacco, Niall was sleeping on the sofa, his breath sounds something Fabia knew by heart, and Justus was scratching the chin of the old tabby cat. Somewhere in the house, Maritza said her rosary, the beads clacking against each other. It was as if the island had been a long, lovely dream.

Holding up her light spell, Fabia led them to Reynaldo's front door, stopping before she turned the knob.

"Are you okay with Reynaldo? With Cadeyrn?" she asked.

She listened to his mind, feeling all his reactions. His anger, his fear, his distrust, his sadness. She saw his father, Hadrian, felt the missing narrative his death had left in the Valasay family's story. But then she saw herself, standing straight and tall in Rufus's thoughts, her hair blowing back behind her, her arms outstretched, ready for anything.

"No," Rufus said. "But I might get there eventually. As long as I'm with you."

"You're with me," she said. "Aren't you standing right here?"

"I wish we weren't standing," he said. "But I've heard of stranger things."

Fabia smiled and shook her head. She wanted to tease him, to laugh at his need for her, but instead, she flushed, knowing she'd rather not be standing either.

She snapped away her magic light and took his hand, opening the door with the other. "Since I was among the first to arrive," she said. "I have my own room. If you're lucky, I'll let you stay with me."

"That would be lucky," he said, and he was serious. *That would be the best luck of all.*

Fabia woke to the sound of a rooster, the noise of which she associated with cartoons and tacky western movies. As she lay curled against Rufus in one of the creaky twin beds in the room, she waited for the sound again, opening her ears wide to catch the first rumble in the rooster's throat. She almost laughed when it finally came, thinking about the rooster and his scratching dominion over the hens, all of whom were probably laughing at him just as she was.

Without disturbing Rufus, Fabia sat up and got out of bed, putting on her clothes quietly, and then leaving the room. She closed the door quietly and padded down the hall, carrying her shoes, knowing that any amount of heel would clack and echo on the thick Spanish tile. By the front door, she slipped on her shoes and went outside, blinking against the flat white sun. Even at this hour and in this season, the heat felt dry and crackling, the air and dirt and plants all seconds from flame. The sky above her seemed to go on forever, the clouds like large creatures ambling across the atmosphere, in no way intending to let loose an ounce of rain.

"It's amazing, isn't it?"

Fabia jumped, shrieked, "Crivvens!" and then when she realized who was at her side, almost barked out a surprised laugh. For the first time in her life, she'd forgotten to check for Niall. He smiled and then looked up, blinking into the same sky.

"You don't write, you don't call." He squeezed her arm.

"You didn't say much this morning, either." Fabia felt her jeans pocket for her sunglasses and put them on.

"Let's walk," Niall said, and took her hand, leading her around the house to the chicken coop, where a large red and black rooster fluffed itself up and leaned his head back, pushing forth a huge wave of sound.

"Pompous ass," Fabia said. "Pawky bugger."

"Just guarding what's his," Niall said, pulling her on.

"His," Fabia repeated.

Niall didn't reply, taking her past the garden that Maritza had dug out of the hard soil, the last of the summer squash and pumpkins ripe and orangey yellow on their dying vines. By the house, staked green, red, and yellow tomatoes of a variety of hues and shapes pulled at the tired shoulders of the plants.

But the flowers were all in full bloom. Clusters of chrysanthemums, tall stands of sunflowers, and a wash of marigolds fanned out from the garden. After they'd walked a bit, Fabia turned back, seeing how Maritza had surrounded the house with color, marking its place on the desert map. Even the pendulous cloud creatures above would see this spot as a rainbow bull's-eye in the middle of nothing.

"Where are we going?" Fabia said, taking her hand back and twisting her hair into a temporary knot. "Are you sure you should be walking so far? Did Justus say you were good to go?"

"Good to go," Niall mused, nodding. "I'm good to go."

Neither of them had opened their minds to each other, and Fabia felt a stirring in her chest, a slip of fear sliding down her throat. This was ridiculous. She should open up and move into him, finding out what this walk was about, what he was about. But even as she thought about it, she heard Rufus's voice, his words from last night: *He's like a response to a question you haven't even asked yet. Something you have before you even want it.*

They kept walking, over a small uprising and down into a vein of brittlebrush and ocotillo, her pants rubbing against leaves and branches. Finally, they came to a long, bleached-out rock.

"Look at this," Niall said, pointing to the glyph carved into the rock.

"What is it? A man?" Fabia asked. "A man with a spear. And what's that?"

She pointed to a round shape, a basket or a bowl or a stone.

Niall shrugged. "I don't know. Maybe it's a prehistoric cartoon. He clearly has some troubles there."

Fabia laughed, sitting down on a section of the rock far from the glyph, as if her weight would erase history. Niall sat down next to her.

"So," she began. But then her tongue couldn't find new words. Yesterday, she'd poured out all that she'd held in since he'd been kidnapped. After Justus had healed him, she'd cried and told him how much she missed him, loved him, worried about him. He told her and the entire group about how Cadeyrn and Kallisto had taken him, explained the whirl of spell that kept him from communicating with anyone. Cadeyrn had filled in what Niall hadn't known, most of which he'd told Fabia earlier. So what was left was new. What remained. For the first time since their birth, Fabia found that neither her words nor her thoughts were good enough to communicate to Niall, to her twin, what she knew she had to explain. And from the way he was acting, Niall was having the same trouble.

"So," he said, his voice falling on the O. He kicked at the dirt, surprising a lizard that flicked around the stone and disappeared. All around them, the desert shone with morning sun, and Fabia felt sweat prickle on her hairline.

"I'm going to stay here," Niall said, just as Fabia said, "I'm in love with Rufus."

Fabia turned to Niall, her breath hanging in her mouth. He was looking at her with the shock she felt inside, his face flushing from heat and their words.

"You're going to stay here? In the desert?" she said finally. "With Reynaldo?"

Niall nodded, taking a big breath. "That I am. I haven't been—I mean, I just have felt there was something else I had to do. And yesterday, I felt it, you know? I know there are things he can teach me that I can bring back into our lives, all our lives. *Croyant* and *Moyenne* lives."

Fabia nodded, but Rufus's words about Reynaldo from last night hit her ears again. She disagreed with how Rufus felt, but one thing was true—they didn't know Reynaldo well at all. She wasn't sure that Niall would be safe here.

Niall shrugged as if he'd heard her, but she knew his mind was not in hers, and wouldn't be, not for a while and not ever in the same way. "There's so much we don't know. And I think we've forgotten that, Fabs. Most *Croyant* pretend that *Moyenne* are only necessary. Not important. Not needed. All the work I've done in Europe is just pro forma. No one's paying us much mind. Mum and Dad feel the same way. We haven't made much headway at all, and now the *Croyant* world is split in two, hacked apart like a melon."

"But is staying here the answer?" she asked.

"Who knows? And maybe something worse will have to happen before we really change things. Maybe Quain will go at us stronger, harder. But I have to try. Just like you have to try with Rufus."

Just as Niall said Rufus's name, Fabia heard Rufus wake up in the twin bed, heard his long muscles stretch out the night's sleep, heard his yawn and then his thought, *Where are you?*

Talking with Niall.

Talking?

Yes, talking. I'll be back soon.

Rufus turned over and closed his eyes, sending her an image of herself. Or rather, a feeling of how she felt to him, soft and warm and wet.

I'll be back very soon.

Niall turned to her, smiling. "He's a good man,

Fabs. You'll be able to share everything with him. More than you ever could have with Fletcher. And more than you did with me. You and I . . ."

Fabia picked up a small desert stone, turning it over in her hand. "It's like there were two umbilical cords, you know? One to Mum, and one between us. We never thought to cut that second one, did we?"

He shook his head. "I wouldn't have wanted to. I guess I thought it made us special. Better. Stronger."

"It made us reliant. It made us half."

"Oh, Fabs," Niall said. "I don't think that. We just never grew up in a way."

She knew everything they were saying was true, but Fabia felt something gripping her insides, a terrible dark hand with its evil fingers around her stomach. She didn't know how to go on without Niall, but she knew she couldn't go on with him the way they'd been all these years.

Fabia?

I'm okay, she thought, sending Rufus an image of the perfect desert sky before shutting down her mind.

"Listen, though," she said, lifting the imaginary fingers one by one off her stomach. "I can't do this all at once. It's got to be a process. There have to be steps."

Niall laughed. "Hi, my name is Niall. I'm a telepathy addict."

Fabia punched him lightly in the shoulder. "Hi, Niall."

But then Niall moved into her, holding her close. "Dates. We'll have specific dates. Once a month on Wednesday evenings. We get it all. The whole story. The thoughts and images. But that's it. Unless it's an emergency or aught. So doona be getting yourself in a right fankle except on Wednesdays."

Fabia kissed her brother's cheek, wishing for him what she'd found with Rufus. Maybe now that they were separate, living their own lives, he would be free enough to fall in love.

She smoothed his hair off his face, and then pulled away and stood up. "Come on. I'm dying to see if those chickens have a product. Maybe that horrible cock-a-bendy's all for show."

Niall took her offered hand, and they walked back toward the house, which was, Fabia now clearly saw, the only house for miles and miles, the desert the largest yard she could have imagined. *What will Niall do out here?* she wondered. There was nothing but beavertail cactus and soil and scrub and sky.

Once they reached the chicken coop, Fabia saw that the lord of the manor, the protector of all femininity had wandered off, pecking the ground by the front door. Quietly, she and Niall slipped inside the coop, the chickens rustling their gold and white and brown feathers.

"So how do you go about putting your hand in a nest?" Niall asked. "Should we sing them a proper cornkister?"

"I don't know any songs like that. What about '*Twinkle-twinkle*'?" Fabia moved slowly toward the nesting hens.

"Okay," Niall whispered. "We stick a hand in, cowp them over, and grab."

Fabia smiled and then did just what Niall suggested, the hen squawking once but then sitting right back on top of her nest. Fabia pulled her hand out from under the warm feathered body of the hen, and in her hand was a small white egg.

"Breakfast," Niall said, turning as the rooster crowed and began a silly quick walk toward the coop.

"Let's get out of here." Fabia cupped the egg, and they both pushed out of the coop and headed around the back of it to escape the rooster's attack.

As they walked toward the front door, Fabia looked at the egg, smooth and warm in her hand. Turning to Niall, she asked, "So what's going to happen to Cadeyrn? Is he going to be punished?"

Niall stopped walking, and she turned and came back to him. "What is it?"

"He's going to stay here, too," he said. "We're both going to learn from Reynaldo."

Her tongue moved against her teeth and palate, searching for a response. Stay? Here? With no punishment? No Council tribunal? No explanation to the *Croyant* world?

"I don't want him punished, but he does have some explaining to do," Fabia said finally.

"I know, I know," Niall said.

"He did so much wrong," Fabia said.

Niall nodded and started walking again. "A black hen can lay a white egg, Fabs."

That was Donoch's favorite saying. Their father always saw the best in everyone, believed in redemption for all but the worst of the worst. That's why he could forgive *Moyenne* for their past fear of *Croyant*, wanting an integrated world. Donoch could forgive burnings and torture and manipulation in order to have a better present and a peaceful future.

"But what does Mum always say? 'A crookit stick will thraw a crookit shadow'?"

"He's not a bad man, Fabs. He fell under a brilliant, evil spell." Niall shrugged, and kicked at the dirt.

Fabia herself had told Rufus last night that Macara had been enchanted, charmed by a powerful *sorcier*. Something that could happen to them all. Had, really, happened to her, the fire's voice still a sound she could hear. Fabia looked down at the little egg in her hand.

"Well," she said as they reached the door. "Keep an eye on him."

"Believe me," Niall said. "I'm keeping my eyes wide open. I'm going to take in everything."

Fabia was sure that the house grew, or how else could she explain that Donoch and Xanthe, Zosime, Sariel, Felix, and all who had arrived earlier suddenly had rooms and beds? She walked down the hallway later that night, staring at the bedroom doors, counting them off in her mind. There had only been four. She was certain of that, but now she kept walking past the sixth and seventh doors, shaking her head.

But in the kitchen, it was clear there was nothing but ordinary culinary magic going on. Maritza, glowing and rushed, made tamales, enchiladas *verdes*, *sopa de hitomate*, arroz con pollo, mole, and tortillas, blending the masa, and baking them on the heated comal herself.

Fabia stood at the doorway, amazed. Felix had offered to help and had forced Sariel into the task as well, both of them sitting at the counter, their hands holding corn husks.

"You see? *Mira*, like this." Maritza put a lump of masa in the corn husk in her hand and spread it out. "*Muy fascile*."

Felix spread his just right, but Sariel put down his spoon and shook his head. "Is there anything you can't do, Felix? I mean, really. Rumor has it you have good hands, but this is ridiculous."

Felix smiled, patting a bit of pork filling onto his spread masa, and smiled. "I've said this before, and no one ever seems to get it. But it's still true. Mom and Dad saved the best for last."

Following Maritza's example, Felix folded up the corn and meat into the husk and tied it perfectly. Laughing, he held it under Sariel's face.

Sariel shook his head and turned to Fabia. "Actually, I think you got the smartest Valasay. He's the only one not in the kitchen."

Fabia smiled and then backed up, not wanting Felix to lure her into a cooking experience. She could whip up a soup or green salad and could toast brown bread and fry eggs, but anything that had more than five steps was beyond her. Maritza's creations had taken all day and contained more magic than Fabia hoped to learn in a lifetime.

Looking for Rufus, she passed by the living room where her parents and Zosime as well as Adalbert, Niall, Cadeyrn, and Justus were talking with Reynaldo. Someone had conjured a map that hovered in the middle of the room, and Adalbert was pointing to areas and describing *Croyant* populations. Her mum waved quickly at Fabia but then turned right back to Adalbert, her face intent. This coming together of *Moyenne* and *Croyant* was her parents' dream, and Fabia knew that they might be staying in Arizona for a while, too.

Outside, the sun was tipping toward the west. Fabia put on the large woven hat she'd taken from the hallway rack and walked past the chicken coop, the rooster staring at her with his dark, mean eyes. Just past it, Rufus was standing facing the desert, his hands behind his back.

"Don't tell me," she asked. "You want to stay here

as well. You love the desert and want to learn everything you can from Reynaldo and his magic pot."

Rufus turned, his hair swaying as he moved. She felt her skin come alive as he looked at her, nerve and hair and cell prickling and tingling. As she came close, he grabbed her and held her against his body, her hat tipping a bit on her head.

"No."

"No?" Fabia wished she could see his face. She took off the hat and held it in her hand.

"Not at all. The desert isn't what I love."

She felt her heart jab an extra beat against her ribs. "What do you love?"

She could hear Rufus's smile even though she couldn't see it. "Let's see. I love . . . the cold. That's it. Constant cold weather. Rain. Endless days of fog and damp. Horrible coffee."

Home, Fabia thought, feeling him enter her mind.

"What else?" she asked.

"Some bad food. Mealy sausage sandwiches with butter. Blood pudding. A boiled brisket. Hard, barely cooked potatoes." He laughed, squeezing her tight. "Haggis!"

"Now if you mean to insult me!"

"And newspapers. Lots of scandal. Attacks on the royal family."

Fabia pushed away and then faced him, holding his arms with her hands. "Is that what you love?"

Rufus shook his head, his thought coming to her as he did. *No, I love you.*

She breathed in, letting his words float around her mind, wanting his declaration to sink in all the way to her brainstem and spine, needing his love to become part of what kept her upright.

"I love you, too." She'd never said those words to

anyone but her family and maybe a pet or two. This time, the words sang in her ears, weighed nothing, meant everything. "I have since I met you."

"On the street?"

"No," she said. "In my room. When I was five years old and you kept me company."

Rufus bent down and kissed her and then hugged her tight. "Let's go home, Fabia Fair. Let's go home and start our life."

Chapter Fourteen

That night, Rufus sat between Fabia and his mother at Reynaldo's large dining room table. Somehow, and Rufus wasn't sure what magic was involved, everything seemed to grow in this house. Not only did there seem to be more space in the living room and additional bedrooms, but the dining table managed to fit thirteen people, when the night before, it had appeared to be a nice enough piece of furniture for about six. Rufus glanced in the middle of the table, searching for leaves or additions, but then he gave up, figuring that if the table hadn't grown for people it would have had to for food. Cooking all day, Maritza and his brothers had made just about every kind of Mexican food Rufus had ever heard of, and he'd eaten more than his fair share of it. Next to him, Fabia leaned against his shoulder, almost dozing in an after-dinner food and wine glow. Across the table, Niall shook his head and smiled. "My sister's right foonered," he said. "All this excitement."

Rufus nodded, and then turned to glance at his

mother, who sat on his other side, whispering to Xanthe, and while Rufus knew he should pay attention to *that* conversation—maybe even slipping into his mother's thoughts—he was too tired himself, too foonered. And the only thing he wanted to think about was tomorrow. He and Fabia were going home.

At the other end of the table, Reynaldo poured out slightly chilled Patron Reserva de Casa into thick green shot glasses. Maritza set down a plate of sliced lime wedges and two saltshakers.

Adalbert, his glasses slightly crooked on his face, raised his glass of tequila and said, "We are all of us in the gutter. But some of us are looking at the stars."

Reynaldo nodded. "Salud." He licked the curve between his index finger and thumb, sprinkled salt on it, and then punched back the tequila with ease, biting into a lime wedge.

The room filled with citrus as everyone followed suit, and Reynaldo poured again. This time, Felix stood in a slight wobble (from the huge amount of dinner wine the table had consumed, Rufus surmised) and said, "Here's to all of the women who have used me and abused me. May they continue to do so!"

"*Dios mia*," Maritza said, finishing her drink and biting down on a lime. "*Hombres*."

"Men, huh? Listen to this," Niall said, picking up his full glass. "Here's to heat. Not the kind that ignites and burns down shanties. But the kind that excites and slides down panties!"

"Son!" Donoch said, his face reddening. But then he picked up a glass as well, and after thinking a moment said, "May the ships at sea never be bottoms up."

Fabia moved away from Rufus's shoulder and turned to him, smiling. "They're all pished. I don't think anyone will get up before noon tomorrow."

Justus nodded. "I'll be busy healing this sorry lot. But I just might have some kind of hangover of my own and let them pay the price." He sipped his water and then crossed his arms over his chest.

Macara raised a glass. "Here's to those who wish us well. As for the rest, they can go to hell!"

"*Salud!*" Maritza said.

"*Sláinte!*" Niall said, his Gaelic slurry.

Sariel stood up. "There are several good reasons for drinking, and one has just entered my head. If a man can't drink when he's living, then how can he drink when he's dead?"

"Indeed," Adalbert said, who had taken off his glasses altogether. "May the winds of fortune sail you. May you sail a gentle sea. May it always be the other man who says, 'This drink's on me.'"

Rufus watched as everyone—even his mother and Fabia—raised a glass, the tequila, salt, and lime making its way around the table. He looked at Reynaldo, who had been drinking along with the toasts, but he seemed to be the only person other than himself and Justus who was sober.

Rufus shrugged. *We usually aren't like this*, he thought, wondering if the man would hear him.

Who is, mí'jo*? But it is a time for celebration. Celebration after a fight. Celebration before one.*

Reynaldo smiled at Rufus and then took the tequila bottle from Niall. He poured a tiny bit, stood up, and then lifted his hand, the light glimmering in the thick bottle-green glass. "My friends, a final toast for this wonderful evening. I will always be thankful that Cadeyrn, Fabia, and Niall came to my house. I've longed to connect with you. And you all know the saying of my people. My house is your house."

He paused and looked at everyone, his gaze dark brown, strong, and completely sober, finally saying, "Be not forgetful to entertain strangers. For thereby some have entertained angels unawares."

The next morning, Rufus and Fabia awakened early and left, having made their good-byes the night before. Holding her tight against him, Rufus and Fabia traveled home through matter, but at the last minute, Fabia decided she wanted to go to the clinic before heading to her flat.

Do you mind? she thought. *I need to let them know I'm all right.*

Rufus shook his head, knowing that soon enough he'd have her to himself. *Not at all. I can't wait to hear what Gillian will say this time.*

Fabia changed the vision in her mind, brought them out of matter, and took Rufus's hand, leading them to the alley behind the clinic. There, they stepped into Scottish air for the first time in what was either three days or two weeks, depending on if their time on the island had been real.

Fabia smiled as she pulled him in the clinic door, excited to be back at work. Rufus smiled, thinking that no matter how much a big-time *chasseur* Fabia thought she was, she was more like her parents and Niall than she knew, wanting to help *Moyenne*, to connect the worlds, to make everyone safe.

"Well, for the love of God," Gillian said, standing up and dropping a file onto her desk. Her face flushed and then she put her hands on her hips and smiled. "The prodigal daughter and her gallus boyfriend. We'd thought you'd gone and made a wretched hash of your life, missing and all. Actually

I had a more interesting version for your disappearance, but Alan was having none of it."

Gillian moved around the desk and hugged Fabia tight. She looked up at Rufus over Fabia's shoulder, her eyebrows raised.

"You're not going anywhere for a while, I hope." Gillian winked at Rufus.

Fabia pulled away and shook her head, glancing up at Rufus. "No, I think we've had a wee too much travel in recent days. I mean to get back to work tomorrow. Rufus wants to help out, too."

"Fine, indeed," Gillian said, looking toward the exam room door as Alan stepped out, shaking a client's hand. He looked up and saw Fabia and Rufus and strode over, a big smile on his face.

"We were about to put out a poster on you two," he said. "We thought you'd been abducted."

Alan hugged Fabia and then shook his head. "Aye, you could have called, lass."

"I'm so sorry. It was—" She bit her lip. "Work."

"Well, enough of that business." Alan put his hands on his hips, both he and Gillian standing akimbo in front of them. And then for a moment, they both stared at Rufus. Rufus refrained from slipping into their thoughts, but he could see that Fabia already had, a big smile curving on her lips.

Finally, nodding and bringing his hands together in a clap, Alan said, "We could use more help around here, that's for sure. And we noticed how good you were with the kiddies. Books and such."

"Aye, and a grannie sooker like you?" Gillian said. "That we need all the time."

Grannie sooker? Rufus asked Fabia.

Don't ask.

What is it?

Let's put it this way, she thought back. *It's a large minty sweet. Something everyone wants to have in her mouth!*

Rufus blushed, and then, swamped with the notion of himself in Fabia's mouth, said, "Of course. I can't wait to start."

Alan and Gillian relaxed their stances, shook his hand, patted his back, and extracted promises of tomorrow's work and future schedules. Before they left, Fabia and Rufus walked through the dormitory, saying hi to the children, and Fabia pulled him back into the closet that served as a library.

"My master plan worked," she said, kissing him.

"What was that?" he said, moving his mouth to her neck.

"To have you with me all the time."

Rufus wanted to say that she probably didn't have much choice in that matter, but he blocked the thought from her. He would have followed her anywhere, but he didn't say a word. Instead, he nodded, and traced the lovely line of her neck down to her collarbone, tasting her until a couple of books fell off the shelves, and they both heard Gillian think with a snort, *Lovesickness.*

The late fall Edinburgh day was surprisingly fine, the elms and ashes losing the last of their leaves in a slightly warm wind, the dry brown bowls falling to the streets in piles. Instead of traveling through matter, they decided to walk home.

"There won't be many days like this," Fabia warned as they crossed the street and headed down Lothian Road. "We'd better take advantage."

"That's *my* master plan," Rufus said, winking at her.

When she smiled at him as they walked along in silence, he wanted to stop and fall to his knees. He wasn't sure how he ever pulled off this one. Here he was at thirty-four, finally in love. In love with the only woman he could have been in love with. How was this possible? Wasn't the idea of a soul mate or a true love as much a fantasy as the books he would read to the children at the clinic?

But then what about magic? Most of the world didn't think it existed, but then, there it was, as real as anything. Real enough for anyone to find it. And even though he'd only known her for such a short time, he knew that he wanted to be with her forever. Maybe other people needed years of dating and living together and couples counseling to make sure their relationship was right, but Rufus knew for certain that they belonged together. There was nothing fantastical about that notion. It was as solid in him as breath.

He wanted both their master plans to work out.

As they walked, he watched her, following the line of her features, her strong jaw, her full lips, her wide eyes. He let his gaze follow her body, resting on her breasts for a moment before falling to her hips and legs.

"Christ," he said as he almost ran into a bench, ignoring her backward glance and quick smile. He ran to catch up to her.

"Fabia," he said, pulling her up short and taking her in his arms.

"What?"

"Will you marry me?"

"Aye, of course I will."

Rufus gaped, his body filling with buzz.

"Silly, I've been listening to you think for well over three blocks. All those absolutely salacious thoughts." Fabia kissed his chin, and then looked up at him, her eyes Lake Tahoe blue. "I accepted you back by Jenner's Department Store. And if you hadn't proposed soon, I would have. If you weren't going to ask me to marry you after all we went through in my bathroom . . ."

In the middle of Princes Street, Rufus stopped her from saying any more by kissing her for a very long time.

Lovesickness, passersby thought.

A miracle, Rufus thought back to the air, to the wind.

At the flat, Fabia patted her coat for her keys. But as she was about to unlock the door, Liam Macmillan pulled the door open and then blanched.

"Donald. Fabia," he said, backing up.

Rufus moved forward and then stuck out his hand. "It's Rufus Valasay."

"Oh," Liam said, taking Rufus's hand, shaking it quickly, and then dropping it. He mumbled, "Donald my arse" under his breath.

"Hi, Liam," Fabia said, pushing past both men. Liam followed her with his eyes, and then nervously stepped back a few more feet.

Rufus walked in and began to walk toward the stairs. He turned and then looked at Liam.

"We're getting married, you know. You're going to need to think about bothering someone else. *Or* else."

Liam nodded and then walked to the door, pushed through it, and fled without a backward glance. Rufus couldn't help but smile at Liam's sad parting thought of *She'll get sick of him. And there I'll be. Ready to comfort her.*

Rufus rolled his eyes and then walked up the stairs, staring at the perfect back end of his wife-to-be. He wasn't sure how bad magic led him here, to Edinburgh, to Fabia. Maybe, if Rufus looked at everything that had happened since Kallisto dangled Sariel in the middle of the living room, he'd have to say it was good. Sariel was free, Macara was drawn away from Quain, and he had Fabia. If every action had a reaction, evil acts had led straight to good ones, to this very woman who flicked her long blond hair behind her shoulder and turned to smile at him as they climbed the stairs.

Suddenly, he felt a bubble of anticipation push against his ribs. The world was about to make sense, finally, in a way it hadn't since his father's death. Everything seemed just seconds away, and Rufus couldn't wait to have the life that he'd always wanted but couldn't find. All his dreams and hopes and needs seemed to be right in front of him. All he had to do was open his arms and pull them close.

He shook his head, and laughed, wishing that Fabia lived on the first floor. He didn't know if he could wait till the third floor before he kissed her again.

If you liked this Jessica Inclán book, try her other stories available from Zebra . . .

WHEN YOU BELIEVE
Forget Me Not

Running for her life from three thugs, San Francisco poet Miranda Stead plunges through a door to what she thinks is safety. Instead, she finds herself surrounded by a bunch of paranoid, robe-wearing people who seem to read her thoughts. And then he steps up: tall, dark, amber-eyed, gorgeous Sariel Valasay. And Miranda hopes he isn't listening to her mind because the thoughts running through her head are decidedly blush-worthy . . .

Sariel knows no ordinary human—a Moyenne—should have been able to break through to their world, but here she is, all lush curves, red hair, and snappy comebacks. As a member of the ancient Les Croyant des Trois, Sariel is sworn to protect her kind and their world from the dark forces always at work. He never thought he'd have to protect her from his own desires. His job is simple: he is to use the power of his touch to erase all memories of the evening from Miranda's mind. He is to forget hearing her wonderful laugh and funny comebacks in his head, ignore her intelligent questions about his kind and his world, stop feeling the magic of her soul in his veins. But one touch and he knows it won't be easy. There's something absolutely unforgettable about Miranda Stead. Tomorrow, he'll make her forget. Tonight, he only wants to make her believe . . .

BELIEVE IN ME
Charm Me

For a Croyant, Felix Valasay lives a charmed life of blender drinks and pleasuring women, so he's less than thrilled to be interrupted mid-hookup by notorious Croyant straight arrow, Sayblee Safipour. If Felix is pleasure first, business later, Sayblee is business first, last, and always. She'd been the smart one in their magic classes, the one he couldn't impress, couldn't win over with a smile or a compliment or twelve, the one he'd wanted so desperately. Now he has the chance to wake up to her beautiful, calm face, to smell the sweetness of her skin, to be this close to those maddening curves . . .

Lothario. Cad. Casanova. Sayblee doesn't need magic to find the right words to describe Felix Valasay. Figures she'd find him "entertaining" when they have important Council business to attend to—setting a trap in Paris for the most dangerous, powerful *sorcier* their world has ever known. To do that they will need to hide in plain sight, living together like an ordinary Moyenne couple, using no magic at all. Keeping her mind shut against the dark forces trying to find them is tough. But keeping Felix's hot body and make-you-melt smiles out of her thoughts is nearly impossible. And sometimes the only way to avoid temptation is to yield to it . . .

BEING WITH HIM

They are here among us . . .

Far from home, gifted with special abilities, hunted for their powers. And they are desperate to find their other, the one who completes them . . . before it's too late . . .

Sometimes, Time Really Does Stand Still

Mila Adams has always known she was different. For as long as she can remember, she has had the ability to shift time, and who would believe that? Certainly not the obnoxious blind dates her mother keeps foisting off on her. But Mila can't help feeling there's someone out there for her, a soul mate who might understand her unique ability. And when she looks into the dark eyes of financial whiz Garrick McClellan, she can't but feel her time has finally come.

Any man would lust after a beauty like Mila, but the moment Garrick touches her—feels her shifting time just as he can—he recognizes her as his partner in power. Their connection is immediate, passionate, raw, and beyond anything either has ever experienced. But who are they? What is this gift that joins them so intensely? Are there others like them? And why do they feel that time is running out?

Turn the page for an excerpt!

"Your painting," he asked, his words coming from him slow, as if he had to pull each word out of his mouth by a string, "the one with the purple swirl?"

"*The Ride*," she said, changing her gaze, moving it from his hands to his face. She was startled by his pointed expression. "What about it?"

"What does it mean?" he asked. And when Mila looked at him, she could see such an intense curiosity burning from behind his indifference, she wished she could open the car door and fling herself out. No one had ever looked at her like that before, not her parents, not a lover. No one ever paid that much attention to her, all at once. "What is it saying? Where does it come from?"

"It's just something from my imagination. Something I think about. All the time."

"Why? Why do you think about that shape? That color? What do you think?" He was leaning forward now, his face alight, his eyes filled with something like heat. "It's like there's movement there. Like the shape is going some place. Like it's carrying people, important people."

Mila blinked, startled. She'd only ever talked about *The Ride* with her art instructors, the museum gallery director, her classmates. "I don't know why you care. You certainly didn't show any interest earlier."

"I—I . . ." Garrick stopped talking, shaking his head. He jerked his head up and noticed where the car was. "Never mind. I shouldn't have done this. I never should have come, Linda or not. Driver."

"His name is Mr. Henry."

Garrick leaned forward. "Mr. Henry, you can let me out here."

Mr. Henry didn't turn but said, "It's a mile yet."

"That's fine. Right here. Let me out here." And when Mr. Henry didn't seem to slow down, Garrick almost yelled, "Stop."

Mila sat flat against her seat watching this beautiful angry man do everything in his power to get away from her. If it wasn't so upsetting, she thought, she'd be able to craft some kind of story about it to tell her friends at the beginning of open studio, recounting the evening with verve and style, a jaunty yarn about the blind date from hell. The man who endured asphalt raspberry burns rather than ride a final mile in a one-hundred-thousand-dollar limo with her.

"Here we go, sir," Mr. Henry said, and Garrick opened the door, and he started to push through to the outside. He stopped for a second, and she could see him take in a big breath.

"Look," he said, turning back to her, one foot already out on the pavement. "It's not about . . ."

It's not you, it's me. Yadda, yadda, yadda, Mila thought. *Get out of the car, jerk.*

Garrick stopped talking, and she thought she heard him laugh. But his eyes weren't happy.

"Good luck with your painting," he said, leaving for real this time, the door closing heavy and hard.

As the car pulled away, Mila watched him as long as she could, until Mr. Henry turned left down the hill, heading toward the Mission District.

"Well," Mila said finally as they sailed through traffic. "That was so much fun, I hope I can do it again next Saturday!"

"He seemed a little strained," Mr. Henry said. "A little tense."

"He needed—well, he didn't need me, that's all I know."

Mila sat back, letting the ride home take her over. If she wasn't laughing, she would cry. And vice versa. It was too ironic. Here was a man who if he hadn't acted like such an ass, she actually would have loved to see again. And for no good reason, except for a strange feeling she'd had ever since he walked into her parents' living room. Some kind of zing, a flurry of energy in her body.

But his good looks and some kind of chemistry weren't enough to overcome his clear lack of manners or caring. So now it was over. She'd survived the dinner, her mother would likely not try a setup for months, and Mila could scratch another San Francisco bachelor off the long list her mother seemed to keep on file. Maybe now after this debacle, Mila thought, it was a good time to kiss that list good-bye.

She didn't even have a chance to look at the clock before picking up her cell phone, fumbling in the dark bedroom to find the button to answer it.

"What?" she asked, blinking into the early morning light, her blankets piled around her.

"I have to see you," he said.

Mila forced herself into total consciousness, taking in small breaths, keeping her eyes open. What day was it? Or what night? Was it the weekend? "Who is this?"

"It's Garrick. Garrick McClellan."

Mila rolled onto her back. "You have to see me? Didn't—didn't you just jump out of a car to get away from me?"

There was a pause, and Mila wondered if she'd fallen back to sleep, but then he said, "I'm—I'm sorry. I want to explain. And I want to ask you something about . . ."

"What? About what?" Mila asked.

"Us," Garrick said. "Us."

Sitting up, Mila leaned against her pillow, her mouth open slightly. *Us?* What was he doing calling her like this after a night like that? After he almost made himself roadkill rather than sit next to her? She wanted to laugh at him. To tell him to take a hike. But then, through the phone, she felt so much that she wanted to lie down flat on the bed and weep. Images were coming to her, feelings, thoughts. Garrick's. So much hurt and loss and pain. He had been so alone. So afraid.

"Oh," she said, trying to find words. "Oh."

"Can we meet?" he asked, unaware of what she was pulling in from his mind.

"Yes. Yes," she said. "We can meet."

"When?" he asked.

What time was there? she wondered. What time was there but this moment? She knew from wasting time how valuable it was.

"Now," she said. "Come over now."